MAN IN A BLACK HAT

Ernest Temple Thurston was born in Halesworth, Suffolk in 1879 but at age ten moved with his family to Ireland. In 1901, he married Katherine Madden, who went on to become a best-selling novelist in her own right, earning substantial popularity with the publication of *John Chilcote M.P.* (1904). The couple's divorce in 1910 was highly publicized in the newspapers, with various reasons assigned for Thurston's desertion of his wife, including that he had impregnated his secretary, had moved into the slums to research his new novel, or was angry that her books sold better than his. (She died suddenly in a Cork hotel room the following year, leading to some sensational speculation that she had committed suicide or was murdered.)

Thurston published some forty volumes of fiction and also wrote a handful of plays; among the novels, *The City of Beautiful Nonsense* (1909), which was frequently reprinted, is perhaps his best known, while his play *The Wandering Jew* (1921) was performed on Broadway and adapted for a 1923 film. He died of influenza and pneumonia in London in 1933.

Mark Valentine is the author of several collections of short fiction and has published biographies of Arthur Machen and Sarban. He is the editor of *Wormwood*, a journal of the literature of the fantastic, supernatural, and decadent, and has previously written the introductions to editions of Walter de la Mare, Robert Louis Stevenson, L. P. Hartley, and others, and has introduced John Davidson's novel *Earl Lavender* (1895), Claude Houghton's *This Was Ivor Trent* (1935), Oliver Onions's *The Hand of Kornelius Voyt* (1939), and other novels, for Valancourt Books.

MAN IN A BLACK HAT

TEMPLE THURSTON

With a new introduction by
MARK VALENTINE

VALANCOURT BOOKS

Man in a Black Hat by Temple Thurston
First published by Cassell in 1930
First American edition published by Doubleday, Doran in 1931
First Valancourt Books edition 2015

This edition © 2015 by Valancourt Books
Introduction copyright © 2015 by Mark Valentine

All rights reserved. In accordance with the U.S. Copyright Act of 1976, the copying, scanning, uploading, and/or electronic sharing of any part of this book without the permission of the publisher constitutes unlawful piracy and theft of the author's intellectual property. If you would like to use material from the book (other than for review purposes), prior written permission must be obtained by contacting the publisher.

Published by Valancourt Books, Richmond, Virginia
http://www.valancourtbooks.com

ISBN 978-1-943910-08-3 (trade paperback)
Also available as an electronic book.

All Valancourt Books publications are printed on acid free paper that meets all ANSI standards for archival quality paper.

Set in Dante MT
Cover design by Lorenzo Princi

INTRODUCTION

In those days I read four or five books a week. It was sometimes suggested I might like to go outside if it was sunny, that it was a shame to be indoors. But I preferred to be in my room, gazing at pages. The library where I got the books made them seem important. It looked to me like a palace, with its sculpted stone emblems, square towers and rooftop balcony. From a grand arched porch a huge staircase swept upwards with a black iron banister like a great swirl of solidified ink. My footsteps on the marble stairs echoed up to the high vaulted ceiling. I often strode over two or three steps at a time in my zeal to be among the books. I would emerge from the ascent into a vast hall illuminated by tall windows.

The bookshelves ought perhaps to have been of carven oak, with acorns and leaves; but they were made of some light, yellowy plain wood, coloured like candlelight. It was hard to imagine just how many books there were here, but certainly more than I had ever then seen before in one place. The school library was just a cold obscure square room with tin shelving: the mobile library van was a long, but narrow, warm rectangle whose contents I mostly knew too well. Here instead was a vast temple of books, a great solemn ceremonial place where the rite of reading was given its proper respect, and the words of awe and wonder were as if kept within a shrine.

How did I choose which books to read? It was like asking me to select an autumn leaf from the woods. Among all the bronze and golden tongues there would be some more strangely blemished, more curiously shaped, or with a finer glimmer, than the others: but how to find them? I had to rely on a sense I hardly knew I had, a quick instinct: some signal received from the title of the book, the name of the author, perhaps an aspect of the lettering or the colouring of the narrow span of the spine. I would reach in, free the book from its niche, and see if the urge that had drawn me to this volume, among all the thousands, was right.

In this way I encountered *Man in a Black Hat*, the 1930 novel by E. Temple Thurston. I was about seventeen when I found it. Who at that age could resist such a title, or the grand and resonant name of the author? I can still see my awkward form, earnest, tense, gazing at the pages which bloomed in the white light from the tall windows. Absorbed in the opening scenes, I soon found that here was an auction at a country house, a strange book that two collectors both wanted, and it looked like the sinister figure of the title was a magician, an occultist. That was enough to clinch the selection. I had already been drawn to the supernatural in fiction through the dreaming and lyrical work of Arthur Machen: perhaps this might be in the same vein.

It wasn't, but it had other qualities almost as good. The fateful atmosphere of the book stayed in my memory for years until I just had to track it down again and get my own copy. I remembered that air of the sinister in a small, sunlit English town, and the sense of an elusive pursuit. I couldn't even remember the ending then, but I did know that (though it was clearly not as ardently written as the Machen book) it held a distinctive aura for me, and remained talismanic when many others had faded away. I would keep remembering the title, a few incidents, but most of all its slow-burning sense of strangeness abroad in quiet streets.

Its author, Ernest Temple Thurston (1879-1933), was born in Suffolk but his family moved to Cork when he was ten and he seems to have celebrated most the Irish dimension in his upbringing. His first book, *The Apple of Eden* (1905), came out when he was twenty-six, and he soon became a popular and versatile author and journalist. He was a novelist, poet, playwright, short story writer, essayist, travel writer, a professional with an easy style, and with progressive social ideas and broad human sympathies. During the First World War he worked for the Department of Information.

He first made his name with *The City of Beautiful Nonsense* (1909), a romance set in Venice, and always the words "charming", "whimsical" and "sentimental" hovered about his work. Another success was *The Flower of Gloster* (1911), in which the author and a hired hand travel the canals of England, celebrating their quiet, lonely waters many years before two other writers of supernatural fiction, Robert Aickman and L.T.C. Rolt, would take up the cause of preserving them.

He earned a huge popular hit with a play, *The Wandering Jew*, in the West End and Broadway in the early 1920s. The lead role was first taken by the Canadian-born Scottish author Matheson Lang, who recalled that as a character cursed with immortality for insulting Christ, he had "a different leading lady in every act and I have to wear a different beard in every act". Lang remembered its success was "immediate and tremendous" and noted that "during the long London run Temple Thurston used to come frequently to my dressing-room to see me during the performance", chafing the actor, who had predicted it might only last three weeks. Another visitor, one among many eminent enthusiasts, was Asquith, then Prime Minister.

"There was about *The Wandering Jew* something curious—even uncanny," Lang later wrote, in his memoir *Mr Wu Looks Back* (1940), named after the Chinese character he played to great acclaim for many years. "It had the most extraordinary effect on some people," he continued, and explained that one woman, who had seen the first act over thirty times, presented him with a family heirloom, a small casket they called "the Wandering Jew's box", which had reputedly been given to an ancestor about a hundred years ago in return for a kindness given to an ill and weary Jew in Tunis—who had revealed that he was indeed the Wandering Jew of legend.

Following the friendship arising from the play, Thurston dedicated *Man in A Black Hat*, which has the theme of immortality and strange powers in common with it, to Matheson Lang. Noting the actor's variety of roles, from Mr Wu to The Wandering Jew, he asked "Why should I not explore fields between realism, romance and mystery?" This story, he continued, "having its basis in actual character and fact, I felt to be too exciting to leave untouched". His lead character, the malevolent magician Gollancz, "needless to say . . . had another name. But he himself is not merely fiction, and when I heard of him, he sounded too good to lose." The book is presented to Lang, concludes the author, because of the interest he has already shown in it. This was not surprising, because Lang's memoirs are laced with other recollections of the mysterious and uncanny that had happened to him.

Man in A Black Hat was by no means the first work of fiction to feature a black magician. Two celebrated examples are Somerset Maugham's novel *The Magician* (1908) and M. R. James's story "Casting the Runes", collected in *More Ghost Stories* (1911). Aleister Crowley has for obvious reasons been suggested as the model for both Oliver Haddo and Mr Karswell, the villains respectively of these works. In the case of the M. R. James story, the identification is not really proven and may be unlikely, but it seems pretty clear that Maugham did have Crowley in mind in his book, and indeed Crowley responded to it on that assumption.

Was he also the original of Gollancz in Thurston's story? Certainly something of Crowley's self-assurance, his mesmeric quality and his reputed ruthlessness in pursuit of what he wanted may also be seen in the character Thurston presents. Gollancz, we learn, had been a "marked man at Oxford" forty years ago: whereas it was the authorities at Cambridge that Crowley had goaded in the Nineties. A simple fictional change to prevent too close a resemblance?

But it might be thought that Aleister Crowley would be too obvious a model for the story, given his notoriety. Another, more likely, candidate could be the Reverend Mr Montague Summers, deacon in holy orders in the Church of England but also a learned demonologist and editor of medieval works on witchcraft. Though he may later have recanted his youthful dalliances with devil-worship, which apparently included conducting a Black Mass in the garden of his Hampstead home in 1918, dark rumours ever swirled around this picturesque figure, who was noted for sporting a large black wide-awake hat, not unlike the sombrero habitually worn by Gollancz.

And Montie, as he was affectionately known to his friends, had indeed been noticed at Oxford, as Roger Dobson, an expert on his life and work, has commented:

"Summers's exotic tastes emerged when he went up to Trinity College, Oxford, in 1899. Assuming the role of a decadent, he burned incense and dressed extravagantly. His ebony cane's silver handle bore 'an extremely immodest representation of Leda and the Swan'. Like his idol Oscar Wilde—who had paid the penalty for flouting Victorian morality—Summers was brilliant and witty: though his perverse and obscene conversation, delivered in a piping voice, was obviously calculated to shock" ('The Mysterious Montague Summers', *Antiquarian Book Monthly Review*, July 1986, collected in *The Library of the Lost*, Tartarus Press, 2015).

Montie published *The History of Witchcraft and Demonology* in 1926, just four years before Thurston's book, and noted that it "caused a sensation and was an immediate best-seller": it was followed by several similar studies. But perhaps most persuasively, Montie was closely involved with the theatre and moved in the circles of most of the eminent actors and directors of the day, where Thurston could easily have encountered him, or stories about him. He founded and ran The Phoenix Society, dedicated to reviving Tudor and Restoration plays, which presented some twenty-six productions in the period 1919-26, just the time when Thurston was having his great success with *The Wandering Jew*.

And indeed, like Gollancz, Summers was not a man who liked being thwarted in matters about books. Roger Dobson gives us an example: "In his third volume of memoirs, *Drink and Ink* (1979), Dennis Wheatley tells how he met the scholar while researching his first Black Magic novel, *The Devil Rides Out* (1934). Staying with Summers at Wykeham House, Alresford, Wheatley was disturbed to find large spiders on his bedroom ceiling. In the garden his wife 'came upon the largest toad she had ever seen' . . . Summers flew into a rage because Wheatley refused to buy an old book. 'Never have I seen such a complete change of expression,' Wheatley wrote. 'From having been normally benign his face suddenly become positively demonic.'"

Of course, whoever Thurston had in mind as the original of Gollancz, he also applied his own imagination to the character. The real interest is in how Thurston handles what could be, less subtly presented, a crude caricature. This I think he does very skilfully. Though his narrator is convinced that Gollancz has stopped at nothing to secure the rare Rosicrucian book he seeks, proof is another matter, and the gentleman himself is urbane and courteous. So what on earth do you do when you think occult powers are in play, and a crime has been committed, yet you are the only one in possession of the facts, and there could be other explanations? The police are tolerant but unconvinced. His protagonist's dilemma is convincingly depicted and the book's sense of remorseless pursuit conducted using uncanny powers is well sustained. We sympathise with the harried Dr Hawke, while also finding ourselves fascinated by the sinister Gollancz, that suave figure who seems to have defeated time and space.

E. Temple Thurston died of influenza in London on 19 March 1933, aged 53, and not long after the popularity of his work waned. Every so often one of his titles has been revived: the vivid Venice setting of *The City of Beautiful Nonsense* has found a few new admirers drawn to its period charm, and the revival of interest in the English canals has brought *The Flower of Gloster* back into print. But until now *Man in A Black Hat* has eluded most admirers of the dark fantastic in literature. It is surely time for it to take its place alongside other much-relished occult romances of the Thirties such as those of Charles Williams, Dion Fortune, E.C. Vivian, Mary Butts and David Lindsay. Even in such thrilling and mysterious company it will still stand high.

MARK VALENTINE
June 2015

TO
MATHESON LANG

My dear Lang,

You explore the variety of your art between such disparate parts as "Mr. Wu" and "The Wandering Jew." Why should not I explore fields between realism, romance and mystery? Here, anyhow, is a story, which having its basis in actual character and fact, I felt to be too exciting to leave untouched. Needless to say the Gollancz of this tale had another name. But he himself is not merely fiction, and when I heard of him, he sounded too good to lose. Whether I have done him justice or not, I present him to you, because of the interest you have already given him.

Yours always,

E. Temple Thurston

MAN IN A BLACK HAT

CHAPTER I

The sudden and tragic death of Crawshay-Martin at the "Scarlett Arms" on the last day of the sale of his property and effects at Malquoits, attracted but little attention, except in the immediate neighbourhood of Bedinghurst.

In these days of evening papers, the material of a piece of news soon wears. Like a remnant appearing at a millinery sale, it is handled and pulled over by a thousand fingers directly it appears upon the counter.

Two reporters from London papers were down at the "Scarlett Arms" the next morning soon after breakfast. I succeeded in avoiding one of them. The other buttonholed me as I was walking aimlessly towards the village.

He raised his hat, which should have impressed me as to his diffidence, and said:

"I beg your pardon—I believe Dr. Hawke."

Probably I was surprised at a complete stranger having my name in Bedinghurst. One is humanly disposed to a sensation of flattery at being recognized. I ought to have known better. I ought to have guessed at once. Directly he said: "I understand you were with Mr. Crawshay-Martin yesterday at his sale——" then at once I realized. Here, no doubt, my face betrayed my annoyance at being caught like this. I probably gave him some warning from my eye. But he was quite imperturbable. Probably a very decent fellow at his job. It is the job itself of prying into the troubles and tragedies of others I can't stomach.

"If you think you're going to get any information out of me," I said sharply, "you've made a considerable mistake."

He replied he was very sorry to have troubled me.

"It was only," he added, "that when a man commits suicide, his friends generally——"

"Who told you he committed suicide?" I demanded. "There'll

be a coroner's inquest. Hadn't you better wait for the findings of that? Isn't that enough for your beastly paper? Or can't it wait?"

He apologized again. In fact the apology was, so to speak, his constant idiom.

"They told me at the 'Scarlett Arms,'" he said, "that it was unquestionably suicide. I didn't know there was any suggestion of foul play."

It was not difficult to see the kind of invitation that was being offered me. He didn't mind my losing my temper. Indeed, he wanted me to lose it. Already I had said something which had been farthest from my intentions. But it was not for his benefit I was prepared to voice my suspicions, and I pulled myself together.

"Look here," I said, "it is part of your job in life to extract news from people, indiscriminately of their feelings. It is part of mine to respect the private affairs of my friends. Our objects in life are diametrically opposed. Down the road this way you come to the 'Scarlett Arms.' That way leads to the village. Which way are you going?"

"I was going to the inn," he said.

"Then I'll say good day," said I, "because I'm going to the village."

As a matter of fact I wasn't going to the village at all. I wasn't going anywhere. I was in that frame of mind when a man can find no satisfying purpose for his actions. The sudden death of Crawshay-Martin, the finding of his body with the throat cut at that hour of the night, had not exactly unnerved me. I don't indulge in nerves. But it had left me in an aimlessness of mood. I could not entirely account for the loss of my friend. There were my own peculiar feelings about the disappearance of that book. That, and nothing but that, restrained me from the conviction that Crawshay-Martin had committed suicide. But for the vanishing of that book, I should have been convinced his end had been that of self-murder. Everything pointed to it. His distress at leaving Malquoits, which his family had owned for so long. And added to that, his parting with all his possessions at the sale. A man who has lost all association with the past and has nothing in the future to look forward to, is in a fair way towards thinking that life is intolerable. But if it wasn't suicide, then what was it? Not murder. There was no one in that room when we entered it. I hadn't thought it was murder. And yet the book was gone.

Suicide, at any rate, was the impression the police had taken with them that morning, in those early hours when they had been summoned to the "Scarlett Arms" to see the body of Crawshay-Martin lying there in the stagnant stream of his own blood.

Certainly they had asked me questions, and I had told them about being wakened at two o'clock by the sound of Crawshay-Martin's voice in the room next to mine.

"Who was he speakin' to?" asked the constable.

"I don't know," said I.

Why couldn't I bring myself to say that I thought it was Gollancz? Somehow, I couldn't. Gollancz wasn't at the inn. He had gone back to town the evening before. More than that, the room, when we broke down the door and entered it, had been empty. How could it have been Gollancz?

"I can only assure you," I had added, "that I distinctly caught the sound of Crawshay-Martin's voice."

When pressed to tell him the actual words I had heard, they sounded ridiculously inconclusive: "So there was relation."

"And you heard no reply?" asked the constable.

"None," said I.

"Anything else?"

"Just—'This is the end.'"

I also told him of that final exclamation—the "My God!" which I had heard in the choking cry out of Crawshay-Martin's throat.

"But all in his voice? Not anybody else's?"

"No."

"And the room when you got in was empty—'cept for the body, I mean?"

What was the good of saying any more? What was the good of telling him about the book?

"Obviously talkin' to himself," the constable had said. "Temporarily insane, you see. Likely a man would talk to himself at a time like that. Not responsible."

To which he added the suggestion that I knew what he meant.

It was quite obvious what he meant, but it did not convince me. I ate an apology for a breakfast, and was strolling out in the road, uneasy and dissatisfied in my mind, when that reporter tackled me. Somehow this clinched my mind. If there was anything in the disappearance of the book, if there was anything in my feeling that Gollancz was in that room when Crawshay-Martin died, I had better go and tell the police quite frankly about it. I walked on through the village and stopped a passing bus on the road to the little town of Shipleigh, two miles away. The police-station was in the main street.

"I want to see the sergeant-in-charge," I said, and was shown into a little bare room behind the outer office.

There was a table covered with brown shiny oil-cloth, and four wooden kitchen chairs. While I was waiting I speculated upon the various confessions and statements that had been made from time to time in the small space of those four walls. Had there ever been any, I wondered, quite as strange as mine? Even if there were, how little was the trace they had left behind. The walls were distempered. The oil-cloth covered table wore the shine of its daily washing. The wooden chairs were varnished. There was not a speck of dust anywhere. Could these things be wiped out as simply as all that? Would the mystery of this man Gollancz present no difficulties to them? Whether my ideas were foolish or not, I felt I had to voice them.

The door opened and the sergeant-in-charge came in.

"Good morning, sir. You wanted to see me."

It was so sharp and to the point that I felt my suspicions out of place. Was this the place to say what I was going to say? The office of a small country police-station. I stared a few moments at the healthy complexion and clear eye of the police-sergeant, wondering if he would begin to understand the almost shapeless conjectures of my mind.

"I've come to see you about this affair at the 'Scarlett Arms,'" I said at last.

"Oh, yes. We had the report in this morning. Mr. Crawshay-Martin. Killed himself last night."

"That's what it looks like," said I. "But Mr. Crawshay-Martin was a friend of mine, and I'm not at all certain he did kill himself."

The difference between the sergeant-in-charge and the constable was encouraging to what I had to say. A look of intelligent inquiry took possession of his face. He pulled out one of the varnished chairs and sat down.

"Do you wish to make a statement?" he asked.

Well—I did not exactly want to make a formal statement. To begin with, it sounded a serious undertaking. But directly I had made this clear, his interest slightly abated.

"You just want to tell us something?"

"Yes."

"But you don't want to take your oath about it?"

An oath. What was one's oath on a matter like this? I had nothing to take an oath upon. There was only what I felt in some restless corner of my brain.

"All right," he said. "Go on. Only we're rather busy this morning."

How was I to begin? Obviously with Gollancz.

"Were you at the sale yesterday?" I asked.

He said he was. On occasions like that, when there were a lot of valuables, bits of silver and so on, knocking about, they generally had a couple of men on duty. People with light fingers had a fancy for coming to those auction sales that were held out of doors.

"Then you may remember," said I, "the sale of a small bundle of books, apparently valueless, which created some interest because they went up to fifty pounds and then were knocked down to Mr. Crawshay-Martin."

He remembered the incident quite well.

"The man who was bidding against my friend for that lot was a Mr. Bannerjee. Dark-skinned man—a Eurasian, from the look of him. I know his name because he was stopping last night at the 'Scarlett Arms.'"

The sergeant even remembered Mr. Bannerjee.

"Well, Mr. Bannerjee was not bidding for himself."

"Indeed?"

"No—he was bidding for a man named—Gollancz."

There was his name. I had said it. And so strong an effect had it upon me that I looked up at the sergeant, as though I expected an immediate reaction. Of course, there was none. What was the name of Gollancz to him, any more than the name of Smith? His face was still healthy and imperturbable.

"They often do it like that," said he.

"Yes—but this man Gollancz, I must tell you," I went on, anxious now to justify my impressive use of his name, "had a particular reason for wanting one of the books in that lot."

"What reason?"

"He is a Rosicrucian."

"A what?"

"A Rosicrucian—and one of the books in that bundle was a priceless document, compiled some time in the early sixteenth century, dealing with the rites and mysteries of the Brotherhood of the Rosy Cross."

With the expression that passed across the sergeant's face, and in that little room with its distempered walls, its oil-cloth-covered table and its varnished chairs, I almost began to feel I was talking nonsense myself. In the Haymarket that day when first I had heard Gollancz was a Rosicrucian, it had seemed unbelievable enough. Here in the office of the police-station in a little one-street town in Surrey, it sounded preposterous. I might have been talking of King Arthur's Knights of the Round Table. I might have been trying to rouse his detective suspicions about Merlin.

"Brotherhood of the Rosy Cross," repeated the sergeant.

In self-defence I hastened to inform him that this Brotherhood was very like the order of the Freemasons. He had heard of the Freemasons? Oh, yes, he had heard of the Freemasons. There was a lodge in Guildford. I went on quickly but with increasing confidence to explain that they were an order practising the same kind of mysteries as—well, as the Spiritualists. He'd heard of Spiritualism?

He nodded his head.

He knew the Spiritualists claimed to be able to place themselves in communication with the other world?

He nodded his head again.

"I suppose you do believe there is another world?" I said.

Put to him like that, in the daily course of his business as a police officer, he didn't seem to know quite how to answer me.

In the privacy of his domestic life and going to church regularly with his wife every Sunday, he would undoubtedly have said he believed in another world. But to introduce these celestial affairs into his weekday life was another matter. He appeared reluctant to admit it. As though, if he did, it might make him look ridiculous.

"Supposin' you leave this out of it," said he. "We're dealin' with what happened to Mr. Crawshay-Martin up to the moment his throat was cut. I don't see what the other world's got to do with it. If it's the other world you want to talk about, I expect you'll find Mr. Hallows at home in the Vicarage."

I had guessed it was going to be as difficult as this, and yet the more I realized its difficulties, the more I felt determined to go on. Probably I was involved in that fear of being made to look ridiculous myself. There was no good in getting heated about it, but I saw no harm in just giving him a glimpse of the narrow prejudice of his mind.

"This isn't a case for your vicar," I said flatly. "If you believe in another world at all—and I suppose you do—I presume you'll admit it had its existence before Mr. Crawshay-Martin died as well as afterwards. What I'm telling you relates to it. You can take no account of it, if you like. But don't tell me I ought to have gone to the Vicarage when I'm at the police-station. My name's Hawke. I'm a doctor. I live in London. There's my card." I took the slip of pasteboard out of my letter-case and pushed it towards him across the shine of the linoleum. "If you don't want me to go on, say so, and I'll take my information elsewhere."

Anyhow, I had preserved my dignity. Which is one of the first considerations of man. He became apologetic with slight puffings of his cheeks, and said of course he was ready to hear what I had to say. So I went on.

"Well—this man Gollancz was a Rosicrucian," I repeated—a little to rub it into him. "And that book was of inconceivable value to him. Like the Freemasons, only infinitely more so, the Brotherhood of Rosicrucians is a secret order. They have rites and mysteries that go back to periods of time and civilizations of which we know very little."

I looked up into his face as I said that. It had the expression of one who has been told to prepare himself for an anæsthetic. There was a certain amount of bewildered anticipation about it. Otherwise it was entirely compounded of a kind of bovine stupidity and ignorance.

Indeed, as I looked at him, this man occupying a responsible and intelligent position, as far as the inhabitants of Shipleigh were concerned, I wondered whether, with all the advantages of education, the human mind in any general sense had advanced since the terrestrial sensitiveness of the Greeks and the celestial consciousness of the Egyptians. Exact science to the exact mind may be the highest function of the intellect. But is the exact mind necessarily higher in the scale of human progress because it appears in the latest civilization? Is mankind the end of man? Is anthropology the religion of life? Is there not just as much evidence of the promise of a spirit creature, toward which all these long paths of the many civilizations are leading? A creature infinitely more conscious than our most hopeful divines of a world beyond? An astrologer whose imagination can more nearly approach the celestial being of the stars, than this latter-day astronomer of exact science, whose mind is imprisoned in the unescapable vaults of mathematics.

It was obvious to my glance, as I considered the mind of that sergeant of police at Shipleigh, that there was little sense in my going any further on that tack. It would have been a waste of time to try and explain to him the mystic character of Gollancz as Crawshay-Martin had presented it to me that morning outside the clockmaker's shop in the Haymarket, and when I had lunched alone with my friend afterwards at his club. I might as well have tried to explain to him the Einstein theory, which it is always a relief to hear that Einstein only on lucid occasions understands himself.

And yet without it, it seemed impossible to convey what was at the very root of my mental disquietude about the death of Crawshay-Martin; namely, that in some way or other, whether by natural or supernatural means, Gollancz had been concerned in it. However, a fixed determination had brought me there, and I meant to go on with it. By some means or another I wanted the police to be persuaded to examine Gollancz, if only on suspicion.

If I could bring that about as a first move, I should be satisfied. With that fixed intention at the back of me, I tried to rouse this man's mind.

"Whether or no," I continued after that glance, "you appreciate the possible value such a volume might have in the mind of a Rosicrucian, you may take it from me that this man Gollancz wanted that book. He secured this Bannerjee to bid for him so that his interest in it should not be detected. And afterwards, when by a mere fluke he lost the purchase of it, he came up to Mr. Crawshay-Martin, who had carried the bundle of books away, and asked him to let him have a look at it. I was there with my friend at the time."

"Was this in the house or in the garden?"

It didn't seem to matter to me. However, I was pleased to see his interest was beginning to be roused.

"It was in the garden," said I. "My friend was very cut up about leaving Malquoits. I have a fancy for thinking he never intended to go into the house again."

"Did Mr. Crawshay-Martin show him the book?"

"The cover of it only. It was tied up in the middle of the bundle."

"And did he know the kind of book it was?"

"Not until that moment. It was the interest of this man Gollancz and the way he had bid for it at the sale that made him suspect."

"What happened then?"

"Mr. Crawshay-Martin took the whole bundle down with him to the 'Scarlett Arms,' where we were both staying. I remained in the garden. The sale was still going on. The auctioneer had come to the furniture, and there was a piece—a Queen Anne knee-hole desk—I wanted to buy."

"When did you see Mr. Crawshay-Martin again?"

"He came back later to the sale, and then I noticed something—well—peculiar about him."

"What?"

I hesitated.

"He gave me the impression," I said, "of a man who feels he's being followed."

The hopelessness of that suggestion was apparent directly I'd said it. His immediate question was:

"Did you see anyone? Behaving suspiciously?"

"Not anyone actually," said I. "The impression was in his mind, at the back of his eyes, rather than in anything he did."

The sergeant made a screwed-up grimace of his mouth. Only that I had given him my card and made a show of being somebody of substance, I believe he would have ended the interview then and there. As it was, in a tone of voice whose interest I felt to be in jeopardy, he said:

"I don't see as how we can take any notice of that. You didn't see anyone following?"

"No."

"Well—what then?"

With a desperate effort to make myself convincing, and to rouse in him the same disquietude as was in my own mind, I told him as briefly as I could the story that Crawshay-Martin had told me in his club. The story of what happened in Rennet's rooms that night in Oxford, nearly fifty years ago. A few moments before, I had decided it would be no good. Now, in self-defence, I was giving it.

I did my best to picture to him those young undergraduates in Rennet's rooms in Corpus College. Crawshay-Martin a young student. Gollancz one of them, sitting at the edge of the circle listening, while McEvoy, the firebrand of their debating society, was holding forth on the possibilities of a personality of evil. I remembered and repeated Crawshay-Martin's account of what McEvoy had said:

"Most religions," he had shouted with his revivalist voice, "have their conception of a personal God. It is in human nature for us to personify, for means of recognition, those forces which influence and control our actions. Well—evil is a force. Look at War!"

I have no doubt the sergeant of Shipleigh police-station thought he was dealing with a lunatic. His eye by this time had that half wary, half apprehensive look with which I am sure one must regard the inmate of an asylum. But I had plunged and could not draw back. I knew I was swimming dead against the current of his intelligence. But once in the stream, I had to go on.

That was the kind of talk, I informed him, that was going on that evening in Rennet's rooms between those scatterbrained undergraduates, when suddenly Gollancz had said:

"Would any one of you have the courage to see the devil if you could?"

And McEvoy had taken up the challenge. At Gollancz's suggestion, having informed them he could not do these things for the multitude, the young firebrand had gone off with him to the seclusion of Gollancz's rooms. The others had remained with Rennet and waited. And then, from the silence of those empty passages outside, had come the inhuman cry of McEvoy's voice. With hurried glances at each other, they had sat listening to the clatter of McEvoy's feet as they tumbled down the wooden stairs. Looking out of the window into the quadrangle, they had seen him with his long, spidery legs, tearing, galloping round the grass square, a demoniacal figure with his wits gone.

"Mad," I concluded—just as Crawshay-Martin had told it me. "Shouting mad."

It is difficult to describe the effect of that story in the clean, distempered atmosphere of that little room. It sounded both preposterous and convincing. I could see at once the sergeant didn't believe a word of it. And yet in the back of his mind he was struggling with an irresistible feeling of mental discomfort. There was a silly sort of grin on his face—the sort of look you would have expected him to wear had he suddenly been told that the Christ he believed to have the power of rising from the dead, was waiting to see him in the next room. With that grin, he said:

"Well—had he seen the Devil?"

"Is that the real question at issue?" I asked. "He was mad. Isn't that sufficient? He was put away in an asylum. That was a fact. What he said about what he'd seen can scarcely be taken seriously. Even the information Gollancz gave to the council at the inquiry that was held, that the devil had materialized, wasn't accepted. Of course not. Even fifty years ago, exact science wasn't to be disturbed from its facts as easily as that. But one fact remained—didn't it? That young man McEvoy was mad."

"And what," asked the sergeant with a stubborn effort, "has all this to do with the death of Mr. Crawshay-Martin?"

It seemed hopeless. And yet now, having got the impetus, I struggled on.

"That happened," said I, "about 1875. Three years ago, 1927, I was talking to my friend, Mr. Crawshay-Martin, in the Haymarket. You know the street in London?"

He nodded his head.

"We were looking in a shop window when a man, dressed in a peculiar black cape, with a faded black Mexican sombrero hat, came up and stood looking into the window beside us. I don't know why I mention his appearance, except it was the first thing that arrested my attention. That cape and the faded black sombrero hat. Not the sort of costume one associates with broad daylight in the Haymarket. Rather a night effect, if you know what I mean, and scarcely English at that. Anyhow, Mr. Crawshay-Martin thought he recognized him. He was a young man—about twenty-five. My friend thought from the likeness he must be a son of that same Gollancz with whom he had been at the 'Varsity. He spoke to him. I overheard the conversation. You must accept this how you wish. He was not a son of that Gollancz. It was Gollancz himself. Unchanged from the time he was at college. There was not a year's difference in his appearance."

"Queer, that—wasn't it?" said the sergeant.

"You mean you don't believe it?"

"Well, it isn't believable—is it?"

"But I saw him with my own eyes."

"Yes—but you hadn't seen him those years before."

That was a fair retaliation. I couldn't complain of it. All I could do, as I did, was to ask him if he considered that Crawshay-Martin had a fantastic mind.

"No," he replied. "Mr. Crawshay-Martin, whenever I met him, seemed to me a nice, sensible-spoken gentleman."

"Then just as it is," said I, "you can take that story as coming from him. Gollancz had told my friend, while they were at college, that he was a Rosicrucian. One of the claims of the Rosicrucian Brotherhood is that they have the secret of perpetual youth."

But that was more than he could swallow. Of course, I knew

it would be. A sergeant of police in this year of grace 1930, in a little Surrey town, being asked to accept the mystic principles of the Philosopher's Stone! But there at the back of it was the death of Crawshay-Martin, found with his throat cut in his bedroom at the "Scarlett Arms." That must have been just the one thread that held us together. I was suggesting there was something queer about it, and no matter what I said, the fact was there, still with us. Crawshay-Martin was dead. I could see the sergeant's mind struggling with the impossibilities of this story I had told him. At last he said:

"What is it you want to suggest? That this man Gollancz had something to do with what happened last night?"

"Yes."

"But he wasn't there. You told me yourself he went up to London last evening."

"I know that. But is it impossible for you to believe in the power of a man like that being able to operate without his actual presence? You're overlooking the fact that I heard Crawshay-Martin's voice, as though he were speaking to someone. And you forget the book—the book that he wanted. When we broke down that door and went into the room last night, there were books from one of his trunks strewn all over the floor. But that book—was gone."

For a moment or two he looked me straight in the eyes, as though at last I had stirred in him some kind of unrest.

"Is that Mr. Bannerjee still at the inn?" he asked.

"He was when I left. I believe he was going up by a midday train."

The sergeant looked at his watch. It was not quite eleven. He stood up sharply from his chair.

"I haven't properly grasped what you've been telling me," he said. "I'm not educated in those kind of things. But if this Mr. Bannerjee had anything to do with Mr. Gollancz, there's no harm in my goin' over with you to Bedinghurst and puttin' him a few questions."

Well, my persistence had achieved something. If I had done no more, I had roused his curiosity. At my suggestion we got a taxi from the nearest garage and drove into Bedinghurst.

It was a glorious day. Just as it had been at the sale, in the old garden of Malquoits, the day before. Hard to believe as we passed the gates of the house and I glanced down the drive between the avenue of maples, that my friend who had walked with me there a few hours before was dead.

Signs of the auction that had taken place were still in evidence. Carriers' carts were collecting the larger pieces of furniture that had not been removed at once. The gravel had been cut into rails with the motor-cars and vehicles that had passed in and out. Malquoits was sold to one of the new rich gentlemen who had grown into money. After three centuries it had passed out of the hands of the Crawshay-Martins. There were, so far as I knew, none of the family left, except for a man named Weaver, his sister's child. On the few occasions I had met Crawshay-Martin, he had sometimes spoken of him.

The tragic element of this finality possessed me as we passed the house. An old Brittany armoire that had stood in the hall was coming down the drive on a local carrier's van. I had seen it so many times. Its departure from that house seemed in that moment as eloquent to me of the end of things as the sudden death of Crawshay-Martin himself. And yet it was but being removed. It was setting out for its journey to another life in another household.

The sergeant had fallen into an abstraction since we had got into the car. We had said nothing. I didn't feel inclined to talk myself. The effort of convincing him that there was something strange in the death of my friend, even if I had not succeeded in persuading him of the occult character of Gollancz the Rosicrucian, had left me uncommunicative.

As a matter of fact, there was not a word that passed between us from Shipleigh into Bedinghurst. Then, as we drew up at the door of the "Scarlett Arms," he said:

"Bannerjee—was that the name?"

I nodded my head, and we walked into the hall. There, in the very entrance, I stopped.

The antlers of a stag—surely not suggesting that it had been shot on the Surrey hills—were hanging on the wall just inside the door. It was used by victors as a hat-and-coat rack. I believe the proprietor was rather proud of it.

It was before this I stopped and stared. The sergeant had stopped as well.

"Look," I said. "Look!"

For there, on one of the points, was hanging a faded, black, Mexican, sombrero hat.

CHAPTER II

He looked first at the hat and afterwards, with a blank expression of inquiry, at me.

It was obvious how little of my story of Gollancz he had assimilated. There was the actual hat I had described to him. The hat I had first seen three years before, that day in the Haymarket. The very same hat that had suddenly startled my attention in the garden at Malquoits, less than twenty-four hours before, as I caught a glimpse of it in the crowd of people round the auctioneer's table.

"Don't you remember!" I exclaimed. "I told you. How he was dressed. Gollancz. When I first met him. A faded, black, sombrero hat."

He snatched at this fact from a slender memory. At least it was something substantial. For a moment his eyes sparkled with material intelligence, as though it were a clue. Then it clouded with confusion.

"But I thought you said he was in London last night."

"So he was. At least, Mr. Sankey told me he understood he'd gone back by an evening train. I certainly never saw him in the hotel. But whether he did or he didn't, there's his hat. He's come back again. The very next morning."

For a moment or two the sergeant stood regarding that faded black object, as though, if he looked at it long enough, it might of its own accord reveal some explanation of its presence there. Presently he returned his glance to mine.

"He's here in the hotel?"

"Obviously." I was inclined to get impatient. "There aren't two men wearing a hat like that. Not in Bedinghurst."

"What do you make of it, then?"

He was certainly impressed, but so far as it had gone the whole thing was much too abstruse for the limitations of his exact intelligence. He was looking to me to clear the ground a little before he put his foot down.

Still, I didn't mind that. He was roused. And the fact of that hat being there at all was quite enough to distract my mind from any close observation of the sergeant's psychology.

"There've been two or three trains in from town," said I. "He could easily have come down by one of those. But why? Has he heard that Crawshay-Martin is dead? If he has, then who's told him? It isn't in the papers yet. Reporters are here. I've seen them. But they're only just collecting the story. How did he know?"

This was going much too fast for the sergeant. My mind was already calculating possibilities outside the region of his particular mentality. At the police-station in Shipleigh, I had asked him whether it were impossible for him to believe in the power of a man being able to operate without his actual presence. I hadn't gone further and given it a name. I hadn't called it telepathy, thought-transference, or tried to explain to him the occult belief in the astral body. The expression on his face had been quite sufficient when I said that. His mind was only capable of dealing with exact facts. He had fastened on to the disappearance of that book. And now I could see he was concerned with the presence of the sombrero hat. That it would be possible for Gollancz in London without definite communication to be made aware of what had happened that night in Bedinghurst was never for a moment in the province of his thoughts.

I knew just what he was thinking. There was sufficient evidence that Gollancz wanted that book. And the book had gone. The owner of it had been found with his throat cut. Yet Gollancz himself had been thirty miles away. With this alibi the sergeant was quite satisfied that Gollancz had not murdered Crawshay-Martin. Nevertheless, the book had gone. By a process of reiteration, I had forced him to acknowledge the importance of that fact and the light it cast upon the suggestion of my friend's suicide. And now he was certainly intrigued by the idea that so soon after the death of Crawshay-Martin, Gollancz had returned to the "Scarlett Arms."

"Then I suppose he's about the place," he said; "and if he is, we'd better go and find him. I should like to ask him one or two questions."

As far as that went, I was satisfied. I wanted no more than that. Just that they should question Gollancz. I was determined he should not merely be lost sight of in this matter without giving some explanation of his movements.

"Do you want me to come with you?" I asked.

"Don't see any harm," said he. "You know about the book. He knows you know. Didn't you say you were with Mr. Crawshay-Martin when he came up and spoke in the garden?"

"Oh, yes. I heard the whole conversation."

"Did he let this man Gollancz see the book?"

"He let him take the bundle in which it was included. But they were all still tied up with string. About half a dozen books in all."

"So that you can't say he knew it was there?"

"Not exactly. But he drew Crawshay-Martin's attention to it. There was one volume, he remarked, which had no title on the cover. And that proved to be it."

"And Mr. Crawshay-Martin knew?"

"Not definitely at that moment. He told me he had his suspicions as soon as he had heard that Gollancz was bidding."

"Mr. Crawshay-Martin wasn't bidding for the book himself, then?"

"Oh, no. There was another volume in the lot which he particularly valued. He wanted to buy that in. It was only when the bidding had gone over twenty pounds, and I told him I had seen Gollancz in the crowd, that he began to be suspicious. Later, in the garden, after Gollancz had gone, he undid the string and examined the volume with no title on the cover. There it was. A manual. In Latin. The Rosicrucian mysteries. Setting out all the rites and practices of the Brotherhood of the Rosy Cross."

"And that was worth more than twenty pounds?" inquired the sergeant.

I looked at him helplessly. It was obvious he was still labouring with the calculation of exact fact. Had I told him the book was worth a thousand pounds, he might have been satisfied there was a *prima facie* case for murder. The intrinsic value of the book to a

Brother of the Rosy Cross was beyond him. As much beyond him as were all those vague conjectures that had disturbed my mind from the moment when I had wakened up the night before to the sound of my friend's voice in the room next to mine.

"Oh, let's come along and see if we can find this fella," I said impatiently. "See him for yourself, and then perhaps you'll get some idea of whether a monetary value would mean anything to him."

It was not yet midday. The bar, of course, was closed at that time of the morning. Mr. Sankey was not anywhere to be seen. A tabby cat sat on the bar counter near the beer handles, washing her paws. Except for this occupant and a little maid-of-all-work, brushing the stair carpet, the house appeared to be empty. Not a pleasant or peaceful emptiness. There was an air of unrest about it. One felt conscious of oppression in the place. It was a bright day, but the blinds had been drawn in all the rooms. And when the sergeant inquired of the maid where Mr. or Mrs. Sankey was, she said she didn't know. In a whisper, as though the dead might hear her.

"Has there been a visitor to the hotel this morning?" I asked.

"Yes, sir."

"The gentleman whose hat is hanging up in the hall?"

"That big black hat."

So she had noticed it.

"That's the one."

"Yes, sir."

"Where is he now?"

"He's out in the garden, sir."

We made our way through a kind of small back sitting-room with a French window leading into the garden. Down in that part of the world, the country inns are proud of their gardens. The "Scarlett Arms" was no exception. There was a nicely-kept lawn with flower-beds surrounded by a high yew hedge. Circular, painted, iron tables dotted about the lawn for open-air teas did not improve its appearance. They gave it a public air. But one had to expect that.

No one was there. The garden was empty.

But through a cutting in the yew hedge there was still a further part of the garden beyond. The bowling green. Except for the bowling-club members and people actually staying in the hotel, this was private. A notice attached to the yew arch over the entrance informed the mere visitor for tea that it was not for him.

We crossed the garden to the cutting in the yew hedge. Beyond it the rink of Cumberland turf, over a hundred years old, spread like a baize-covered table down to a long, thatched arbour at the other end. This was used as a club house. Members had lockers there where they kept their woods. The whole green was surrounded by a high hedge. In contrast with the other part of the garden, it had the very air of privacy. And there, seated on a low form intended for players at the other end of the green, were the figures of two men, as incongruous in that peaceful English scene as it is possible to conceive.

One was the Eurasian gentleman, Mr. Bannerjee, who had bid for that lot of books at the auction. The other was Gollancz, whom I had seen on those two occasions. In the Haymarket three years before. And for those few moments in the garden at Malquoits.

I snatched a glance at the sergeant, and I think that even his unimpressionable mind was stirred by the irrelevance of their appearance to their surroundings.

Mr. Bannerjee was possibly a figure with which one has become acquainted in these days of cosmopolitan education. His sallow, æsthetic features are to be seen in the neighbourhood of Gower Street where there is a college and hostelries for the Asiatic imbibing Western civilization. He is to be found, sitting round chilly coal fires "supplemented" with coke, in Bloomsbury boarding-houses. He appears at small tennis clubs in St. John's Wood in white flannels, looking as English as it is possible for an Oriental to look.

Seated on that form at the end of the bowling green, the figure of Mr. Bannerjee certainly did not look in keeping with the place, but it was nothing to the impression of incongruity one received of that other—of Gollancz.

He was still wearing that peculiar kind of evening cloak, which would have given any other man a sort of *opera bouffe* appearance. Yet the suggestion about him was anything rather than fantastic. There was nothing carnival or festive about him. This was the first time I had seen him without his hat, and the high intellectuality of his forehead was remarkable, even down the length of that bowling green. It rose from the straight eyebrows like a dome built upon the deep, arched sockets of his eyes.

His dark hair was not long, but it was thick, and clustered at the nape of his neck. And it was not, as one first saw him, that he was not English. Not (as with Mr. Bannerjee, who belonged to another place) that he belonged to another time. It was as though, when one looked at that long, impenetrable face, one felt that these dimensions were immaterial to him. He might be sitting by an old English bowling green in the garden of an English country inn, but it was not the haphazard of chance that brought him there. His surroundings became translated to the needs of his personality. It was not the bowling green that made him look ridiculous. It was he who made the bowling green appear absurd.

We had stopped for a moment at that cutting in the yew hedge to take stock of them. At that distance they had not heard our approach. Mr. Bannerjee was talking excitedly, but failing to rouse the imperturbable attention of Gollancz to anything more than an occasional inclination of the head.

I had that feeling then—one does sometimes when the occasion warrants it—of the mysteriousness of people's conversations one cannot hear. Some people one watches talking, and from the most casual observation of their gestures, their facial expression and general personality, it is possible almost to repeat the things they say. But with these two no mind could have imagined what they were saying. I did not conceive it to be the death of Crawshay-Martin. I could even believe that that was trivial to them. If only we could have approached from behind the high hedge and listened.

"That's the one, is it?" said the sergeant. "The one without a hat."

Of course it was the one without a hat! Hadn't he seen the black sombrero hanging up on those antlers in the hall! I felt it was well-nigh hopeless. An intelligence like this matched against the mind that operated behind that lofty forehead.

We began to move in their direction. I was just stepping on to the bowling green. The direct line of approach. But the sergeant caught me peremptorily by the arm.

"You can't walk on the green with your heels," he said.

So it was still a bowling green to him. The presence of that man there, who more than ever I felt in some way to be associated with the death of Crawshay-Martin, had not made it absurd in his mind. He was probably thinking of the match that Shipleigh was to play there against Bedinghurst that summer. I followed him down the cinder path at the side.

At the sound of our feet on the cinders they both looked up. I fancied I saw a look of perturbation in the face of Mr. Bannerjee. I was not sure. But as far as Gollancz was concerned, the sight of a sergeant of police disturbing his peaceful occupation of that garden might have been the very thing he expected.

"You gentlemen will excuse me interrupting your conversation," said the sergeant amiably as he reached the form where they were sitting; "but we're concerned here with this death of Mr. Crawshay-Martin."

Gollancz nodded his head, and then turned his eyes, without recognition, upon me. Why I say without recognition, I don't exactly know. That was their expression, and yet, with an inner perception, I felt him to be associating my presence there, not only with our meeting in the garden the day before, but as far back as that morning in the Haymarket three years ago.

"There were some books," continued the sergeant in a tone of voice as though he were talking about a batch of modern novels, "which Mr. Crawshay-Martin bought in at the sale yesterday. They were found scattered over the floor when the police arrived early this morning. But one amongst them was missing. I've brought this gentleman along with me because he happens to know something about the book in question, and he tells me you were bidding for this lot at the sale."

"I was bidding," said Mr. Bannerjee.

"Yes—but wasn't this other gentleman associated with you? You were bidding for him—weren't you?"

A smile gleamed in Gollancz's face. I can only describe it in that way. It was more like a light thrown by some ray upon his countenance than an actual parting of the lips or a showing of the teeth.

"This gentleman," he said quietly, and I confess to hearing a note of decided beauty in his voice, "was bidding for me. Unfortunately through some mistake he lost the purchase. It was knocked down to Mr. Crawshay-Martin. Hearing of his sudden death, I came down this morning to see whether there were any possibility of acquiring the book I wanted. In view of his unfortunate——"

He spread out his hands. It was as though, partly because of the unpleasant sound of redundancy, and partly out of respect for the deceased, he did not wish to repeat that word—death.

"Yes—but how did you hear?" asked the sergeant. "It only happened at two o'clock this morning. Even the papers haven't got hold of it yet."

"Oh—that is quite simple," said Gollancz gently. He might have been endeavouring to allay the worries of a child or a nervous old woman. "My friend Mr. Bannerjee was speaking to me on the telephone this morning just before breakfast. He told me. You will confirm that, of course, by inquiries at the telephone office in the village."

Why should we confirm it? I asked myself that as I stood silently at the sergeant's side. Did he know already what was in our minds? At least, in mine? If Crawshay-Martin had died by his own hand, where was the necessity for this confirmation?

"And you haven't found the book?" I said.

He looked up at me as though he was conscious of my presence for the first time.

"Is this gentleman an inspector of police in plain clothes?" he inquired quietly.

"I'm a doctor," said I, before the sergeant could explain. "Dr. Hawke. Mr. Crawshay-Martin was a friend of mine. I was with him yesterday at the auction. Possibly you don't remember my sitting with him in the garden after the purchase of that lot in which the book was included."

"Oh, yes, I remember," he said pleasantly. "We met before, too, on another occasion, in the Haymarket. Three years ago. Mr. Crawshay-Martin did not introduce us. Still, it was an encounter."

Peculiar choice of phrase that. An encounter. As though he had realized in that chance meeting the predestination of this conflict, this clash, which was now in me a conscious state of mind. Encounter. And yet his tone of voice in the use of that word had been as far from expression as was possible. He had looked up at me pleasantly, but with the deep regard of his eyes as he said it. I knew that never for one moment had he thought I was an inspector of police.

However, I did not feel my mind deflected in any way by this calm admission of his recollection. Why should he hesitate to admit that?

"I was staying at the 'Scarlett Arms' last night," I continued. "My friend's room was next to mine. I heard the sound of his voice as though in conversation with someone just before he died. It was at the sound of something he said that I tried the door. It was locked. Mr. Sankey, the hotel proprietor, came, and between us we burst open the door. But it was too late. By that time Crawshay-Martin was dead. His throat was cut."

I was closely watching him all the time I was saying this. The expression of his face had never changed from that of mere attention. And when I had finished, instead of making some oblique remark, as, for example, how distressing it all was, he said:

"And who had he been conversing with?"

For a moment the calm frankness of this question disarmed me. It was the sergeant who to a plain inquiry gave a plain reply.

"Oh—there was no one there," said he. "It's fairly clear that in a moment of temporary insanity he was talking to himself just before he committed suicide. Still, that book has disappeared, and that is what we can't quite make out."

I waited a moment to see how Gollancz was going to answer that. Whether, not being an actual question, he was going to ignore it altogether. But ignoring even the most delicately implied suggestions was not apparently a process of his mind.

"Do you mean it's lost?" he asked.

"It can't be found," said I.

"Then that seems to me to make my journey down here rather a waste of time," he replied.

"Might I ask," the sergeant interposed clumsily at this point, "what you consider that book to be worth?"

Gollancz looked up at him. This time he was actually smiling.

"Do you mean in money?"

"Yes."

"To a bibliophile?"

The expression of suppressed ignorance on the sergeant's face was comical. For one moment Gollancz enjoyed it. It was too profound to waste any time pitying it. With an almost generous consideration, he helped him out.

"You mean to a collector, like Pierpont Morgan?"

"Yes. That's what I mean."

"Oh—it might be worth twenty thousand, fifty thousand pounds, or it might not be worth more than ten, as a mere antiquity."

The sound of these prodigious sums obviously impressed the sergeant. He was also none the less impressed by the casual way in which Gollancz had admitted them. If he had ever had any suspicions about Gollancz from my statements in the Shipleigh police station, they were almost entirely allayed by now. Gollancz had offered an alibi and it was easy enough to prove it. Now his frank admission of the value of that book had almost removed all grounds of suspicion in the sergeant's mind.

I could see what he was thinking. If, as seemed likely, the book had completely disappeared, then there undoubtedly was a case of theft somewhere. I saw a glance of his eye at Mr. Bannerjee, and for a moment even my own thoughts wavered from their convictions. Had Crawshay-Martin indeed only committed suicide? And had this Eurasian stolen the book in that interim between the discovery of my friend's death and the fact of the missing volume?

But if that were so, why were they still there? Why were they sitting quietly in that garden when by all computation of the reasonable acts of human nature, they should have been off and away with their spoil?

"There's just one other question," said the sergeant. "If you don't mind."

"As many as you like," replied Gollancz.

"Then can you tell me what this book was, that might have been worth ten pounds, or might have been worth fifty thousand?"

And this, as far as I was concerned, was the first intelligent question the sergeant had put. I watched Gollancz's face closely before he replied. It was inscrutable, but its very inscrutability was arresting. The actual absence of emotion in the lustre of his pale eyes, suggested such supreme control as that any emotion there might have been was upon a plane beyond my comprehension. His face could almost have been an instrument recording sounds which the human tympanum is incapable of registering to the brain, or which, as is just as likely, the fallow faculties of the brain are incapable of receiving. It was impossible to say what he was feeling. And yet I had a distinct impression he was feeling deeply.

Nevertheless, his voice conveyed nothing when he replied:

"I don't fancy a description of the book would help you. To tell you that it was a manuscript written in the middle of the sixteenth century will justify my contention that it was worth at least ten pounds. Any manuscript of that age is worth something as a curiosity. That it was an unknown manuscript by Simon Studion, the author of the known '*Fama Fraternitatis Rosea Cruce*,' will mean nothing to you. That it expounded principles of the Chemical Nuptials, the inter-reaction between the base chemicals of the earth and the more refined chemicals of the body, as they concern the mystical spirit of man, will mean still less. In fact, that it was a work only to be understood by alchemists, will show you that its value is not computable in terms of pounds, shillings and pence. I have said fifty thousand pounds because I thought you would appreciate that. And I mentioned Mr. Pierpont Morgan because I fancied you would recognize his name as a collector. Probably Mr. Pierpont Morgan would not give two pence for the book. And I think, from his point of view, he would be quite right."

Having delivered himself of all this, he smiled distantly at the sergeant and added:

"Is there anything more I can tell you?"

And to that the sergeant, who by this time was a little confused, replied:

"No—thank you very much. Good morning."

And then we left them.

I must confess myself I would like to have stayed. There were many other questions I should have liked to put to him. But I was quite conscious of the fact that between himself and me he had raised an impenetrable and resistant screen. Whether because I was Crawshay-Martin's friend, or because I was a man of science, I can't say. I could only feel the antagonistic barrier. He would answer the sergeant any question that simple-minded creature would have liked to put to him, as, out of compassion, one might feed a bird in a cage. He would have said nothing to me had I stayed.

Accordingly when the sergeant walked away, I went with him. We left those two still sitting in the incongruous sunlight at the end of that bowling green. It was incongruous! The more I saw of Gollancz, the less I could associate him with the bright air of daylight.

Once we had passed through the cutting in the yew hedge, I said:

"You're going to verify that statement, I suppose?"

"What statement?"

"About the telephone message this morning?"

"I will," said he, "if you think it worth while. I'm going past the telephone exchange. You can come, if you like. But I have no doubt it was true. A peculiar looking gentleman, I'll admit. But you can't deny he was pleasant spoken. If anyone's been stealing that book, I shouldn't be surprised to find it was the other dark-skinned one."

I smiled to myself at this exhibition of racial prejudice. It was no good saying anything. We went through the village to the telephone exchange. This was quite primitive. It was in a private house. A Mr. Nugent had been engaged by the post office authorities. The call office and switchboard were in his front sitting-room. His daughter assisted him in the work of operator. She was at work at the switches when we went in.

"Did you take a call early this morning, about half-past seven, from a visitor at the 'Scarlett Arms,' a Mr. Bannerjee?"

"I took a call for him, not from him."

"Where did it come from?"

"London."

"What name was it?"

"Gollantz, or something like that."

The sergeant looked at me with a smile. He might have been telling me that he knew his job better than I did. But I wasn't concerned with his satisfaction.

"Do you hear the conversations that take place?" I asked.

She simpered.

"Sometimes. When there's not too much work going on."

"Did you hear this one?"

"Bit of it."

"What did they say?"

"Couldn't tell you. It was in a funny language. I didn't understand a word of it."

"Thank you," I said, and we went out again.

In the road I stopped in front of the sergeant and looked straight up at him.

"In a foreign language," I repeated. "And does it strike you as at all peculiar that Gollancz rang up Mr. Bannerjee and not the other way about?"

"What's peculiar about that?" he asked.

"How did Gollancz know?" I said.

A butcher's cart sped by in a cloud of dust. He shrugged his shoulders and turned away from me.

"You'd better say all this at the inquest," said he.

CHAPTER III

The whole trend of my mind was to receive a considerable set back when I returned to the "Scarlett Arms" that morning for lunch. Mr. Sankey, the proprietor, was standing on the doorstep, waiting to see me as I came up.

"Can you spare a moment?" he said.

I hung up my hat on a point of the antlers and followed him to his private sitting-room.

"A little short drink?" he suggested. "Sherry?"

I told him he would have a sherry with me. I make no criticism of his character when I suppose he had considered that possibility. Anyhow, he did not stop to argue the matter. Opening a glazed hatchway that communicated with the bar, I heard him say: "Two sherries, miss. For Dr. Hawke."

After all, why not? Some ways of doing business are more pleasant than others.

He waited there until the two glasses were placed on the sill. Then, closing the hatchway door, he brought them across to the table and sat down.

"Yours," he said, lifting his glass.

Sipping mine, I nodded my head and waited. He wiped the bottom of his glass and put it down.

"Did you ever hear Mr. Crawshay-Martin talk of a nephew of his? A Mr. Claude Weaver?" he began.

"Occasionally. Yes, often."

"He's coming here. He's written for a double room. With his wife, I suppose."

"Has he heard?"

I admit I put this question in some surprise.

"No. That's just the point. Apparently he's made a mistake about the date of the sale. He thinks it's to-morrow. And he wants to be present. So he's written for a double room, and says he'll be here by the one-thirty."

"Where does he write from?"

"An address in Hampshire."

"Then there's not the faintest chance to let him know. He'd have to come up to London and would have started long before this. Well—you can't do anything. You must just wait until he arrives and then tell him—what's happened."

"Yes—awkward—unpleasant—isn't it?"

"I don't fancy it will be actually unpleasant," I said. "A bit of a shock, of course. But I don't imagine there was any love lost between nephew and uncle. It was not like my friend to give expression to his feelings, but I've noticed a tone of contempt in his voice whenever he spoke of Claude Weaver. Mrs. Weaver, his sister, married a man, I believe, whom Mr. Crawshay-Martin strongly disapproved of. Of course, that's more than thirty years ago. He's dead now. Mrs. Weaver is a widow. But this man is the offspring, and apparently takes after his father. My friend never saw him more than he could help. No doubt that's why he suggests staying here at the inn. He'd know his uncle wouldn't care to put him up."

"Ah, well, then that's not so bad as I thought," said Mr. Sankey, and he drained off his glass of quite excellent sherry. "But that's not all. You started talking—you know, this morning, in the bedroom, after we'd burst open the door—about a book that was missing."

I was just about to raise my glass. I put it down. It must have intimated to him that I knew what he was talking about, because he went straight on.

"There's a loose floor-board in that room," he continued, "near the fire-place. It's gone a bit rotten at the edge. Wants a new board in. There's no proper holding for a nail. I was up there when they were moving the body away to the mortuary, and somehow my eye caught sight of that board. I can never remember about it. You know. One of those little things you're always remembering just at awkward moments when you can't attend to them. I could see then how loose it was. They were carrying the body downstairs, I stayed behind to have a look at it. I pulled it up. Intending to leave it like that, you see, so that I shouldn't forget it again. It was a short board. Didn't even reach the carpet. It was all loose. I only had to lift it out. As I did so, I thought I saw something between the joists underneath. Almost tucked away out of sight under the floor boards it was. Just a sharp corner of it catching the light."

He stopped there, and walked across to a desk the other side of the room. I could only sit, without speaking, and watch his movements. From a drawer of the desk, he produced a book and brought it back to me, putting it in my hand.

"This was what it was," he said. "A book."

I knew before I had opened the untitled cover of heavy, dark red morocco. I recognized it. And when I turned to the first page, there it was, in old, handwritten characters, the ink of which, on the parchment-like paper, was faded to a faint vandyke brown.

"*De Philosophia Harmonico-Magica Fratrium Roseæ Crucis.*" To which was also attached the name of Simon Studion. There was no date.

Turning over the fragile pages, there were to be found extraordinary illuminations executed evidently by the hand of the writer. What in a modern volume we should call illustrations now. But no telling what they meant. One was an elaborate drawing of the Apocalyptic Lamb. Another described itself as *Tabula Smaragdina Hermetis*. Still another, a mystic circle of flames, centred to the form of a rose, in the midst of the stamens of which was a cross. To this were attached the words—*Rosa Caeli*. All these were cabalistic signs. And in front of the volume, on a page by itself, was a coloured illumination in faded golds and glaring blues and reds of the Rosy Cross.

I looked up from these antiquated pages at the attentive but bewildered expression of Mr. Sankey, the proprietor of the "Scarlett Arms." And just for a moment I could not avoid a sudden perception of the miraculous quality of life.

There was this book in my hand by Simon Studion. Obviously an alchemist. One of the masters, perhaps, of magic of the Middle Ages, before men turned their gaze from the dust of stars to sift the dust of the earth in their search for the mysteries of life. Which were right? Exact science had driven away the occult practices of the ancients and locked them up in the dark vaults of superstition. But did all that knowledge, accumulated and then destroyed in the vast library of Alexandria, mean nothing?

Here was a volume that had escaped destruction at the hands of modern science. What sort of a man was the man who wrote it? What a chain of adventures it must have forged, since first in that dim past of the Middle Ages it had lain under his hand while with an infinite patience he had drawn those now-faded characters on the then virgin page!

And there it was, after all those three or four hundred years, lying in my hand in the proprietor's sitting-room of the "Scarlett Arms" in the year 1930. And we had no more knowledge of its history than that it had been in the library of Crawshay-Martin's father and now, after passing through a modern auction sale, had been lost and discovered again under the boards of the room in which my friend had been found that morning with his throat cut.

I say that just for the moment I could not avoid a sudden perception of the miraculous quality of life. It was barely for a moment. An instant later it had given way to the realization that all my suspicions of Gollancz had fallen to pieces. The Shipleigh sergeant could laugh at me now. The book had not been stolen.

But even as that consideration took hold of my mind, I became conscious of another.

Why had Crawshay-Martin, just before his self-inflicted death, behaved so extraordinarily as to hide this book under the boards of his room? Who was he hiding it from? What did he hope to gain by its concealment? And there my mind was confronted by the inevitable answer. The answer which the exact science of the law would provide at once. Crawshay-Martin was temporarily insane. He had no rational motive for his actions.

All of this having passed through my mind in the space of a few moments, I closed the volume and looked up at Mr. Sankey.

"Yes, this is the book all right," I said. "What are you going to do with it?"

"I suppose," said he, "I ought to give it to this Mr. Claude Weaver when he comes."

"Then you'd better get a receipt for it," said I. "I've never met Mr. Claude Weaver, but I'm not disposed to a high opinion of him from all Mr. Crawshay-Martin told me. Of course, I suppose whatever property my friend has left will go to his sister, who's the next-of-kin. Unless he's left a will to the contrary. All the same, I'd get an acknowledgment, if I were you. Because obviously that book is of some value."

I told him the story then that Crawshay-Martin had told me. How in one of the vacations down from Corpus when he was a student, he had taken this same volume out of his father's library and had commenced translating it for a holiday task. And how his father, finding him at it, had snatched the book away with unexplainable anger.

"Mr. Crawshay-Martin," I concluded, "had never seen the book from that day till the moment when he discovered it in a lot put up in the auction yesterday. There's evidently some interest or value attached to it. You'd better get an acknowledgement."

Concerning my suspicions about Gollancz, I told him nothing. Probably because by this time I felt a bit of a fool. It seemed quite sufficient to me that I had to humble myself by confession to the Shipleigh sergeant. Therefore I let him put the book back again in his desk, contenting myself with his promise to get an acknowledgement from Mr. Claude Weaver when he handed it over.

"And now," said I, "can you tell me what that gentleman, Mr. Gollancz, wants down here? He was at the sale yesterday."

"He's come down," replied Mr. Sankey, "apparently to see his friend, that coloured gentleman. They're staying the night. He wanted me to give him Mr. Crawshay-Martin's room. Of course, I couldn't do that. Matter of fact, when he asked, the body was still up there. They hadn't removed it to the mortuary."

"Asked you to give him Mr. Crawshay-Martin's room?" I repeated.

"Yes. Described it. The big panelled room."

I cannot explain the effect this had upon my mind. Irresistibly, though without any justification for it, the whole force of my suspicions, tidal, like a wave, came back over me.

"How did he know what the room was like?"

"Well, as a matter of fact, we advertize that oak-panelled room. There's some linen-fold carving, you know. Probably you didn't notice it. But it's considered rather unique."

"All the same," I exclaimed; "asking for that room when he knew Mr. Crawshay-Martin was dead in it. Dead, with his throat cut."

"Oh, he didn't know at the time. Not till I explained my reasons for refusing."

"But he did know!" said I emphatically. "He'd been on the telephone to his friend, Mr. Bannerjee. Mr. Bannerjee had told him. I heard him say so. Just now. Out in the garden."

"Well—he didn't say nothing to me," persisted Mr. Sankey. "But he quite understood when I explained."

"That satisfied him?"

"Oh, yes."

"He's not having the room?"

"No."

I finished my glass of sherry. I can't say what had become of my suspicions then. Everything I was told seemed designed to disperse them. And yet they were there, about me. Vaporous, invisible, like chill currents of air. I could not wholly throw them off.

"Well, I think I'll go up and get a wash," said I. "And then I'll have some lunch."

I recollect Mr. Sankey's voice as I departed, informing me there was a nice joint of silverside of beef which he had specially ordered for Mr. Crawshay-Martin. And I remember thinking as I mounted the stairs how ironical that sounded.

There was a long, narrow passage to my room. It was heavily carpeted with a red and blue Turkey strip. My feet made no sound. I was considering all I had heard from Mr. Sankey. The thought of Gollancz was vivid in my mind when, as I approached the door of that fatal room, it opened silently and Gollancz himself came out.

We met face to face in the passage.

I cannot describe my sensations. I cannot begin to fathom the depth of my surprise.

I stopped. In the act of closing the door behind him, all but the movement of his hand was suspended. Contact between us was unescapable.

I suppose at moments like these one's voice utters words as involuntarily as the body, to save itself from falling, performs certain instinctive preservatory movements. Until I heard the words immediately afterwards, I scarcely knew that I had said:

"Were you looking for something?"

He turned half round from the door and directed the sharp angle of his pale eyes upon mine.

"Why should I be looking for anything?" he said.

"Then why should you be in that room?" I replied.

There was no time to consider the advisability of controlling the temper of my voice. That encounter—I use his word now—was like the fortuitous striking of two flints. I must confess I did not feel mine was a match for hardness or sharpness with his. But I could not restrain it from emitting the spark of my rekindling suspicions. That was the difference between us. He could restrain his from whatever it was he felt.

"I understand the panelled room is open to visitors," he answered quietly. "I saw by a pamphlet they have downstairs that it's considered one of the sights. Beautiful linen-fold. Pity we've lost the art of Patience."

I write that word—patience—with a capital letter, because that was the way he said it. As though he were warning me that I had none. That I was going too fast.

The worst of it was, I felt he was right. I was impatient. My impatience had given me away. Ever since that moment when I had heard my friend's voice in that room next to mine, I had been pursuing this man Gollancz in my mind. And now, just when I thought I had come up with him, caught him so that he could not escape, he had got away. Without a wrench, he had slipped out of my hands. For what more natural than he should have wanted to see that room? Far more natural, for instance, to the mind of a sergeant of police, than that he had been looking for something hidden under a loose board, when, within all the bounds of possibility, he could not have known it to be there.

And so I felt I could say no more. The quietness of his voice and the plausibility of his explanation had disarmed me. I was about to pass on to my own room when he laid a detaining hand on my arm. I looked at the hand. I suppose I was going to suggest by my glance that I resented it. Even that suggestion failed me. It was the most perfectly moulded hand I had ever seen. Capable of anything. Of the most exquisite execution upon a violin, at the same time that it conveyed indomitable strength. A medical friend of mine looks first to the hands of his patients for indications of character. Ridiculously he came into my mind then. I wondered what he would have thought of that hand of Gollancz.

With that thought passing across my mind, I looked up expectantly into his face.

"You are a doctor," said he.

"I am," said I.

"Might I add the inquiry if you are a Freemason?"

"No, I'm not," I replied.

He nodded his head as he looked at me.

"I thought not."

This assumption on his part astonished me. I knew enough of that Brotherhood to realize its relation to the Order of the Rosy Cross. But on what grounds did he suppose I was not a Freemason? I asked him that.

"Only," said he, "that had you been a Mason, even only one of a lower degree, you would not have interfered."

"Interfered with what?" I demanded.

"I am only speaking of your attitude of mind," he replied quietly, and then, with a smile, he added: *"Vel sanctum invenit, vel sanctum fecit."*

Still smiling, he withdrew his hand from my arm and walked away down the passage. I was left to pursue the direction to my room, puzzling out that sentence in Latin with rusty memories of Tacitus and Virgil creaking in my mind. *Vel sanctum invenit, vel sanctum fecit.* Did he mean by that, that mine was merely vulgar curiosity? Vulgar suspicion?

I pondered over it as I washed my hands. Was that, indeed, all it was? A pursuit of something I did not understand for the mere earthly satisfaction of revenge?

It was something like this, he thought. And seeing me accompanied by that sergeant of police, hearing his questions in the garden, he was probably justified. But even he, with the disquieting perception he possessed, had miscalculated one aspect of my mind. The fact that I was not even a Freemason of a low degree did not prohibit the inclination of my instinct from feeling there was something behind and beyond the death of Crawshay-Martin which touched realms of life unapproachable to the ordinary being.

Being a doctor, he assumed I was only capable of dealing with the exact sciences. He had not made allowance for that faculty of belief—a faculty in all of us in varying degrees—which is aware of the unknowable mysteries hidden away behind the superficial and attainable facts of life.

The Spiritualist with his planchette and his mediums endeavours to reach them. I am not saying whether he does or does not. Personally, I will not touch these things, because it seems to me that that way madness lies. Yet my very apprehension constitutes a proof of my belief in their existence. And Gollancz, the Rosicrucian, I knew instinctively to be a man quite unlike ordinary men. It was obvious that the common ways of life were not his ways. He did not begin to think as, normally, I thought. His impulses, his acts were not to be judged with mine. They were on another plane. I knew that. Even the finding of that book under the loose board in Crawshay-Martin's room had not entirely destroyed in my mind the association between it and my friend's death.

Gollancz wanted that book. I was still convinced of it. Finding him coming out of that room had reinforced my conviction. His explanation of his presence there, plausible though it had been, had not convinced me. He wanted that book. Probably from his point of view for the most sacred and importunate of reasons. What was more, in the end, I had a persistent apprehension that he would get it.

Why apprehension? It is difficult to explain that. My friend, Crawshay-Martin, had evidently determined he should not have it. Possibly that determination had descended like an heirloom to me. Like a trust. And, so far as I could, I had made up my mind to keep faith with it. In any case, it would soon pass out of my region of interference. In the possession of Claude Weaver or his mother it would no longer have anything to do with me.

But the suspicion of Gollancz causing the death of my friend still remained. Nevertheless, I knew, now that the book had been found, that I could not bring it home. What proof had I? None.

The fact that he looked no older from the time when Crawshay-Martin knew him as a student at Corpus would not arouse the suspicion of authority, even if it were believed. And did I believe it myself? That is an extraordinary fact about the mind. To Crawshay-Martin, I have no doubt, meeting him again in the Haymarket after all those years, it presented in itself the nature of an actual miracle. But to me, though I did not for a moment discredit my friend, I could only think of Gollancz as an extraordinarily well-preserved man of, say, sixty years or so.

How else could one think of it? Eternal youth, the Philosopher's Stone, what else can they mean to one these days, more than does the legend of the Wandering Jew? Frankly, I did not believe in his immunity from death. Who would? And yet I was far from satisfied.

With these thoughts revolving incoherently in my mind, I washed my hands and went downstairs to lunch.

As is the custom in some of these country inns, there was one big table in the coffee-room. On busy days one found oneself sitting there with commercials who had no other conversation than to relate their most memorable orders for the goods they travelled in. Not interesting topics to the outsider.

On this occasion there were no commercials, and apparently Gollancz and the other man, Bannerjee, did not indulge in a diet of silverside of beef. I should hardly have supposed they would. I did, however, expect them to be eating the vegetables of the course. But the room was empty. I took a seat at the end of the table farthest from the door and began my meal alone.

I had just finished the first course, an excellent soup, when the coffee-room door opened and a lady and gentleman came in.

It was obvious at once to me that they were Mr. and Mrs. Claude Weaver. And all my instincts of natural curiosity were to look at the man. But my eyes reached the woman first and there they stayed.

She was a supreme example of the modern type. I don't fancy myself it has anything to do with the War. A new generation was in its infancy, its childhood even, before the War began. Theosophists say there is a new root race in existence. Its characteristic quality is intuition and imagination. I don't know that I credit these sweeping statements. But I am fully aware that the children of this last generation have been quite different from those I knew in my own childhood. There is an independence of spirit about them. Certainly they do live more imaginatively in themselves. For this reason there is a kind of loneliness about them which is sometimes almost pathetic. Often to their own parents they are complete strangers.

It struck me at once that this young woman—she could not have been more than twenty-six—answered to this description. There was an unsatisfied look in the cold, contemptuous glance of her eyes. She had none of the late Victorian submissiveness to the stronger sex. She would even have denied its superiority of strength, except, perhaps, that of mere muscularity. Endurance, courage, daring, none of these qualities of masculine vitality did one feel she would allow to be superior to her own. Utterly she rejected the nineteenth century woman's ideals of men.

And yet, notwithstanding all this, the make-up of her face and the highly-polished scarlet of her finger nails declared the admission of her femininity, in which one could so clearly see she felt herself to be unapproachably alone.

I realize now my first actual thought as I looked at her was that she had no happiness in her married life. It would, indeed, have been difficult to imagine the kind of man who could make her happy. It is this common state of affairs, in my opinion, that is largely responsible for these modern friendships between women. They have little respect for men as the active male. Passivity is ceasing to be a fundamental characteristic of their sex. I do not mean that they want to dominate. But they do desire to participate. And this, it seems to me, is responsible for much of the prevailing antagonism between men and women.

Certainly when I turned my glance to Claude Weaver himself, I was not surprised at the look of disillusion and inquietude in her face. I came to the conclusion that Crawshay-Martin had been particularly restrained in his remarks about his nephew. The man was more than weak. There was a vicious quality in his weakness. Certain nervous movements of the eyes and involuntary, neurotic gestures with the hands—which even at that distance I could see were dirty—led me at once to the conclusion that he indulged in drugs.

I had no inclination to delay my glance at him, and certainly I was not eager just then to introduce myself. That could wait. Mr. Sankey would be sure to contrive that after lunch. The whole current of my interest had gone back at once to her. Indeed, it was difficult to take one's eyes from her. Not that she was actually beautiful. But a more striking figure of a woman I have seldom seen.

They had taken two seats at the end of the long table nearest the door. He was actually facing me down the length of the table, and once she was seated opposite one of the windows that looked out on to the garden, I could only see her profile. That was interesting enough, and I waited in curiosity to hear her voice. It was some time before I did. A facetiously-minded person would have said it was obvious they were married from the fact that they had nothing to say to each other. For nearly the first five minutes of that meal they were silent. But even that silence was interesting in its way, and then at last he said:

"I don't think there's any necessity to stay the night now."

He had been informed then, already, of his uncle's death. I wondered if he had been given the book. For a moment or so she went on eating in silence, and then she replied:

"You'll have to pay for the room. You ordered it. And I thought we were going to see the house."

Her voice was what I had expected. Attractive, but not clear. A kind of husky petulance that had the quality of concealing rather than expressing her thoughts. For instance, I had a distinct impression that economy and a desire to see Malquoits were not the reasons that she wanted to occupy the rooms they had taken. Economical! One could see she was not that.

"You want to stay then?" he replied.

"I don't see why we shouldn't."

It seemed as though she didn't care one way or another. Then why was I convinced that she did? That voice. She would never tell the truth about herself to that man.

After that they were silent again for a space. And there must have been something that was attractive in that voice, because I found myself waiting to hear it again. As well it was interesting, sitting there, a stranger to them, listening to what they were saying. Overhearing without eavesdropping. Presently he spoke again.

"Did you notice that man as we came downstairs?"

"What man?"

Again it was no more than an instinct, but I felt even the simplicity of her question to be a camouflage. Impossible to say of what.

"That strange-looking fella, talking to the proprietor in the hall."

My interest quickened at once. Was it Gollancz? They were talking in that somewhat subdued tone people use in public when there isn't the noise of a crowd to hide their voices. I stopped eating to listen.

"Why should I have noticed him?" she inquired.

"He was looking at you."

"A very excellent reason," she replied, "why I shouldn't have looked at him."

He gave expression to a smothered ejaculation of laughter. It was quite eloquent. If I had not been there, he might instead have muttered, "You cold, contemptuous little bitch!" That was the tone of it. It made you feel they were on those terms. He would have selected a word like that on purpose. In a lower stratum of life they would have wrangled openly in public.

She took no notice. One felt she would have taken no notice whatever he might have said. It was barely conceivable to suppose that two people so foreign to each other could live together at all in the married state.

And there was no doubt about her frigidity, her contemptuousness. It would have aggravated anyone unless you had had that feeling, as I did, that it was a kind of painted mask she wore, as unreal as her painted lips and her scarlet polished nails.

The man who could find the real woman in her could possibly bring her to surrender. But what kind of a man? I confess I should not have cared to tackle the business myself. Any man I had an affection for, I would have warned against marrying a woman like that. The more he loved her, the more hell his life would be. Had she a heart at all? I sat there at the bottom of the table watching that pale profile. And gradually I became conscious of a faint animation in it. As though she were hearing something in a distance that denied the sound to me.

Weaver had brought a newspaper into the meal with him. He had laid it down on the table. Having given vent to that ejaculation of laughter, he picked it up. As though the sight of her was intolerable to him any longer, he had spread open the pages in front of him. His whole body at the table was hidden from me, and must have been from her, by a broad expanse of printed paper.

And she never moved. It was not a startled animation. She was just looking in front of her through the window. From my angle I could see nothing but a vertical strip of the garden.

This was all the matter of a moment. In a moment the animation came and receded from her face. The next, that vertical strip of the garden was obliterated by the passing figure of Gollancz.

For that one moment he must have been there, out of my sight, looking through the window at her.

Not a first look. I saw that in her face. Not startled. Receptive.

He had looked at her as she came down the stairs. Weaver had said that.

And she must have looked back. That was her camouflage. She had seen him. This was already their second meeting.

CHAPTER IV

At the conclusion of lunch, Mr. Sankey looked in at the coffee-room door. Seeing the three of us seated there, still unacquainted, he sidled awkwardly into the room, rather like a fat, good-natured spaniel not quite sure of its right to appearance in the best parlour.

Seeing him approach Mr. Weaver, bend over him and speak in a confidential voice, I gathered from that gentleman's sharp look at me down the table, what he was saying. It was characteristic of Mrs. Weaver that she never turned her head the fraction of an inch in my direction.

A moment later, Claude Weaver stood up from the table as Mr. Sankey came down the room towards me. Unaccustomed to the precise formalities of introduction, the proprietor was mumbling something as he came to the effect that being a friend of Mr. Crawshay-Martin's, it seemed a proper thing to him that I should meet his nephew.

The upshot of these manœuvrings was that we advanced towards each other and introduced ourselves.

"I fancy I must have heard my uncle speak of you," he said.

"I've often heard him mention your name," said I.

He then turned to his wife. She was still sitting at her place at the table. Still looking out of the window. As though this were a business meeting of her husband's and had nothing in a social sense to do with her.

"Juniper."

She turned slowly round. It might even have been an effort—but an attractive effort. The scarcely concealed insolence of it had a quality of grace. With a complete absence of emotion, I could admire it. At the same time, I could imagine how it would have stung a man who wanted to make an impression on her.

And that name—Juniper! Through what chance had she come by it? It suited her. But how had ordinary parents in the early years of the twentieth century ever known she was going to turn out like that? Perhaps they weren't ordinary. Selecting that name and solemnly pronouncing it at the font, they would scarcely have been ordinary. In choosing it, they could certainly never have made allowances for the possibility of her marrying a man named—Weaver. Yet it suited her. Juniper—the tree under which the prophet Elijah rested when fleeing from the persecution of Jezebel.

"This is Dr. Hawke," said Weaver. "He was staying here last night. He was a friend of my uncle's."

She nodded her head to me.

"My God! Young woman!" I thought to myself, "I should like to teach you manners!"

And I was sufficiently aware of my own mood about her to realize that there would have been a considerable amount of interest in the proceeding. It would have taken some time. And that would have meant a fair share of her company.

"And now," said Mr. Sankey with affability; "if you will all come along to my private room, I'll settle up this little affair of that book. I think you'd better be there, doctor," he added, "just to explain."

This I felt to be the precautionary measure on his part which I had suggested. I was to be a witness to the handing over of the book. It was just as well. We followed him to his room. Mrs. Weaver, her husband, and then myself.

Closing the door and offering her a comfortable chair, Mr. Sankey went across to his desk. On this occasion I gave up all idea of entering into any conversation with Mrs. Weaver. It was sufficiently interesting to sit and watch all her attitudes and movements. Impossible to say that every one of them was a pose. That callous indifference of hers was not assumed. It was herself. She lay back in the arm-chair Mr. Sankey had provided her with, lighting a common Virginian cigarette, inhaling deep breaths of the smoke and letting it filter out through her lips and nostrils, as though it could stay there in her lungs for ever for all she cared. Not much graciousness of the shade of the juniper tree about her. But inviting, all the same. No one could have denied that.

Mr. Sankey had taken the book from his desk. He was standing in the centre of the room, clearing his throat before he started on this undertaking, which evidently he considered to be of no little responsibility. Then, as though at the last moment he had come to the conclusion it was beyond his powers, he turned to me.

"Dr. Hawke," he said, "I think perhaps it would be better for you to explain to Mr. Weaver about this volume. I've been thinking over what you said this morning and since we had our little talk, Mr. Crawshay-Martin's solicitors have been on the phone. They tell me he left no will, so that, of course, all the property, such as remains after his affairs are settled, will go to Mr. Weaver's mother. They said that. So what d'you think I'd better do about this?"

"Did you consult them?" I inquired.

"I didn't think about it. A book. Personal effect, as you might say. I presume it will go with other things he had in his room. Watch and chain. You know. Things like that."

"Yes, but this book may be very valuable," I interposed.

At this point, Weaver took it out of Mr. Sankey's hands to have a look at it. A chance look at Mrs. Weaver showed me that even she was mildly interested. She stretched out her hand to her husband, intimating that she wanted to have a look at it herself. He brought it across to her chair. She took it on her lap and opened it while he stood behind looking over her shoulder.

"'Philosophy of the Magic Harmonies of the Brotherhood of the Rosy Cross.'"

He read that out.

"I had a bit of Latin," he said, with quite unnecessary pride, "when I came down from the 'varsity."

In the meantime she was turning over the pages, pausing at the illuminations, frowning at them, and slowly passing on.

"But what's it all about?" she muttered presently. Not raising her head. Not looking at anyone. Not bothering to give her question a direction.

And it was when she asked us that, that an idea sprang with a malicious sense of curiosity into my mind.

"If you have any doubt about the value of the book," I said, "you'd better invite Mr. Gollancz in here to tell you what it's worth. If he told you it was worth fifty thousand pounds, perhaps you'd hesitate before you interfered with what seems to me entirely a solicitor's job."

At the sound of that sum of money, Weaver leant over his wife's shoulder and took the book out of her hands. She let it go without a word. She wasn't looking at it any longer. She was directly looking at me. For the first time.

"Mr. Gollancz?" she repeated. "Who is Mr. Gollancz?"

Sankey seemed ready to explain, so I let him. I was content to watch that same faint animation in her face. From Sankey's description, there was no doubt that she recognized him. The man she had not known when her husband talked about him at lunch. The man she had seen through the window.

"But what does he know about this book?" she inquired. She looked at me. Sankey was not satisfying her.

"That book," said I, "reveals the rites and mysteries of the Brotherhood of the Rosy Cross. Members of that Brotherhood are called Rosicrucians. Mr. Gollancz is a Rosicrucian."

It was the same malicious humour made me tell them this. I wanted to drag Gollancz into it. I wanted to observe his face while he was watching other people handling in possession a thing that was priceless to him. Supposing I had been right about my assumption that Gollancz had stood for a moment watching her through the window. I wanted to see these two together and study their reactions to each other.

"You send for Mr. Gollancz," I repeated. "He knows all about it." Then I looked directly at Weaver. "Ultimately," I said, "it'll come into your possession, even if you don't take it away with you now. So ask him what he'll give you for it."

I realize more even now than I did at the time the kind of devilment in me that was at the back of these suggestions. How could I have imagined all it might lead to? The antagonism between myself and that man which seemed inevitable, and yet had no foundation in actual reason, was at the root of my mood. I resented his contempt of exact science. I had been aggravated by his suggestion of my interference. Had I been a Mason, even of a lower degree! Somehow, that had rankled. The more so because I felt he had intended it to. As well as that subtle comment of his on my impatience. The more stinging to me because I knew it was justified. All this, in addition to my apparently unfounded suspicions about the death of Crawshay-Martin, had created a vindictive mood in me which the more I felt, the less I was proud of. In this respect I was aware of his superiority, and did not enjoy it. I can admit it now. Looking back. I couldn't have done so then.

And so it was, that afternoon in the "Scarlett Arms," I persuaded them to send for Gollancz. Of my own accord and will I contrived that first meeting between him and Mrs. Weaver. Sankey was indifferent to the suggestion. But, then, he did not know all I knew. Weaver was in complete agreement. The possibility of an offer of money had brought a quickening light into his eye. It was easy to realize he was avaricious. The more I saw of him, the less I liked him. As for Mrs. Weaver, I had the distinct impression she was the most eager of any of us to meet Gollancz. Not that she said so. She did not say a word. Probably once she had seen that look in her husband's eyes, she knew there was no need of persuasion.

Mr. Sankey opened the hatchway door and asked one of the girls to see that the message was taken to Mr. Gollancz.

"Say that Mr. Weaver, who is staying in the hotel, would be very glad to make his acquaintance in reference to a certain matter. Very glad. Don't forget that."

I smiled. From his point of view, Mr. Sankey evidently knew the kind of man he was dealing with.

We hadn't long to wait. Weaver was still turning over the pages of the book, and now with renewed interest. Sankey was asking me some foolish questions about Rosicrucians, as though he had suddenly discovered he was harbouring some extraordinary animal under his roof, and did not know whether it should be allowed the ordinary amenities. Mrs. Weaver had risen from her chair. She was casually examining some advertisement cards stuck in a mirror over the mantelpiece, when the door opened and Gollancz came in.

"A Mr. Weaver sent for me," he said. He looked straight at Weaver. Not at anyone else.

The effect of his entrance was peculiar. Even I, who had met him two or three times before, felt that the angle of this discussion about the book was suddenly twisted into another and unexpected direction. Assuming the possession of it now to be technically in the Weaver family, we had been deciding what it was worth and what should be done with it. The moment Gollancz brought his presence into the room, all that seemed to be immaterial. Despite my own determinations, I could not deny a feeling of his right to the book. But it was not likely I was going to give way to sentimentalities of that nature.

It was Weaver himself who answered.

"My name's Weaver," he said. "My uncle who died last night was Mr. Crawshay-Martin. We were discussing this book."

He held it out in his hand. Gollancz did not look at it. I saw that. I was watching his eyes.

"Dr. Hawke, here," continued Weaver, "says that you know something about the value of it. And it's a question as to whether I should take it away myself as a personal effect of my uncle's, whose entire property goes to my mother, or whether I should leave it to be dealt with by the solicitors. Is it a fact you do know what it's worth?"

A peculiar light, half-cynical, half-understanding, appeared to pass over Gollancz's face. This was apparently a characteristic of his features. They did not so much register an expression. A light passed over them and faded away. You could never say exactly what it was he thought.

"You mean its worth in money?" he said.

Much in the same way as he had said it to the sergeant in the garden. With a kind of acid amusement.

"Naturally. Yes. In a round sum."

"I've been asked that question already to-day," said Gollancz—

but did not look at me. "I can't do better than give the same answer. It might be worth twenty thousand pounds. It might be worth fifty. It might be worth no more than ten pounds for its antique value as a specimen of sixteenth century manuscript."

No one could have failed to see the look of greed in Weaver's eyes at the mention of that considerable sum. Fifty thousand pounds! Notwithstanding the perfection of his wife's taste in dress, I had reason to know he was not too well off.

"Who'd give me fifty thousand pounds?" he asked.

"Well—not *you*, would it be?" suggested Gollancz. "I thought you said the entire property went to your mother."

"Same thing," said Weaver. "My mother's an old woman. She wouldn't stand in my way over the realization of a sum of money like that. Would *you* give fifty thousand pounds or anything like it? I hear you were interested in it yesterday at the sale."

I had not mentioned this, so I presumed Mr. Sankey must have told him. Anyhow, he brought it out quite casually, as though fifty thousand was a sum any man might offer for a book if he wanted it badly enough.

Another man in Gollancz's position might have laughed. But I can't associate Gollancz with laughter. Not because I think he had no sense of humour. I can believe his sense of humour to have been acute. More subtle and perceptive, indeed, than most people's. But laughter, however much you may extol it, is an immoderate thing. It requires a certain degree of abandonment. And for Gollancz to abandon his will to any sensation would be an inconceivable thought to anyone who had once met him.

He did not laugh here, though I am confident his sense of the ridiculous must have been profoundly moved. He just shook his head at Claude Weaver as though he were refusing a beggar in the street whose claim to charity he knew to be bogus from start to finish.

"I have never had fifty thousand pounds in my life," he said quietly. "Money is not a possession of mine. A man may turn the base metals of the earth into gold, but the moment he possesses that gold for himself he is no longer free. I have my freedom. If I wanted that book, I should be free to take it. To buy it from you would not make it mine."

We were all staring at him from the different angles of our astonishment. Sankey probably was wondering whether he was going to be paid his bill. Weaver himself was clearly fuddled. His brain, obfuscated with drugs, was incapable of assimilating these anomalies.

And, as far as I was concerned, my surprise was not so much at what he had said as the fact that he had said it at all. This was his philosophy of life. There was the Rosicrucian speaking. And in that one sentence about the turning of base metals into gold, he had indirectly laid claim to the alchemical powers of the old astrologers. A man may turn the base metals of the earth into gold. That was the way he had said it. It couldn't mean anything else. If a man might, then he could. That was how I understood him. And yet here, in this twentieth century, I found it impossible to laugh at him.

But the one whom these remarks of Gollancz seemed to affect most of all was Mrs. Weaver. Recovering a little from my surprise, it flashed in my mind: "I wonder what she makes of that."

I turned to look at her. She was still over by the fire-place, but leaning no longer on the mantelpiece. She was standing erect and quite still, with her eyes fixed upon Gollancz. It was an extraordinary expression that was in her face.

Women, as one realizes in a practice like mine, are just as liable to sudden physical attractions as men. The old idea that a woman must fall in love with a man before she can experience the desire and infatuation of sex has been exploded. It was fostered by our fathers, who needed special licence for their own infidelities. The equalizing of the divorce laws on this matter is a legal recognition of that fact.

And so far as Gollancz was concerned (even regarding him as I did as a man of more than sixty years), there could be no doubt of his physical attractions. To begin with, you did not in any accepted sense think of his age. He might have been thirty. He might have been less. He might have been more. It was strange. Age was not a consideration that applied to him. His attraction was not a question of youth. Youth was the last quality by which you would have described him. Certainly there were no marks of age about his face. His figure was as erect as any man's I have seen. The whites of his eyes surrounding the pale pupils were as clear and transparent as a child's. From my point of view, as a medical man, he must have had an extraordinarily healthy life. But of the callow impulses of youth, the last recommendation I imagine Mrs. Weaver would have looked for in a man, there was none. The eyes that belonged to Gollancz had seen a share of life that would not be generally the experience of a man of thirty. And yet there was nothing of disillusionment about his expression. Life, as it had passed into his knowledge, had not hardened him. Antagonistic though I felt to be everything he said and did, I should have had to admit the presence in him of an idealist.

Nothing of what I have just written suggests a purely physical attraction. And, indeed, it was not that I saw in Mrs. Weaver's face. That she was infatuated, I had no doubt. That meeting which I had not seen in the hall. Their second meeting when she saw him pass by the window. These were indications of it. But it was not the common infatuation of the susceptible woman for the comely attributes of the opposite sex.

She was more—fascinated. Extravagant though it is, I could almost use the word—bewitched. Not that she displayed obviously any such abnormal condition of mind. The animation in her eyes was too slow to register anything startling like that for the casual observer. She might merely have been interested in the peculiar and unexpected things he was saying. But, accustomed as I was to studying women of her class and hearing the confessions of their most intimate affairs, I had no doubt of my impression. Had she, for instance, looked at me like that, I should have realized there was little escape from the ultimate determination of her passions.

"Do you mean you wouldn't make an offer for the book?" inquired Weaver, when he had recovered from his mental confusion.

"My friend, Mr. Bannerjee, who bid for the book yesterday at the sale," said Gollancz, "might be persuaded to offer the sum which Mr. Crawshay-Martin paid for it."

"What was that?"

"Fifty odd pounds, I think. Less than sixty. I say, he might be persuaded. I've not consulted him. But, as for myself, I should not give anything."

"In fact," said Mrs. Weaver, and we all turned to look at her. This unexpected sound of her voice from the other end of the room. There was a wry expression about her mouth. A kind of comic admiration. I don't know how else to express it. A look as though, through the sense of her humour, she was perceiving a quality about Gollancz that had won the full measure of her interest.

"In fact," she said, "you would sooner take it than pay for it."

She said it half in fun. There was a laugh through the thread of her words. But it had its meaning. The intent of it was there, even if her husband and Sankey were unable to appreciate it.

And Gollancz understood it. I could see that. His eyes turned from Weaver's face to meet hers, and I was conscious that it was a meeting. An encounter, as he would have said. If I were to say that in that moment they understood each other, I do not mean exactly that she understood him. It is inconceivable. The man was not easily to be understood by anyone. It was more that she realized he understood her.

A dangerous realization for a woman. For, as I appreciate them in my particular walk of life, a woman has little but her mystery, her unknowableness, to stand up with against the desperate inclinations of human nature. Mere force of character will seldom save her, once she has nothing left to conceal.

And that, it seemed to me, in one moment as their eyes met down the length of Mr. Sankey's private sitting-room, was what was happening between herself and Gollancz.

I had had proof myself that he could read the thought passing through the mind of a mere stranger in the most casual of meetings. Then why not, when the meeting was far from casual, in hers? As he looked, and as she looked back, I could sense the consciousness in her face of what was the stark nakedness of her mind to him. He knew her then better than she knew herself. But what it was he knew, it was still less possible for me to say than her. Her eyes narrowed and then fell away.

"Mrs. Weaver," he said, "may not know how delicately accurate she is. But it explains my attitude precisely."

"I shall keep it then," said Weaver at once. "If that's the sort of figure it's worth, I shall have to wait till I get a purchaser."

Gollancz looked from one to the other of us. Imperceptibly perhaps his eye rested a little longer on hers. Then he bowed. There was the faint suggestion of Orientalism in the inflexion of his body.

"That is all I can tell you," he said, and without another word he withdrew. I use that word with consideration. Withdrew. I did not feel he had departed from the lives of Mr. and Mrs. Weaver.

CHAPTER V

The inquest on the body of my friend, Crawshay-Martin, took place at the coroner's court in Shipleigh. I was called, of course, to give evidence.

The discovery of the book by Mr. Sankey had naturally entirely upset all foundations of the suspicions I had entertained of Gollancz. Logically I admitted that myself. What had I to say in support of them? Nothing.

The Shipleigh sergeant smiled at me when we next met. It was on the day of the inquest.

"I hear the book's been found all right," he said.

I acknowledged the accuracy of his information.

"I thought at the time," said he, "the vicar 'ud have been more interested in what you had to say."

He said it with pleasant good nature, or I might have lost my temper. As it was I had to smile in amusement at his harmless little jest as convincingly as I could. There was no sense in pursuing the matter any farther. The proceedings of the inquest went through in the normal way. There was plenty of evidence that a man under such circumstances might have had his mind unhinged. He had lived at Malquoits all his life; his father and grandfather before him. Of course, it was a wrench to sell the place and all the pieces of furniture he had known from childhood.

But when I was called upon to give evidence, I was determined to say all I could to rouse the coroner's mind. I wanted him to think it was not all such a simple matter as it looked.

"Mr. Crawshay-Martin," I declared, "was one of the most level-headed men I know. And though I realize he was distressed at having to sell all his property, it was not the kind of distress which, as a member of the medical profession, I should ever have associated with a brain storm such as develops into suicidal tendencies. He was certainly inclined to be quiet, not talkative, that night when he went to bed. But suicidal! It's incredible to me."

I put it as strongly as that. I couldn't put it stronger. I had no evidence even to suggest murder against someone unknown. And when it came to my hearing Crawshay-Martin's voice those few moments before he died, I might swear a thousand times that I felt his words to have been addressed to someone, but if I heard no one else's voice, then what was the good?

From the coroner's point of view, and, of course, from everyone else's, those things Crawshay-Martin said that night in the solitude of his own room were only an additional proof of his temporary insanity.

The verdict was according to that, and I went back to London.

I live in one of those old houses in Arlington Street, close to where Mrs. Kelly employed the divine Emma, and Captain Willett Payne first set desiring eyes upon her beauty.

The ways of London life, I fancy, have not changed much since then. The Abbesses of Arlington Street, as they called Mrs. Kelly, still maintain their establishments of slender reputation in Mayfair. Though in these days of amorality there would appear to be less occasion for them.

Ladies, such as those who masked their faces for an evening at Mrs. Kelly's, call upon me now in the broad light of day to tell me their troubles with husbands and lovers. Were I a Doctor Graham of that period, trading upon the foibles of feminine human nature (as am I not?) I should probably recognize but little difference in the patients that come to me with their secrets in the twentieth century.

For all the changes that take place in the city streets and the country roads, the signs of transmutation and progression in the human mind are extraordinarily faint. Indeed, when one considers the quality of intellect in the Greek drama two thousand years ago, and compares it with the plays in the modern theatre, one is inclined to wonder what progression there has been at all. And in that age, science, as we understand it now, was unknown. The minds of the scientists in those days of highest intellect in art, were all trained in the occult.

Whenever that thought occurs to me, the strange figure of that man Gollancz rises in my mind. Is he right? And am I all wrong? I ask myself that and wonder. If occultism satisfied the powerful intellects of the Greek philosophers, why should the mind of the modern scientist so contemptuously disregard it?

Exactitude is a well-intentioned principle. But is it paramount in a world where the shifting sands of fact can alter in a night the entire features of our belief? Any morning we may wake up to find that an astronomer has discovered a new planet, an Einstein a new theory, a mathematician a new formula, and our whole conception of the origins and processes of life that has been so fixed the day before may be changed.

In my own profession of medicine, this blatant inexactitude in an exact science is constantly reduced to absurdity. What the doctors recommended last year, they will abuse to-day. Does anybody know anything? Do facts really help us? We live in a world of bewildering uncertainty.

There is no necessity for me to pursue this any further. I am not writing a thesis upon metaphysics. I am writing the story of Gollancz, the Rosicrucian, and that book revealing the rites and mysteries of the secret Brotherhood of the Rosy Cross. I can only set forth what I know.

And of what happened for the next six months after the death of my friend Crawshay-Martin, personally I know nothing. I returned to London from Bedinghurst and heard no more of Claude Weaver and his wife.

Whenever I sat down at the Queen Anne knee-hole desk which I had bought at the sale at Malquoits, it is true my mind reverted to that extraordinary happening at the "Scarlett Arms." Again and again those same suspicions returned to me about the death of my friend. Why had he spoken as he did just the moment before his death? Why had he hidden that book under the loose board in his bedroom? Why had Gollancz come down the very next day, telephoning to his friend, Mr. Bannerjee, before that gentleman had acquainted him with what had taken place overnight? And why had he visited that room before he knew that Mr. Sankey had recovered the book?

All these questions, as and when they returned to my mind, still remained unanswered. But after a while the urgent sting in them had gone. In six months' time I had practically put them out of my consideration, when one morning, in a pause between the appointment of one patient and another, my maid brought a card into my consulting-room.

Picking it up off the salver I read:

Mrs. Claude Weaver
The Court House,
Stoke Charity,
Hants.

"Is the lady in the waiting-room?" I asked.
"Yes, sir."
"What did she say?"
"That she wanted to see you."
"Professionally?"
"She didn't say."

I was amused. Possibly more. I may even have been intrigued. Quite vividly I recalled her attractive insolence that day in Mr. Sankey's private room at the "Scarlett Arms." What could she want with me? For the short time I was in her company, she had scarcely condescended to allow me more than a passing glance. I remembered my impression that she needed a little instruction in the matter of manners. Was this going to prove my opportunity for giving it?

"Ask Mrs. Weaver to come in," I said. And the maid retired. I looked at my appointment book. I had another patient in half an hour's time. Well, half an hour should be sufficient for me to get an outline of the medical history of her case.

I was writing when the door opened and she was shown in. Intentionally I was writing. Intentionally I delayed one instant before I looked up. The first lesson in my course of instruction in that matter of manners. I did not intend her to suppose that I was interested.

A second later I laid down my pen and stood up. She was standing in the middle of the room. As well dressed as ever. And my first thought as I looked at her face was:

"This is not the same woman. This is another woman. What's the matter with her?"

Diagnosis is largely a question of intuitive inspiration. Here is a function in medical science in which facts help, but undoubtedly facts are by no means all.

The imagination of the discoverer in chemistry is suddenly lit, illuminated with a flash of thought, and in the glare of it a new metal, unknown to science, is brought to light.

Where does the ray of that thought come from?

A musician hears out of the void a sudden phrase that becomes the *motif* of a magnificent symphony.

Upon what sound wave do those vibrations come?

A doctor, looking in a patient's eyes, suddenly divines the root of a disease.

How has that inspiration reached him?

I looked at Mrs. Weaver. From whatever it was she was suffering, I could see she was not in essence quite the same woman I had met at the "Scarlett Arms." But what was her complaint? No inspiration reached me. I could not tell.

We shook hands, and I indicated a chair for her to sit in. When she was seated I went back to my desk.

It is not often necessary to beat about the bush with a woman. Having determined in her mind to come to a doctor, she makes no bones about it once she is there. Over personal matters, women are clearer in their purpose than men. They are less sensitive. I am not sure that they are not less modest. I mean nothing uncomplimentary by that. When it comes to consulting a doctor, modesty is a waste of time. It is more. It is a pure sentimentality.

But in the case of Mrs. Weaver, who, I should have imagined, had little consideration for the feelings of others, we talked about various things before I could begin to get an idea of what it was she wished to consult me about. I asked after her husband, and her replies were guarded. In the six months that had passed, I gathered that his condition which I had suspected that day when I saw him at the "Scarlett Arms" had not improved.

"Do you ask because you noticed anything about his health that day?" she inquired. "When you met him at Bedinghurst?"

"What should I have noticed?"

"Oh, you can be as brutal as you like. Being a doctor, I suppose you realized he took drugs?"

"Yes—I did notice it."

"Heroin?"

"I imagined something like that."

"Had you bought anything the day before at Mr. Crawshay-Martin's sale?"

I pointed to the knee-hole desk.

"Charming," she said. "Nearly a collector's bit. I suppose he had some priceless stuff?"

"Supposing," said I, "you told me what you had come to see me about?"

She had still been looking round at the desk while she spoke. Allowing her words—in that same kind of indolent manner—to fall over the back of her shoulder for me to pick up. If I liked to take the trouble. But when I said this she looked round quickly. Her eye had no insolence then. It was brought up sharp against the fact of her being there, like a horse that shies at a jump.

"I take it," I added quietly—much in the way the rider might pat the horse's neck to give him confidence—"I take it you came to see me professionally?"

She pulled herself together. Whatever the jump was—and I was soon to learn—she set herself at it again and cleared it like a thoroughbred. For all that insolence of her manners, there was no wanting of spirit about her. She probably had the hell of a life with that husband of hers, but in the little she had said about him there was no sign of whining. It was not really that I conceived her funking anything. There was even a species of courage in her insolence.

But here, to the sudden directness of that question of mine, she had certainly swerved. What she had to say was evidently not easy. There was some inhibition in her mind about it. She was in conflict with a kind of nameless dread, harder to conquer than a normal fear.

"I haven't exactly come to see you professionally," she said at last. Before speaking she had begun taking off one of her gloves. There were her fingernails with the same high-polished scarlet. She was looking down at them, and when she spoke she lifted her head with an apologetic laugh. Apologetic, that is to say, for her. There was the note of a defiant gesture about it. That was that, and if she were wasting my time, I could say so.

"Well, another patient is coming to see me in about twenty minutes," said I. "Till then, of course——"

"Oh, I'm not trying to wangle the fee," she interrupted with a laugh.

I felt I could have smacked her face for that. Some of these women can be damned rude. I am forty-eight years of age, but apparently a woman can still make my blood go suddenly hot. At least, she could. I probably looked annoyed as I said:

"If it's anyone's job to talk of fees, possibly it's mine. If I can be of any help to you in any way, I shall be delighted. And if twenty minutes now isn't enough, perhaps you'll give me the pleasure of dining with me to-night at the Bath Club."

I said that with the same tone of insolence as she had in her voice. If she liked to insult me by suggesting that I was the kind of doctor who cadged for his fees at the slightest provocation, then she might as well realize that I considered her to be the kind of married woman that would dine with a man on the slightest acquaintance.

"I shall be very pleased," she said casually, taking it for granted, as though I had merely suggested the proper thing under the circumstances. I couldn't help smiling at her effrontery.

"Well, what is it you have to say?" I asked.

She looked up directly at me for a moment with that different expression in her eyes, and then she said:

"You told us that day at the 'Scarlett Arms' that Mr. Gollancz was a Rosicrucian?"

"I did."

"How did you know that?"

"My friend, Mr. Crawshay-Martin, had told me so. Three years before his death he told me. On the first occasion when I saw Mr. Gollancz. It was one morning in the Haymarket. A casual meeting."

She nodded her head. In a serious kind of way for her. Then she put a question which was ordinary enough under the circumstances, but which, coming from her, was the last I should have expected. In somewhat of a tense voice, she said:

"What is a Rosicrucian?"

I sat up in my chair. Involuntarily I sat up. I was not only surprised at her being sufficiently interested as to want to know. I was at a moment's loss to know how to answer her.

From her, the question was decidedly singular. And it was then, as she said it, that I realized this was the change that had taken place in her. That quality of insolence she still possessed. As I said before, it was not a pose with her. It was her natural self. But that she should ever have evinced an interest in occult matters, was the last thing I should have expected of her.

That immediate world in which she lived—so it seemed to me—was all she cared about. There was, I should have imagined, that modern contempt in her of anything relating to the spiritual. I made certain that, as is characteristic of these young women to-day, she had none of what is called religion. Their type of intelligence does not admit of it. It produces a cynical, an Epicurean view of life. Certainly their wits are all about them. They know, more shrewdly than most men, the artistic value of plays and books. It is they who make the startling successes of the playwrights and the authors these days. To have read the latest audacious novel and seen the latest suggestive play is the celebration of a sacrament to them.

And beyond this, in their own particular ways to get the best out of life while it lasts, is their faith.

They have no morals. This is as I have seen them in my profession. Yet they are far from essentially immoral. To bear children is largely an imposition upon their brief but valuable time. A great emotion is a state of mind of which they are predisposed to be suspicious. They know it is still an inherent weakness of their sex. And they escape it whenever they can.

To hear this young woman, then, asking me, and in that tone

of voice, what was a Rosicrucian, for a moment upset all my calculations of her. The only thing I appreciated was that it was in this the change in her was revealing itself. Had she found a sense of the spiritual? It seemed incredible. And all the time that these impressions were passing across my mind, I was aware of her question, waiting to be answered.

I leaned across my desk and looked at her closely.

"Do you want the picturesque answer to that," said I; "or something as near to the truth as I can get it?"

This was the first time I had seen her display a sign of some kind of emotion. She was annoyed. I was secretly amused.

"Is that an opinion of my intelligence?" she asked.

"It's in consideration of the effect you produce," said I.

She thanked me. "All the same," as she put it. Evidently still annoyed and by no means mollified by the complimentary twist of my explanation.

"Do you imagine I've come here just to waste your time with idle questions?" she added.

And I could see she was really serious then. The expression about her eyes was strained. She looked anxious. It is the best way I can describe it. As though there were something to it far more than mere curiosity. Upon what answer I gave, apparently depended some action she had in mind. I thought for a moment of the simplest way I could put it, and then I said:

"Well, a Rosicrucian, as you might find it in the encyclopædia, is a member of the Secret Brotherhood of the Rosy Cross. Is that sufficient?"

"No. I gathered that from what you said at Bedinghurst. What is the Brotherhood of the Rosy Cross?"

"It's a society, like the Freemasons, instituted to promote the universal welfare and brotherhood of mankind."

"That's rather vague—isn't it?"

"Very."

"Most of the people I know who are Freemasons join it because they think they'll do a bit of good for themselves."

I smiled.

"You might say that of any body—social or religious," said I.

"Yes. Idealism is bunk. Isn't it?"

I couldn't help laughing. It was so characteristic—even to the use of the word "bunk"—of the casual impression she gave you in that—altogether—of herself.

"Well—I don't know that it's—bunk—to the genuine Rosicrucian," I replied. "I rather fancy if he isn't an idealist, he isn't anything. Do you recollect what Mr. Gollancz said about the possession of money? He has none. He prefers to be free. In this twentieth century, the common opinion is that a sufficiency of money buys for us the only freedom that is possible in a peculiarly circumscribed civilization. Most people work themselves to death in order to get enough money to be free. A Rosicrucian might be considered to be an idealist, in that his entire mind functions on absolutely reverse principles to that. He claims the power of being able, like the alchemists in the Middle Ages, to turn the basest metal into gold. But for him to possess that gold and use it in the form of money would be the unqualified negation of the whole of his conception of life. His freedom would be gone. He would become subservient to the petty tyrannies of existence which make us all the slaves that we are."

"Do you believe in all that?" she asked me eagerly.

"I believe that slavery is the most prevalent factor of human existence," I said. "But I'm not prepared to say that Rosicrucianism is the way to escape from it. I don't think there is any escape."

"But the Rosicrucian does!"

"Oh—yes."

"And is that all? Just a secret society like the Freemasons?"

"Oh, no. That, you might say, is only the beginning. I believe there are different degrees in the Rosicrucian Brotherhood, just as there are in Freemasonry. The higher you reach in those degrees, the more nearly you approach to the mystic, the occult, all those things which ordinarily are hidden from the more common and mundane understanding of men."

"What sort of things?"

I played about for a moment with a silver paper-knife on my desk before I answered. I didn't really want to answer. I didn't want to involve myself in any foolish and unreliable statements. But she was become so eager. She was leaning forward in her chair and her eyes were searching up—almost pathetically it seemed—into mine.

"Well," I said carefully, "such as a power to prolong youth."

She stared at me. She stared so hard that in defence of my reason for that statement, I told her about my first meeting with Gollancz, and the story about that affair at Corpus which Crawshay-Martin had told me subsequently at his club.

"And he was the same man! Not a year older!" she echoed when I had finished.

A very different reception for my story than that which the police sergeant at Shipleigh had accorded me.

"Look here," I said. "Before I tell you any more, will you explain to me what is the meaning of this violent interest of yours? Why do you want to know all this?"

"Because I've been dreaming," she replied. Her voice had fallen almost to a whisper.

"Dreaming? What of?"

"Of that man—Gollancz."

"When?"

Before she could answer a knock fell on my door.

"What is it?" I called out.

The maid entered. She mentioned the name of my next patient.

I looked at Mrs. Weaver.

"It's not half an hour, is it?" she exclaimed.

"Must be," said I.

"Then it's the Bath Club—to-night," she said at once.

"The Bath Club," said I. "Eight o'clock."

She did not stop to shake hands. She just nodded her head to me and went out.

CHAPTER VI

The Bath Club has as much, if not more, air about it than any club in London. You know what I mean by "air." I belong to it for the squash rackets and the swimming. It is convenient to Arlington Street. As well as that, in the course of my practice and since my wife died twelve years ago, I have found it the best possible place to dine a lady who does not want to be entertained with the alimentary distractions of a band and a kind of mannequin parade of the latest fashions.

At the Bath Club you can talk to a woman without treating her as though she were the transmitting apparatus of a loud speaker. The air of the place dispenses with the mechanization of life. All of which is to say that, without any necessity for the amplification of existence, one can merely be oneself.

I like that.

It was particularly, then, at the Bath Club that I invited Mrs. Weaver to meet me for dinner. What arrangements she had made for staying in London, I did not know. I hadn't inquired. Stoke Charity, in Hampshire, is not a place I imagine you can get to by a late theatre train. But that was her affair. Possibly they had a flat in London. I didn't know. In any case I assumed that young woman was quite capable of taking care of herself.

Whatever arrangement of domicile they had for occasions like this, she arrived at the Bath Club very beautifully dressed. When I say beautifully, I don't mean in the picture fashion. Her clothes were an expression of her personality. I can't pretend to describe them. There was a daring exposure of her back. Fully justified. But not daring to the point of blatantly absorbing one's attention. It was all in the scheme she had conceived about herself. I dislike the type of woman who has a throat or a chest or a back and, in the manner of her dress, insists upon telling you about it.

This frock Mrs. Weaver wore that night—some kind of dull, black silk—had nothing insistent in it to distract one's mind from the essential character of herself.

I may as well say what I mean. I thought she looked damned smart. I can't say I liked the scarlet finger-nails. They always suggest to me someone who has been clawing raw flesh. But otherwise her make-up was not artificial. She was naturally pale and, like a sensible woman, she used herself as a model for her employment of cosmetics. It is the woman who tries to make up as someone else who does not begin to know the secret of it.

To my surprise, she refused a cocktail, and in answer to the lift of my eyebrows explained that it was because of her health.

"I told you," she said. "I'm not sleeping well."
"You said you were dreaming."
"Same thing. I never used to dream. I find it queer."

Well, if she didn't want a cocktail, I was not going to insist upon it. A doctor must put up with the consequences if a patient actually does what he is told. We went without cocktails and sat down to dinner.

Here again, during the first course, as in my consulting-room, it seemed to be difficult to get her to centre her mind. We talked about all sorts of things rather than the actual subject which was the purpose of our meeting. But through this haphazard conversation I was beginning gradually to get a different impression of her. There was a depth beneath that insolence I had not suspected. Isn't there something that Browning said about a man having two faces?

"God be thanked——"

I have looked it up:

"The meanest of his creatures
Boasts two soul-sides, one to face the world with,
One to show a woman when he loves her."

It was something like that I could feel in her. She was facing the world with her insolence. With that she was showing the casual observer how little it meant to her for her body to be sold to a degenerate. For her whole life to be the ghastly chaos that it was. And the other soul-side, as we talked at the opening of that dinner, I could suspect. It was there, little though she would admit it, ready to show some man when she loved him.

At last, when the second course was put in front of us and she had collected beside her plate three little pellets of bread out of the soft part of her roll, she said:

"You said this morning that was only the beginning of your definition of a Rosicrucian."

"I did."

"Then what more?"

But I did not exactly want it this way. To describe the occult meaning of Rosicrucianism to a modern woman is somewhat of a thankless task. It was quite apparent that her interest was in Gollancz the man. I could not suppose she was really interested in Gollancz, the Rosicrucian. And my eagerness to hear what she had to tell me I felt to be far more important than hers to hear a description of a mystic Brotherhood. Especially when I found it impossible to believe she had really given her interest to that kind of thing.

But there was no dissuading her from her curiosity. I had to go on with my definition of a Rosicrucian, but making it as brief as I possibly could.

"It all goes back," I said, "to periods of time when science, as we know it now, was unheard of. Knowledge, wisdom, to us is the accumulation of facts. We believe nothing which cannot be substantially proved. The ancients believed in manifestations of a nature which now would be met with open contempt. Though one has to admit there's a definite sign of change in the trend of mental processes. Even the most established scientists are beginning to allow for unknown and unknowable factors. Your dreams, for example. Psychologists are definitely taking the interpretation of dreams into serious consideration in their study of the inhibitions and complexes of the mind."

"You think my dreams have meanings?" she interposed quickly.

"I don't know," said I. "I haven't heard them yet. But you see what I mean?"

"Yes."

"The Rosicrucian puts these unknown and unknowable factors first. He works from them. Not to them. Like the Spiritualists. They don't say—not really—we will discover if there is a life after death. They say—there *is* a life after death. Let's get in touch with it and find out what it's like. And it's that kind of attitude of mind that leads all sorts of people into all kinds of malpractice."

"Do you mean the Rosicrucian is a fraud?" she asked. "A charlatan?"

"No. I'm not saying that. Seeing the constant and ineradicable belief of human nature in a hereafter, he is entitled to his premise about the unseen world and the unseen powers of life. I only suggest that sort of thing can lead to chicanery."

"Do you think this man Gollancz is like that?"

She asked it so sharply, so intently, that I could see there was more than mere inquiry in her question. There was a personal animation. But, then, most women are like that. Their inherent inclination is to take sides. I did not, perhaps, take so much notice of that sharpness as I might have done.

"I don't know anything about Gollancz," I replied; "and that's a fact. Not personally, anyhow. All of what I have told you about him so far is secondhand. I heard it from my friend—your husband's uncle. Naturally it's impossible wholly to accept the impression of one person from another. Crawshay-Martin said he had not changed in appearance in those forty years. Well, to Crawshay-Martin's particular vision that may have been so. But it doesn't justify us in the assumption that Gollancz has the power—the magic power, because, as we understand things, it would be nothing but magic—of prolonging youth."

"You're very sceptical—aren't you?" she said.

And that made me laugh. But directly I had heard the sound of my laughter it evaporated. Wasn't she sceptical, too? I asked her.

"I should have been," she replied enigmatically, "a few months ago. I don't know whether I am now."

"Look here," said I abruptly. "The sooner you tell me about these dreams of yours, the better. We're talking at cross-purposes. We might as well be talking different languages. The only way when one's discussing an elusive subject like this is to put all the cards of one's experience and beliefs on the table like a game of patience, and see what cards you can get out, and what cards are left with no place to fit them into. Come on, Miss Milligan. That's what it amounts to. My red six on your black seven. And there's bound to be an ace hidden away somewhere we can't get at."

She smiled at that. But very unlike herself. It was merely a smile to acknowledge that she knew I was doing my best.

"I know you're quite right," she said. "But there is just one thing I want to know first."

"What's that?"

"These men—these brothers of the Rosy Cross, when you say they're idealists, that their values—as of money—are the utter reverse of ours, do you mean that—that—they haven't the same conception of—of human relationships as we have?"

Those little hesitations of hers were most noticeable. In the same manner as her smile, they were unlike her. I should never have conceived it as characteristic of her to mind what she said, or how she said it.

"Idealism is bunk—isn't it?"

She had said that that morning in my consulting-room. And that was the sort of remark I should have expected of her. But here she was stammering and indecisive. And what was I to take as the meaning of her—human relationships? I should never have believed that to be her kind of phrase. Surely, if she had intended to convey their real relationship with the opposite sex, she would have said so. Straight out. Do they ever have anything to do with women? Something like that. And probably even less fastidious if that was her mood at the moment.

Yet, somehow, my instinct inclined me to think this was her meaning. And it is difficult to describe the impression it produced. I felt a kind of heat of anger stirring me to a call upon what, in the male animal, you would call the protective impulse. If this was the effect that Gollancz had upon her—and I had not forgotten those preliminary meetings at the "Scarlett Arms"—then the sooner she was put on her guard against a man like that, the better.

"If by that you mean," said I, "what is their relation to women, then I should imagine it doesn't exist. Mind you, I haven't made a study of Rosicrucianism. I'm not an authority. Being a secret brotherhood, I should be surprised to find anybody who has. But you haven't forgotten what he said that day at the 'Scarlett Arms'—have you?"

"What?"

"What he said about freedom. That he must be free."

And then she said a thing that for some reason or other made me feel cold in my blood. I don't know why.

"What's that got to do with it?" she asked. "I didn't mean, do they marry. There's a relationship between men and women without marriage, isn't there? At least I seem to have come across it fairly frequently."

I looked at her steadily across the table and, with a kind of defiant indifference, she looked back at me.

"Do you imagine it's only marriage that makes the servitude?" I asked her.

"I imagine it's a pretty considerable part of it," she said bitterly. And in that one sentence I had learnt all I wanted to know of her affection for Claude Weaver. But bad enough business as that seemed, the suggestion conveyed all through what she had said of her interest in Gollancz seemed to me the more unthinkable. The tragedy of her married life at least was capable of being faced and seen. This other was in the dark.

"Well," I said presently. "I can't tell you whether the Rosicrucian is a celibate or not, but I'm quite sure of this, that if a man like Gollancz desires to keep the complete essence of his freedom, he doesn't allow himself to be tied up by the bonds of sex. To you it may be marriage that is the epitome of bondage. Believe me, I don't want you to confide anything in me. Possibly I understand more than you tell me. But, then, your whole concept of life, as it is with any normal person, is based on a relationship of the sexes. To face the emotions and the desires of love is not a thraldom to you. It's a kind of enfranchisement. I don't want to pretend to be romantic about this, because romance, I fancy, is the last sort of thing you'd have any truck with."

"Why?"

"Well, there's not much room for romance nowadays, is there?"

"No. Precious little. Go on."

"Well—it is—a sort of enlargement of experience, anyhow. But to the Rosicrucian, I imagine, it's exactly the reverse. He doesn't begin to reach the higher degrees of his calling until he has risen above and completely mastered his physical desires. And, when you come to think of it, it must be like that. He's a kind of Mahatma."

"What's that?"

"A master amongst the Buddhists. A man who has followed in

the steps of Gautama Buddha until he has left all earthly desires behind him. A Mahatma, by the exercise of will and concentration, can release his spiritual from his physical body. He couldn't possibly do that if there were any ties left between his body and his mind. If a man desires a woman, there's no human possibility of his putting her completely out of his thoughts. When the spiritual—what they call the astral—body of the Mahatma leaves its earthly shell, there's nothing to draw it back. It can travel wherever it wills."

"Do you believe that?" she asked me quickly.

"How's one to say—believe?" said I. "Years ago, when I was in India, I saw one of these men put himself into a trance. Knives were put into him and he did not bleed. Apparently he felt nothing. To all intents and purposes his body was dead. And what had become of his consciousness, or his spirit, or whatever you like to call it, how could I say?"

"Did he come back again?"

"Oh, yes. Three or four days later I saw him. Spoke to him. Beyond the fact that it was impossible to feel oneself in ordinary communication with a human being, he was as normal again as we are. He fed himself on meagre quantities of rice."

"And you say the Rosicrucians are like that?"

"I never said anything of the kind," I replied, laughing at her—trying to rouse her out of this intensity of her mood. "All I can tell you is that a Rosicrucian, by the very nature of his aspiration, is a man who has forsworn the desires and the pains of the flesh. What powers he gains by that, I couldn't say. I don't pretend to know. Now, what about these dreams? And if you're not going to tell me about them, let's talk of something else. I make no pretensions to be anything other than a man of the world. I was born into it, and so long as I'm in it, it's quite good enough for me."

We sat for a little while eating in silence. By that time the dinner was practically finished. We were at an ice. She was dipping her spoon into it, taking up minute quantities and conveying them almost automatically to her mouth. I doubt if she realized it was cold.

At last she looked up and said:

"I began dreaming about Mr. Gollancz directly we got back to

Stoke Charity. My husband took that book with him. The solicitors didn't seem to think much of the value of it. So they let him have it. But, of course, you must have known that. You stayed on for the inquest, didn't you?"

I nodded my head.

"Well, the dreams began directly we returned."

"What sort of dreams? Nightmares?"

"No—not at first. At first it wasn't even Mr. Gollancz himself. I mean not the man I could recognize. One night it might be one kind of man. One night, another. Never him in appearance. But him in my mind. Do you understand?"

Provided one knew anything about dreams, it was quite easy to understand. The physical resemblance in a dream is immaterial to the psychologist. Dreams have fourfold meanings. It is the consciousness of the dreamer that is of importance.

"What kind of dreams were they?" I asked.

"Oh, nonsensical dreams," She laughed. "You couldn't have made head or tail of them. I could scarcely recollect them afterwards. Only the sense that he had been present in them remained after waking. And then, as I tell you, not him to look at. Once, for instance, I dreamt of the butcher at Stoke Charity. But it wasn't the butcher, though it looked exactly like him. It was Gollancz."

Our ices were finished. They brought the coffee. It broke into the conversation. We were silent for quite a long time. At moments when I thought she was unaware of it, I snatched glances at her, bent over her coffee, staring down into the bottom of the cup. Was it possible that a few dreams could have made that difference in anyone? There was an abstraction about her as of one who against their will is looking over an edge into a disturbing depth. What did it remind me of? It had the impression of a likeness. To whom? With an uncomfortable jolt of my memory, I realized it was to Crawshay-Martin. Not the man himself, of course, but to the look he had had in his face that afternoon in the garden at Malquoits. The look I had tried to explain to the sergeant at Shipleigh. As though he were being followed.

"And did you see anybody?" the sergeant had said.

Hopeless ass: It had been no good trying to talk to a man like that. Of course, I had seen no one. That was just the point of it. There could have been no one. Yet there, as visible as a cast shadow, had been that look in my friend's face. And there again it was in hers.

"What are you thinking about?" I asked sharply, to rouse her.

She looked up.

"I was wondering," she said, "why I'm telling all this to you. Is it part of it?"

"Part of what?"

She tried to laugh herself out of her mood. A flash of her former insolence. I could see the effort. It was no longer offensive, or even annoying. It was more like herself. I welcomed it. But it was only momentary. Her eyes returned to the bottom of her coffee-cup as though it were the bottom of a well. She went on:

"That sort of dream lasted for about three months, only becoming more and more vivid."

"How often did you have them?"

"Oh, sometimes every night. Never more than a week between one dream and another. Then there was a kind of pause. I didn't dream at all for nearly a month. I supposed it was a condition of my health, and that, whatever it was, it was gone. And then, one night, I dreamed of Gollancz himself. Actually him. I saw him plainly——"

She looked up across the table.

"As plainly as I can see you."

"What was the story of the dream?" I asked.

She looked away, frowning. Obviously it hadn't occurred to her to think of it constructionally. I could see her wrestling with her memory and unable to get a grip of it.

For that one instant as she turned her head away, I saw the quarter profile of her face. I was seized by an impression of her as she was, apart from all this business of her dreams. Apart from any question of Gollancz. And I found myself thinking:

"My God! She's lovely."

It was like a discovery. Why hadn't I seen her in that particular light before? When she turned back, it is quite probable I was looking amazed. But she didn't seem to notice it. She merely said:

"I can't remember. There was a story. There must have been, of course. Something mad. But I don't remember it. I only remember him."

Something had happened to me. I couldn't tell what it was. But I found myself becoming intense in my questioning of her. From being a kind of interested spectator—as it might have been, a Freudian student of dreams—I found my interest actually involved with hers. For some reason or other, I felt her to be in some kind of danger, and there came upon me the vital necessity to save her at all costs.

"Had anything happened that you can remember?" I asked.

"Where?"

"At home? Where you live. Stoke Charity."

"Do you mean in the house?"

"Not necessarily. Anywhere. The place doesn't matter. Some event, I mean. Your husband? Yourself?"

She looked about her. As though her memory were a confused collection of objects scattered about over the floor and she were trying to pick one out of the jumble.

"I don't know what sort of thing you want me to remember."

She was frowning.

"I don't want you to force any memory," I said. "Just tell me if anything happened about that time which you recollect."

"The only thing I can think of," she said after a further pause, "was an American coming down to Stoke Charity to see that book. After what the solicitors had said about it, I think my husband had somewhat lost his interest. My mother-in-law, who lives with us—she's blind, you know—remembered the book being in the library at Malquoits, and I fancy the realization that it had been about all that time without anyone trying to sell it, made him think that all the talk about its being worth fifty thousand pounds was ridiculous. He'd simply put it away in a drawer in his desk. And then one day he got this letter from an American, saying he had heard about the book—how, he never told us—and asking if he could come down and have a look at it. Being so far out of town, my husband invited him to lunch. He was quite an ordinary American. That's to say, he didn't do the things Americans are supposed to do. There wasn't any hustle in his conversation, and he never said a word about New York. He was really a very interesting man, and knew more about the Middle Ages in England than my husband did. Anyhow, he came. He saw the book, and straight out during lunch he offered a thousand pounds for it. A thousand pounds. You can imagine the look in Claude's eye at that."

"Why should I imagine it?" I asked.

"Oh, no good pretending to me you don't see things," she said, with a more friendly intimacy than I had yet heard in her voice. "I saw you look at him that day at the 'Scarlett Arms' when Mr. Gollancz said it was worth fifty thousand."

So she had noticed that. The perfunctory insolence of her manner was not so unobservant. To all appearances that day she had ignored my existence. Then what was I to deduce from this? Browning? "The meanest of His creatures boasts two soul-sides, one to face the world with . . ."

"Go on," I said eagerly. "Did he accept it? A thousand pounds for a book is every penny of a thousand pounds."

"Oh, no, he didn't accept it. Claude's far too wary to take a first offer for anything on its face value."

How she hated that man! It was a fair, a not unloyal definition of any man's business acumen. But as she said it, I seemed to feel all the underlying contempt of her nature beneath it. The contempt for the male sex that some of these modern women have driven into them by the sharp steel of experience.

"From that point," she went on, "Claude started like an auctioneer who's had a first bid at last from a peculiarly sticky audience. He laughed at a thousand pounds. But it was something to begin on."

"And did the American go any higher?"

"Yes. He went to two thousand pounds. Two thousand pounds for a book! Sounds incredible, doesn't it! My mother-in-law was at lunch while this conversation was going on. My mother-in-law, I must tell you, by the extraordinary freakishness of Nature that seems to procreate with the wildest inconsistency, is an angel. An angel gone blind. She had said nothing all through the meal, but when the American offered two thousand pounds, she suddenly said:

"'Sell it, Claude—sell it. It isn't everyone who can dispose of an infliction for two thousand pounds!'"

"What did she mean by that?" I asked.

"I don't know. She had always disliked the idea of that book being in the house since her brother's death. She loved her brother, you know. And I think he was rather hard to her after her marriage."

"Crawshay-Martin hated Weaver," I said.

"Probably—but he might have gone to see his sister sometimes. However, as I said, she's an angel. A blind angel. But her angelic counsels had no effect upon Claude. The American wouldn't go higher than two thousand. Not that day, anyhow. And after he'd gone, Claude locked the book away in a safe in his study. He was beginning to believe in its value again. Catching a glimpse of that fifty thousand pounds."

She looked up then and studied my face.

"Well, you've asked me to tell you something I remember happening. That's all, in the way of an event, I can think of."

And so, when she'd finished, I sat staring at her. Was it the revival of the book that had brought her mind back to Gollancz? Or was it the threatening loss of that book from the place where he was sure of its safety that had brought Gollancz back again to her? As I sat looking at her, I asked myself that question, and I couldn't answer it. I wanted more facts. I told her to go on about her dreams.

"Gollancz actually appeared in the next dream," I prompted her.

"Yes. But don't ask me the story of that. Except——"

She stopped abruptly and laughed. It was not so much laughter as a breath ejected through her nostrils.

"Except what?"

"Am I to tell you everything that's ridiculous?"

"Unless you tell me everything, I don't see——"

She spoke as though I weren't speaking:

"He kissed me."

But had she thought that so ridiculous? I was conscious of a hot thought that she hadn't. Yet why should it matter to me, one way or another? All the same I felt annoyed that she was trying to hoodwink me about it. And she thought she could get away with it. She didn't know that what one dreams in sleep is frequently what one wants to happen when one is awake.

"Hence," said I, "your question about the human relationships of Rosicrucians?"

She had forgotten that. If these women could blush, she would have blushed then. As it was, she laughed at me.

"Very astute," she said. "I suppose that's what you call a pointer in diagnosis."

"Never mind what I call it," said I. "You go on. He kissed you. Is that the kind of dream you had about him?"

"No. That didn't happen again."

Her voice changed. She dropped the bantering note. Quite suddenly she became intensely serious.

"I began to dream about him," she said, "in places. Different places, but always in London. In different streets. Streets I knew. Oxford Street. Piccadilly. Regent Street. I'd seen him—that hat—you know—over the heads of crowds of people."

She didn't know how vividly she was bringing back my recollection of my first meeting with Gollancz. His departure as he crossed the Haymarket into Piccadilly Circus. That sombrero hat, floating away over the sea of hats until it was submerged and Crawshay-Martin and I saw him no more.

"And did you come into contact with him?"

"No. In my dream I tried. You know the sort of dream when you try to get at something and thousands of obstacles come in your way. People. Taxis. Buses. In the end, he'd always disappear up some side street. And when I got there, no one like him was to be seen. But at last one night I dreamt that I succeeded in following him. It was in the Strand. Extraordinary how clear all these different places were. I can remember the places better than anything else in the dream. Well—you'll see. It was near the Law Courts. Just where the Strand narrows into Fleet Street. You know, where the 'Dragon' is. I followed him through the crowds of people that were outside the Courts. He passed a street called—Fetter Lane, is it?"

I nodded my head.

"Yes, in the dream, I couldn't see the name on the corner

house. Anyhow, I don't think I ever knew there was a Fetter Lane. I never go down into that part of the world."

"No—the dressmakers don't congregate there," said I. "I don't quite see you amongst the little typists. That's their beat. Is that where you caught him up?"

"I didn't catch him. Suddenly he turned up a kind of alley. I saw the name of that. Clifford's Inn. He went in there. It was vivid in my dream. Vivid. I can see him now turning in under a kind of gateway that led into a square—almost like a quadrangle in one of the colleges. There was a doorway in one corner. A doorway with a porch over it, and there was a number at the side. Number eight. He went in there and I ran after him. Ran, in my dream, to catch him up. But the staircase was all dark. I couldn't see where he had gone. I found a door in the darkness and began hammering on it. I kept on hammering and then I woke up. I was beating the pillows. A nightmare."

She stopped to search my face.

"Anyhow, you dreamt of something that actually exists," I said. "There is a Clifford's Inn."

"Yes. I know."

"Oh! You've verified it?"

"Yes. I went down to Fleet Street this morning, before I came to see you. I come up to Town sometimes and stop in a little club I belong to, here in Dover Street. I went there and found Clifford's Inn. I went down into the quadrangle, and stood on the other side staring at the door."

"Was it just the same as you'd dreamt?"

"Exactly. The same kind of door. The sort of porch to it."

Her voice dropped almost to a whisper.

"And while I stood there, on the other side of the little square, he came out. Gollancz. In that hat. And he never looked at me. Or he seemed not to. I was the only other person there and he took no notice. He walked up the alley into the street. I was so dumbfounded I couldn't move for a moment. My dream. Exactly as I'd dreamt it. And when I did pull myself together and went out into Fleet Street, he was gone."

CHAPTER VII

I suppose we must have sat there with our empty coffee-cups for fully a minute in silence looking at each other after those last words of hers:

"And when I did pull myself together and went back into Fleet Street, he was gone."

The greatest significance of all she had told me was the unavoidable impression I received that these dreams were not so much an indication of the state of her mind as the superimposition of Gollancz's will upon hers. Dreams, to the Freudian psychologist, are subliminal pictures on the subconscious brain relating to the person who experiences them. They may refer back to years in the past, but essentially they belong to the state of mind of the person who dreams them.

There was nothing of this about the dreams she had told me. I had got the suggestion from them that it was Gollancz himself who had found his way into her sleeping and unsuspecting mind. Not so much she who had been labouring under an obsession of him, as he who had compelled her subconsciousness to consent to this taking possession of her thoughts.

In those first vague dreams when she had been aware of his presence, but had been unable to recognize the physical characteristics (as when she had dreamed of the butcher at Stoke Charity, feeling all the time that it was Gollancz), it was as though he had been gradually insinuating his will upon hers.

What, then, had changed the character of those nocturnal pictures, so that after the hiatus of peaceful sleep, she had begun to dream actually of him? I had asked her and she had told me. Something had happened about the book. Still, irresistibly in my mind was that old conviction that he was determined to get possession of it. Without my being able to resist the suggestion, it returned to me then.

The American—Mr. Holt (she had mentioned his name)—had appeared. The quiet security of the book down at the Court

House, Stoke Charity, had been threatened. Two thousand pounds had been offered for it. A less avaricious man than Claude Weaver might have accepted that. I didn't pretend to know what powers Gollancz possessed. But it was fairly reasonable to assume that to have it removed four thousand miles to another continent would not make it any the more accessible to him.

How he had come to know it was going to be put up at Crawshay-Martin's sale was not to be reckoned. Certainly Crawshay-Martin himself, until that moment, had lost track of it. Had Gollancz known for certain? I could not even be sure of that. He had asked to look at it there in the garden, after Crawshay-Martin had bought it. As though to verify his suspicions. Without doubt his friend, Mr. Bannerjee, had bid for it. But that didn't prove he knew it was amongst the lot. It was impossible for me to say what I knew of Gollancz's supernormal powers. But upon one thing I could not be shaken. He wanted to get that book, and while it seemed impossible for him to conjure it out of the possession of the person who held it, he was capable, as I believed, of going to the desperate lengths of his supernatural influence to secure it.

Crawshay-Martin may have cut his own throat, but what induced him to it? For what reason had he hidden the book under that loose board in the bedroom at the "Scarlett Arms"? And why had Gollancz entered the room that day? None of these things could I possibly forget. And when I heard the story of Mrs. Weaver's dreams, up to the actual point of her being led to the very place where he lived, these suspicions came back to me with a force that beat upon my mind until, for that minute or so, I had nothing but silence to offer her. Silence and the slow, speculating stare of my eyes.

"And that was this morning?" I said at last.

She had just told me it was. The question was indicative of the preoccupation of my thoughts. She nodded her head.

"And when was your dream? About this place? Clifford's Inn?"

"Three nights ago."

"You woke up?"

"Yes. It was a sort of nightmare. I told you. I was beating the pillows."

"Wide awake?"

"As wide awake as you usually are after a nightmare. A kind of consciousness of terror."

"You could see about the room?"

"It was dark."

"Yes—but when one wakes up, things in a dark room are quite discernible. The night has a sort of visibility about it if your eyes haven't been looking at anything brighter."

"Oh, yes, like that I could see."

"And did you notice anything?"

"Why do you ask me that?"

Well, I didn't exactly want to tell her why I had asked it, I didn't want to frighten her. It was only an idea that had occurred to me; an idea based upon the fact that if you stand by the bedside of a child while it's asleep, and in a low but audible voice tell it something—to correct a fault, for example—it will have a perceptible effect upon that child's waking mind. All its conscious functionings are asleep. The subconscious alone is active. By repeating something audibly while the child is in that condition, it is possible to reach its subliminal self. Had Gollancz by some means done that? In some essence of himself was he there in that room while she slept?

But she was looking at me closely, as I've seen many a patient looking and waiting to hear one's report of an examination. There was a strain of apprehension in her eyes. As off-handedly as I could, I said:

"No particular reason. Only that one's liable to queer impressions when one wakes up out of a nightmare."

"Well—I had an impression. Queer enough."

"What was it?"

"That Gollancz was there in the room."

I controlled my voice to say:

"Because of something you saw?"

"Yes and no."

She had given me an opportunity I welcomed to laugh at her.

"Which?"

"My window was open. It was a very still night. Not a breath of air. And then, suddenly, as I sat up in bed, the curtains swung against the window. Not into the room, as they would have done if a wind had sprung up. But against the window, as though a wind was blowing out. They fell back again at once and were motionless. The room was as still as the night outside. And, I don't know, but it felt as though someone had gone out of it. As though he'd gone out. Of course, I suppose it was the sensation of the dream still about me. That's the worst part of a nightmare. The waking up. Being unable to shake it off."

I pursued that no further. What she had told me, after all, was quite a possible happening. Passages of air play funny tricks. In a very still atmosphere in a room I have seen curtains do that myself. As for her sensations, the nightmare, as she said herself, would have accounted for those.

It was only peculiar that having had that extravagant idea in my mind and put my question, her answer should have corroborated it.

"And have you told your husband anything about this?" I asked.

That question was prompted partly by curiosity. I knew directly I had put it that I had done so for the satisfaction of hearing her say she had told no one but me.

"Do you imagine we have anything in common?" she inquired.

I didn't know. I couldn't say. I could only suppose that the exchange of a common point of view was one of the first essentials of the matrimonial agreement. I ventured to suggest it.

"How charming," she remarked. "Do you imagine then that people actually exchange their real views before marriage?"

"Don't they?"

"They may do. I haven't met them. People before marriage, as far as I can make out, play a kind of a part, as deceptive to themselves as it is to the other person. They may have bad tempers, but nothing appears to ruffle them. They are amazed even at themselves. Unselfishness is a positive joy to them. Demonstrativeness and affection are their most outstanding qualities. Some even acquire a kind of charm they have never possessed at any other time of their life and will never possess again."

There I stopped her with laughter.

"Cynicism brought to a fine art," said I.

"Not at all. You only asked me if I'd told my husband. I thought you might like a comprehensive answer."

And then I felt suddenly sorry for her. Damned sorry. If she had ever been induced to think there was a charm about Claude Weaver before she married him, then I didn't wonder at her cynicism. So long as she could, she had kept up a show of being a reasonably satisfied married woman. But it only needed a couple of hours of understanding conversation, even with a comparative stranger, to break all that down. She was aware that I knew he took drugs. Then what was the good of pretending to me any longer? There was no genuine pretence in her nature. And she said it then:

"You know he takes drugs?"

"Oh, yes. That was obvious to anyone with half an eye."

"Well, then, what's the good of talking about an exchange of common points of view? How can you exchange anything human with a man who sometimes is like a raving lunatic? I have charge of his drug when he's sober, and then when he wants it, it's like living in hell with a madman."

Suddenly she stood up, shrugging her shoulders and laughing.

"I didn't come here to tell you my bothers," she said. "What have they got to do with you? There isn't a prescription for incompatibility, is there? All I wanted to know, you've told me. So they're celibates, are they?"

All that she said, even to the last sentence, in a bantering voice. And, like what they say about a woman's postscript, it was that last sentence which contained the key to her mind. I knew it then, that in some kind of fashion, she was in love with Gollancz. It might be no more than an infatuation. It might even, in some sort of way, be that she was bewitched. In these matter-of-fact days, did I believe that? How could I say? The whole affair was very curious. All the time I found my thoughts tending to speculation rather than to fact. Whatever it was, it was a condition of mind that a good many people mistake for love. And when she said that, with her bantering laugh:

"So they're celibates, are they?"

Then I knew that I was in love with her already myself. And I could as little explain that. Had pity anything to do with it?

Hardly. She was not the type of woman to waste your pity upon. A natural inclination is to give people the kind of thing they demand of you. Pity from anyone was the last consideration she would have asked for. Moreover I was too conscious of the force of her character to make a blundering mistake like that. An emotion about a woman either goes like alcohol to a man's head and makes a fool of him, or it sharpens his wits.

Anyhow, it took me that way. With a quickening instinct I knew that to advance my emotional interest in her at such a stage of what I had not even the justification for calling our friendship, would be fatal to my chances.

What chances?

She was a married woman.

Somehow I suppose when the fundamental impulses get hold of you, a marriage like hers appears to be no obstacle. Could it be called a marriage in any sense? For if the kind of relationship as existed between herself and Claude Weaver is to be dignified by the name of marriage, then it might well be an institution of the Satanists.

No, I was not thinking of her marriage as an obstacle. A woman like her is not tied by conventions. It was the indeterminable figure of Gollancz that stood in my way.

How much there was in her mind of those dreams she had had over the period of that six months since their first meeting, that she had not told me? With all the frankness she had exhibited in coming to consult me in Arlington Street and now out to dine, I had to make allowance for the inherent secretiveness of her sex. A woman never tells you the whole truth. How can she? The whole truth would destroy her.

But that question of hers—"So they're celibates, are they?"—had told me a good deal. And more than that. She had suggested there were other relationships than that of marriage. In one of her dreams he had kissed her. Then, whether she knew it or not, that was her thought about him. The animation I had seen that day in her face as she looked at Gollancz out of the window at the "Scarlett Arms" was an animation rooted in the instincts of her sex. Nothing could dissuade her from it. I knew enough about women and human nature in general to be sure of that.

If, as it well might be, it were the explanation of all her dreams, it was a thing that must burn itself out. I was not fool enough to believe I could extinguish it in her with this emotion of my own. A younger man might have flung himself at her feet. But to do that would only have roused her to a contempt she could never have forgotten. I thanked God I wasn't a young man. Looking at the fascination of that insolent face of hers, I told myself I could wait. But I was determined to keep in close touch with her whenever she came to London. At Stoke Charity with only her dreams, I felt her to be more or less safe. But not here in town.

For, however I argued the experience of her nocturnal pictures to lie in this infatuation, nothing, I told myself, of Freudian theories could explain that dream of Clifford's Inn which had brought her to the very spot where he lived.

But she was standing up and ready to go. A clock had chimed eleven. She was holding out her hand and looking at me with her bantering smile. Insolence, I was coming to understand, was the face she wore with which to meet a world of total strangers. This bantering cynicism was the mask for her friends. I was sure, anyhow after this meeting and her confidences, she regarded me as that. But nothing more. Not then. And it was not easy to let her go with so little to console myself. However, a man is not forty-five for nothing. The only satisfaction I could get out of it was to suggest that if she didn't want to take a taxi that short way down Dover Street to her club, I would walk with her.

"I'm not accustomed to these old-time chivalries," she remarked. "Is it your idea that young women should not be seen alone in the street at night?"

"Oh, no," I said indifferently, "We've been sitting a good while. I just wanted to stretch my legs."

Nothing more was said about her dreams or about Gollancz as we walked down to her club. We did not speak of the book again or of her husband. Only when she stopped outside the entrance and I held out my hand to bid her good night, I said:

"Do you mind promising me something?"

"I've got nothing of value to give away," she replied, smiling.

Very nearly I muttered: "My God! Haven't you!" But checked myself. She was not to be won like that.

"It's not a matter of giving anything away," I said. "But only, whenever you come up to town, I want you to come and see me and tell me what's happening."

"What should happen?"

The same quick note in her voice. She could not keep it back.

"Well, do you imagine that this morning is the last time you'll see Gollancz?"

"No."

She tried, ineffectually, to laugh as she said that.

"No. It won't be the last time," I said. And then I told her, with an intentional note of warning in my voice. "He wants that book," I said. "More than your American does. I expect you'll have something to tell me before long. Write if you want to. But what I'm principally saying is—come and see me whenever you come up to town."

Had she suspicions about me then? Women are quick instinctive creatures. I saw her eyes narrow an instant as she looked at me, and to ward away that glance I added with a smile: "Don't you worry—my fees aren't exorbitant. Only for isolated appointments."

We shook hands and she was gone into the building. I saw her through the glass door talking to a hall-porter in livery, and I envied the beggar having a later word with her than I. Perhaps it was as well she didn't see that glance of mine. I walked away down Dover Street. But when I reached the Ritz, it was impossible to turn into Arlington Street and go to bed. My mind wasn't fit for bed. A man who has made the discovery about himself I had just made, can't lie down as if nothing had happened and go to sleep. Little had I thought my life was ready for an emotional experience like this. Forty-five! It was hard to credit it.

Wondering what it was all going to mean to me, I found myself strolling on down Piccadilly. Crossing the Circus. The theatres were bursting, as the taximen say. The night life of London was in a swarm. At a superior and yet none too contented distance, I passed by men fighting for taxis for their womenfolk. Why hadn't I asked her if she was going to be in town the next night?

Because I wasn't a fool.

The pavements were crowded all the way down Coventry

Street. Shakespeare was brooding over the garden in Leicester Square, and there were hundreds in Leicester Square who wanted no more than their taxi or their bus home. Young women in short skirts with shapely and shapeless legs were hurrying to and fro, skimming the surface like beetles on an agitated pond. I was in that mood of feeling profoundly sorry for everyone and none too certain of myself.

The increasing quiet of Garrick Street was a rebel. Covent Garden was silent as a tomb. Where was I going? At the back of my mind I knew quite well where I was going. I was going down to Clifford's Inn. An insatiable curiosity animated by my emotions was drawing me there like a magnet. With what could I satisfy it at that time of night? Nothing. And yet on I went, choosing the by-streets rather than the main thoroughfares, because, I suppose, they accorded with the isolation of my mood.

The situation was an extraordinary one. I don't consider myself a conventionalist. I see too much of the confusion of human relationships ever to assume that the affairs of men and women can run to the schedule of accepted moralities. But this I realized could only have happened in life. In love with a married woman, I was enforced by the most peculiar circumstances to stand by and wait until her infatuation for another man had resolved itself. And her husband in all this did not count. Claude Weaver himself, as an issue in the problem might scarcely have existed. I never reckoned with him. Divorce is a solution one accepts nowadays with a complacency that reveals the changing aspect of marriage.

But Gollancz was not to be ignored like that. And so far as I could see there was only one solution to the problem as he caused it to be presented. I was convinced of what she called his celibacy. With so little information as I had of the secret Brotherhood of the Rosy Cross, I knew the distractions of sex were anathema to the occult mind. How could a man achieve such power over himself as apparently Gollancz did possess—as one felt he possessed—if he ever allowed the desire of a woman to occupy his thoughts! Yet possibly it was from this very aspect, the irresistible attraction of the man presented itself to her.

What could I do? How should I warn her? I felt her to be even in actual danger, and yet to attempt to drive her from it I knew would only drive her on.

Outside of the freakishness of life itself, I wondered if ever a man had determinedly thrust himself into such a situation as I. And so I went on wondering until I had turned out of Fleet Street under the dark arch of the porter's lodge with its carved coat-of-arms in the discoloured stone and found myself in the silent isolation of Clifford's Inn.

Number Eight was the building from which she told me he had come out that morning. But in the darkness of that place, so near to and yet remote from the highly-lighted streets of civilization, it was impossible to see a number amongst those huddled houses without going close up to the door itself and deciphering the figures dimly painted on the jamb. There seemed to be so little order in their disposition. The whole building, as I realized it then, was like a vast Elizabethan manor house set down there in the heart of London, that had escaped the flux of time and hidden itself from the demolishing hands of the housebreaker. It twisted here and there with projecting wings that formed deep recesses—each a kind of courtyard—still paved with the cobbles of a period unrecognizably removed from the wood-blocked surface of Fleet Street, only a stone's throw away.

Of course, I had seen Clifford's Inn before. But only superficially, as the American tourist sees it. A mere look round in the broad light of day at the dark, red-brick buildings, the small, square, panelled windows, the deep arched doorways leading to the narrow flights of wooden stairs. Conscious all the time of the close proximity of Fleet Street. The convenience of its buses and taxis to transport one back again to the full, noisy stream of civilization. Once I had had lunch there at the little restaurant on one of the ground floors, but had scarcely been conscious in that casual visit of people actually living there. Inside the jambs of some of the doors there were names of solicitors and architects who carried on their daily business and left the place to its silences as the evening rounded off the hours of their work. The place was associated in my mind with people like that.

I had never seen the Inn at half-past eleven o'clock at night like this. The porter had probably long since gone to sleep in the lodge. If that, indeed, was where he lived. But still in upper windows here and there lights were burning. People, whose existence it was not easy to imagine, were living their lives there, in those Elizabethan buildings. Up those twisting, narrow wooden stairs, there were doors that opened into the private life of queer individuals. People one probably never heard about. Struggling artists, perhaps. Obscure journalists. I tried to imagine them. A regular nesting-place for impecunious poets, those upper stories in the buildings of Clifford's Inn.

As I searched for the doorway of Number Eight in the entrances of those dark houses, one solitary man passed by me over the cobbles, and then a moment later a man and a girl. They disappeared under their respective archways. Above the muffled vibration of the traffic in Fleet Street I could hear the sound of their footsteps mounting the bare wooden stairs. I could hear the heavy door slam as they shut themselves away in the privacy of those chambers where they lived.

For the moment as they passed me by in the cobbled courtyard outside they had been fellow human beings, available to the speculating direction of my glance. In my imagination I could follow them up those stairs. But once that door had slammed, a mystery of silence conjured them out of my reach into itself. I was aware of the total ineffectuality of my inspecting glance. I knew nothing about them. The secret purpose of their existence was as hidden from me as though with the closing of that door they had died and the essence of them were in a world of the hereafter upon which we can only expend the most hazardous of calculations.

At last, after a process of elimination, I discovered the doorway of Number Eight. It had actually been the first building as I had entered the Inn, but turning sharply to the right down a narrow kind of passage between houses on one side and railings on the other, it had escaped my notice.

Unlike the other doorways, which were set flush with the face of the building itself, it had a projecting wooden portico, beneath which the stairs vanished into a sort of cavernous darkness, just as she had told me. Approaching the entrance itself, I found the stairs winding sharply out of sight. No names were painted on the jamb of this doorway. I was left in ignorance, even to the mere sound of names, as to the occupation of chambers in that honeycomb of dwellings.

Under any ordinary circumstances, possibly my curiosity might have begun to evaporate by then. Had I been looking just for the habitation of a mere individual I should probably have been satisfied with my discovery of that entrance of Number Eight.

But things had happened to me that evening which, in a man's life when he comes to the age of forty-five, are not lightly to be disposed of. I was far from content with having found the actual place that Juniper had described to me. If there were names on the doors upstairs, I wanted to read them. I wanted to satisfy myself that Gollancz did live there.

The sensation that anybody might appear at any moment and ask me what the devil I was doing, accompanied me all the way up those dark stairs. Conscious, I suppose, of the little right I had to be there, I trod the wooden steps as lightly as I could.

Why, under such circumstances, is one inclined to do the very thing that makes one's actions appear the more suspicious. Thinking of it afterwards when I got home to Arlington Street, I realized I should have mounted those stairs making a noise in Clifford's Inn that night just as loud as those others I had heard ascending to the privacy of their chambers.

At any rate, whatever I should have done I didn't do. I crept up the staircase, dimly lit from an upper floor by a faint electric light. It burnt like a gas-jet in the old glass casing of an antiquated street lamp that had probably been there for a hundred years and more.

On the first half-landing there was a heavy oak door with massive hinges and a brand-new brass knocker. It bore the painted name of a private individual and was ostensibly not connected with any business. On the first floor proper, with two or three separate doors on the narrow landing, were the premises of a firm of architects.

From that upwards the stairs grew narrower and more winding. One door, just beneath the street-lamp lighting one's ascent, opened actually on to the stairs themselves. A visiting-card was pinned with a drawing-pin to the door. A Mrs. Somebody or other lived there. Extraordinary! Who would ever have thought it! Alone in that dark, silent building. A woman living by herself.

I reached the top landing. The ceiling fell away to a tiny window with the slope of the roof. There were two doors here, one facing me, corresponding to the door in the half-landing downstairs. The other on my left. That facing me had a name newly painted on it. A recent inhabitant of Clifford's Inn, proud of his occupation. A journalist, perhaps, eager to see his name in print.

The door on my left had a name as well. The name of a solicitor who had once resided there. It was almost obliterated with age. I say had once resided there. It was obvious he resided there no longer. No one could ever have discovered his place of business from those faded characters on the door.

But the name of Gollancz was nowhere to be seen. Had Juniper been mistaken? It did not seem consistent with her character. She was scarcely the kind to romance about the things that happened to her. But so far as my investigations were concerned, there was no more to be done. I had found Number Eight, Clifford's Inn, and that was about all.

Yet as I turned to go down those narrow stairs again, a peculiar impression invaded my mind. It was not from anything I saw or heard. It came to me through my sense of smell. I was aware of a faint perfume of incense on that top floor. As though, without being actually conscious of its burning, I were in the precincts of a Roman Catholic church.

It was so delicate, so indefinite, that I only paused for one moment, to draw it in with my breath. But in the kind of way that incense has, it lingered in my nostrils until after I had got out in the night air again. I was still smelling it as I passed under the archway of the porter's lodge into Fleet Street.

What had it suggested to me? I couldn't definitely say. I don't know whether it is upon my senses alone that that particular odour has an effect of transportation. It seems to convey my mind into the regions of another world.

Possibly that is what it is intended to do. Probably that is what it does with everyone. In the sacramental and uplifting atmosphere of the Mass, one feels oneself exalted beyond the mundane things of this life. No doubt it is intended that one should be so.

It had, anyhow, that effect upon me. I scarcely realized I was back again in Fleet Street. Like a dreamer I was walking in a mental abstraction. And then, as I turned the corner of the passage into the actual thoroughfare, I bumped into a man who was turning into the Inn itself.

It was only a slight collision. Nothing to interfere with his progress or mine. But sufficient to make me notice him. With a jolt of my memory that carried me back those six months and more to the gracious garden of Malquoits, I recognized the dark, olive-coloured face of Mr. Bannerjee.

With that Oriental impassiveness to the actual facts and people in life, he did not appear to have seen me. He turned up the passage of Clifford's Inn and, as I stood there watching him, his figure was lost under the dark shadows of the porter's lodge.

CHAPTER VIII

By the time I had recovered the full presence of my mind and hurried after Mr. Bannerjee, he was out of sight. Nevertheless, standing down there in the cobbled courtyard outside the doorway of Number Eight, I could hear the sound of footsteps mounting the wooden stairs. They were lighter, quieter than those others had been, but, to my strained attention, audible enough.

At the top floor, where they ceased, I listened with every sense in me lent to the service of my ears. Even then for a moment I could hear nothing. Should I have heard if he had knocked? Was he opening the door himself? Was he waiting for it to be opened for him? Whichever had happened, it had been done in complete silence. All I heard was the noise of it closing. A muffled sound, far less resonant than those other doors had been. As though the edges of it were padded with felt. Baffled, as it might have been the closing door of a church.

Why didn't I go up those stairs after him?

That hour of the night, the secretive sound of that door, a

sense of the barrier of silence that followed it, all these things I suppose made me realize that, whatever was happening in that room up there, not the faintest chance was conceivable for one of my antipathies ever being admitted to it.

That Gollancz lived in those chambers on the door of which I had seen that half-obliterated name of the long-departed solicitor, was quite obvious to me then. Why had I ever expected to find his name blatantly painted up for any inquisitive eye to see? Would his be likely to be the sort of life of which a man would invite inspection? The lives of those occupying chambers in Clifford's Inn, hidden in the heart of civilization, were already remote enough from public curiosity. And behind that undistinguished door, I could imagine him so far removed from the ordinary ways of life as to be almost a recluse, lost in the hermetical solitude.

It was even impossible from where I stood to determine which were the windows of his chamber. Above the wooden portico two faced me, one above the other. But these, as I had discovered when I had been inside, were landing windows giving light to the staircase. Through the top one I could just see that antiquated street lamp casing with its faint electric gleam. And on the right of that the building ended. Such rooms as there were extended in a long wing to the left of the staircase, or penetrated beyond into a farther wing, the windows of which were not to be seen at all from where I was.

In that left wing no lights were burning whatever. It was a blank wall. But, judging by the position of the door, the upper windows were those of the lady whose visiting card I had seen, while those on the first floor below belonged to the firm of architects. In what direction the other chambers extended I had no knowledge of architectural construction to determine. But his windows must look out somewhere and, satisfying my determination to learn something that night of the way he lived, I wandered round into the next courtyard formed by the projecting wings of the building.

It was possible here, even for one quite ignorant of architecture, to conceive a disposition of rooms having their entrance in Number Eight, yet facing with their windows across the space in which I stood. And there, sure enough, on a top floor was a window that was lighted. But not with electric light. There was no sharp glare about it. Only a soft glow that penetrated through the narrow slit of a division between the heavy curtains. By a manœuvring of position, I could just determine the source of light through the interstice. It was a candle burning. I could see the pear-shaped flame. Probably there were others, sufficient to provide the amount of illumination that was coming through. Still, that one was the only flame I saw.

But candles! Candles burning in the heart of London, with the power station of the London General Electric Company probably somewhere in the neighbourhood. Nevertheless there they were. Candles! And then, with a sudden rousing of my memory, I recalled that odour of incense outside Gollancz' door.

What ceremony, what sacrament was being performed behind the heavy folds of those dark curtains? More than ever I realized that, if I went and knocked on that door then, I should not be admitted. But back into my mind, as I stood alone in the dark shadows of the buildings, returned those illuminations in that book of Simon Studion's.

Could it be possible that in this matter-of-fact, irreligious twentieth century, and there in the heart of London, the occult practices of the ancient astrologers were still being carried on? Every natural instinct in me was inclined to laugh at it. It seemed incredible. And yet something of suspicion remained, inseparable from whatever I might think. How could any human purpose so waste itself upon mere folly? I asked myself that question and found it unanswerable. Unless the possessor of that purpose was not in his right senses.

In my imagination I regarded those highly intelligent features of Gollancz' face. Could a man like that be declared to be mad? Were those things that he had said to me in the passage outside the panelled room in the "Scarlett Arms" the sayings of one whose reason was gone? When a man like Nietzsche, of colossal intellect, became demented, it was a complete cataclysm of the mind. He retained nothing that was of service to thought. He became a lunatic.

But who in their senses could have said that Gollancz was anything like that? After all, some of the highest intellects of the present day were claiming themselves to be in touch with the unseen spirit world, and were they reckoned to be mad? Who was to define the means by which the apparently finite mind of man was to bring himself in touch with the infinite? Darkened rooms and spirit writing are more questionable channels of communication than lighted candles and burning incense. Could those who worship in churches be said to be mad? Because that sacramental ceremony was being performed in an unauthorised place of worship, was I justified in condemning it any more than the mysterious and sacred elevation of the Host in an established cathedral?

It would be impossible to say where my thoughts and conjectures led me that night as I stood down there on the cobblestones in Clifford's Inn and stared up at that curtained window. Nothing, anyhow just then, was to be made of them, and in a dazed confusion of mind I turned back again into Fleet Street and went home.

Perhaps it was the unaccustomed exercise of walking at that time of night, perhaps an exhaustion of all the emotions I had experienced, but I slept like a man dead.

The first thing in the morning when I woke, I was conscious of some momentous realization. There is no necessity to romance about it. This is a plain statement of fact, not a romance. I will try to make it appear as matter-of-fact as I can to keep it in proper relation to this story. But there was no doubt about it, I was in love. The insolence, the pride, the indifference of that woman had become characteristics of irresistible attraction to me. Once having thought of those lines of Browning, I could not get them out of my head. There was a soul-side to her. I was sure of that. Reserved for the man whom she would love. And when I thought it might be revealed to Gollancz and not to me, a restlessness came over me it was impossible to subdue.

At ten o'clock I have to visit the hospital with which I am associated. I am usually there an hour. From eleven o'clock till one I go and see such patients as are confined to their own beds or are in nursing homes. There were three or four that morning by whom I was expected. But by the time I had finished my work at the hospital, I knew that nothing short of an emergency could persuade me to see them. Juniper was returning to Stoke Charity that day. I wanted to see her again before she went. What for I couldn't say. I suppose when a man of forty-five comes upon an emotion like this, it is a serious business with him.

With my practice in Arlington Street it was a simple matter to telephone the various nurses in charge, inquire what sort of night the patients had had, recommend this treatment or that according to the reports I received, and trust to my luck that none of them would be urgent.

I suppose the public cherish the opinion of a doctor that he is a man with no imperative impulses to distract him from the plain path of his engagements. They cannot conceive him as being one who is liable, in the importunate desire of a moment, to put his work aside and get away from it all. He could not, in their opinion, wake up one fine morning with the insistent urge to play a game of golf. Least of all could he, as I felt then, be possessed with the irresistible need to meet a woman he loves. A sick man's ailments are everything to him. It is difficult for him to imagine they are not of permanent importance to his doctor.

Yet such that morning was the case with me. And none of the reports I received over the telephone being urgent, I rang up Juniper's club in Dover Street.

"Is Mrs. Claude Weaver there?"

"No, sir. Mrs. Claude Weaver had a wire calling her back to the country by an early train this morning."

I put down the receiver with a sense of defeat and loss. The only satisfaction I had was that she was in London no longer. Poor enough in its way, but it enabled me to realize my fear that she would go down to Clifford's Inn again and that that second time she might renew her acquaintance with Gollancz, begun so briefly at the "Scarlett Arms."

She had not done that. I confessed myself of a sense of relief. But if she hadn't, why shouldn't I? I would have done so the night before had I thought for a moment that anything would have come of it. But now, in the broad light of morning, surely if I went there and knocked on his door in Clifford's Inn, I should be admitted.

How I was to explain the purpose of my visit I did not begin to consider till I was seated in a taxi and proceeding in the direction of Fleet Street. All I wanted was to see him in the intimate surroundings of his actual life and from them determine something of the personality with which, inevitably, I knew I was in conflict.

But once I found myself going there, I realized well enough that some feasible explanation would have to be given. And, even then, it was possible that with those extraordinary powers of his penetrative mind, he would be aware of the invention of my explanation. However, that I could not help. So long as I had some reason I could stick to, he could perceive what he liked of my purpose.

But what was to be my ostensible reason for going there? Certainly I could say nothing of Juniper. Apart from the fact that her dreams had been told me in confidence, it was the last of my intentions that he should come to realize what I had discovered about myself.

There was only one thing we had in common. That illuminated manuscript of Simon Studion's. It had belonged to my friend, Crawshay-Martin. I had been with him at his sudden death in the "Scarlett Arms." Two encounters, as Gollancz described them, we had already had on that subject. I could go to inform him what I had heard, not necessarily from Juniper, of Mr. Holt's offer of two thousand pounds. If he really wanted that manuscript, as I had definite reason to suppose he did, he must make up his mind about it. Claude Weaver was not the man to resist the offer of two thousand pounds for a mere book for long. In what might almost appear a friendly spirit, I could give him this warning. Would he be able to see through that? If he did, I didn't care. I had a solid stratum of fact on which to rest my intentions. Mr. Holt had made that offer. It was not likely to be his last. The taxi pulled up in Fleet Street opposite the Clifford's Inn passage, and my mind was clearly made up as I stepped out on to the pavement.

It was a very different place that morning from the dark, almost sinister building I had visited the night before. Hardly was I able to reconstruct the reality of my sensations then. One cannot definitely estimate the psychological effect of light upon the mind. There, that morning, in the bright glare of day, with the busy rush of people outside the Law Courts, it seemed inconceivable that I should have been impressed as I was by the mere whiff of an odour of incense and the flickering light of a burning candle.

How was it possible, with clerks and messengers running here and there about their business, with charwomen seated in the sun on the parapet of the railings outside Number Eight, consuming what I am told they call their "elevenses," with the sound of the typewriter clicking away in the architect's office on the first floor as I mounted the stairs, how was it possible to believe that only a few hours before I had been imagining myself in the proximity of the occult practices of the ancient astrologers?

Even the solitary lady's visiting card, pinned to the door with a drawing-pin—probably given to her out of the architect's office—did not provide me with the same sense of astonishment. Why shouldn't a Mrs. Somebody-or-other reside there alone in these inconvenient bachelor's quarters if she liked? An original certainly, but a decidedly independent way of living. As for the door, on the landing above, with the obliterated solicitor's name and the faded words—"Commissioner for Oaths"—it presented none of that mysterious character I had discovered in it under the light of the antiquated street lamp on the stairs the night before.

Mounting that wooden flight again that morning, I could afford to ridicule my nocturnal impressions. Knocking on that door with my bare knuckle, I could await, without any misgiving as to my reception, the answer to my summons. Whatever peculiar habits of life Gollancz might pursue as a Rosicrucian, it was impossible that morning in the year 1930 to conceive a man relating himself in any practical way with the unknown and the unseen forces of life. Everything about me in that place was so clear, so definite, so unmistakable. The empty milk bottle from the Express Dairy on the step outside the solitary lady's door. The bucket of dirty water the charwoman had left on the landing for the pleasant interruption of her "elevenses" in the sunshine with her companions outside. These were the things that imposed themselves with vivid detail upon my mind.

I knocked and waited, quite satisfied in myself with the excuse I had manufactured. I knocked, and stood listening to the sound of pigeons making amorous advances to each other on the roof outside the little landing window. Gollancz, I had no doubt, would open the door, and for the first time I should see him in his own personal surroundings. Without that cloak and sombrero hat. As he was, in the peculiar way of living, mysterious or not, that I knew must be his.

For a moment I stood listening for a responsive movement on the other side of the door. There was none. The pigeons continued their reiterative love-making. The typewriter thumped downstairs in the architect's offices. Through the open landing window the nasal and unlovely laughter of the congregated charwomen rose to my ears. Still there was no reply. I knocked again. No answer. Then my mind began to speculate. If Mr. Bannerjee had visited Gollancz the night before at half-past eleven, if, indeed, some ceremony with that burning incense and those lighted candles had been in preparation, then it was not likely to have been concluded till long after midnight.

Under those circumstances, would a man be likely to be up betimes in the morning? Was he still asleep? I knocked again. Still there was no reply. At that moment a burst of laughter from the charwomen in the courtyard below suggested my descending the stairs again and asking one of them. I went down.

In their masculine cloth caps, their grimy blouses, their thick woollen stockings and ungainly boots, they were still sitting there on the parapet of the railings, as uninviting an assortment of the gentle sex as one could well imagine.

"Do any of you know whether a Mr. Gollancz lives here, in Number Eight?" I asked.

An undersized woman with a check-cloth cap raised her eyes from a bitten piece of bread and cheese.

"Top floor," she said mournfully. "Door without a name. Leastways, not 'is."

"I've just been up there," I told her. "I've been knocking and there's no reply."

"I 'eard yer."

"He's out, then, is he?"

"No, 'e ain't out. 'E's in, all right. But 'e's asleep. And some mornin's 'e sleeps 'eavy. Don't even want 'is fruit and 'is glass of water. Writes me an order to leave it there on the table an' dust the room an' get out."

"Eat more fruit," said one of the other women, the only one wearing what you might call a female hat. I suppose it was a species of charlady-like humour, because, for some reason which I could not discover, it raised a general laugh.

"Would he mind if I went in and woke him up?" I asked.

I was in no mood to be thwarted again that day. Of course, I had no real intention of waking him up at all. Scarcely a thing one can do to a man on so slight an acquaintance as ours. Especially a man like Gollancz. But being for the second time come out of my way to investigate his ways of living, I was not going to go back without an effort to see the interior of his rooms.

With her speech impeded by a mouthful of bread and cheese, she asked me if I were a friend of Gollancz's.

"'E ain't got a temper," she said. "Wouldn't mind if 'e 'ad. But 'e can look at yer, enough to make the food turn in yer stummick, if yer does something 'e don't want yer to do. So I ain't goin' to let no touts in nor nothin'. See what I mean?"

I saw quite well what she meant. Not that I knew exactly what a tout was, except to be able to assure her that I wasn't one. And apparently she believed me, because, rummaging in some part of her clothes which, with a woman of daintier proportions would be called her bosom, she produced a key.

"All right. That's 'is door," she said. "I'm comin' up in a minute. That's my bucket out on the landin'."

Why she informed me of that, I can't say. It was like a man giving you his visiting card to assure you he was what he represented himself to be. Such assurance I should have thought she would more likely have needed from me. I could have shown her a stethoscope. Taking me at my face value—evidently not that of a tout—she handed me the key and turned with a bite to her bread and cheese.

I moved away at once into the doorway of Number Eight, before she could change her mind. This was better luck than I could have expected. All the way up those winding stairs, I gripped that key in my hand to reassure myself of it. Now I knew I was upon the threshold of discovery. Even if Gollancz woke up and refused to listen to my information about the Studion manuscript, I should at least have had a glimpse at the life he lived. I should have known more the kind of man he was than on those four fortuitous occasions when we had met. I should be able to tell Juniper more of the private life of a Rosicrucian from actual experience.

A kind of excitement, I confess, at the thought of all this had taken hold of me. I was hurrying up those stairs. Where a person lives and how they live, the books that lie on their shelves, even the kind of furniture they live with and how it is disposed about a room, all provide angles of insight into their character. I am sure I had never entered the habitation of anyone with such vital curiosity as that morning when I inserted the key in that door in Clifford's Inn, turned it, and found myself looking at the place where this man Gollancz lived.

Certainly my first sight of it was disappointing. The door gave entrance to a cramped little room, evidently used as a kind of kitchen. A small, rusty gas-cooker was squeezed into one corner. In the other, for the door allowed of only two in that confined space, there was a shallow sink with a water-tap over it. Above these, fixed with brackets against the wall, was a shelf on which stood a few jars such as one would expect to find in any kitchen. There was no room for a table. Scarcely room indeed to turn round, and no window other than a skylight above one's head, the glass of which was darkened and obscured with all the floating smuts of Fleet Street.

The poverty of it all was the first and clearest impression I received. The gas-cooker was there certainly for the preparation of meals, but it had none of the appearance of being used. Remembering what the charwoman had said, I conceived the possibility of his living alone upon a diet of fruit and water. However, a man might well have less sense than that. The medical profession at the moment approves of fruitarianism. I had not expected to find Gollancz a gourmand.

Still, as I have said, that cramped little kitchen gave me no other impression than that of poverty. Should even that have surprised me? Hadn't he told us that the possession of money was the denial of freedom? With a feeling that at least he was living up to the principles he proclaimed, I turned to the door that faced me. Obviously this must be into the living-room. With a quickening conscience that I was really doing an unpardonable thing in prying like this into a man's private life, yet still with the unshaken determination to persist in it, I opened this farther door.

Should I have knocked? There was a man sleeping there. A man I knew and yet who, to me, was more than a stranger. But I hadn't knocked. A thought that by now he might be awake and, hearing who it was, at the last moment deny me entrance, excluded all sense of propriety from my mind. I was determined to get in. I was in.

At the doorway I paused, looking about me. It was a fair-sized room with two windows giving on to the courtyard where I had stood the night before. To the left of the doorway where I was, it turned off with an L-shaped formation into a space that was hidden from my view by a heavy curtain depending from a rod that stretched from wall to wall. And that was all. Except for a small door opening obviously into a cupboard, this was the whole extent of the place where Gollancz lived. A flat—if that is how they describe their chambers in Clifford's Inn—of two rooms, the rent of which could scarcely be more than forty pounds a year. And with such inconveniences as it presented even to a casual glance, it would be dear at that.

Yet with all the expectations that had been excited in my mind, it was not unlike what I should have thought. If the utter denial of the desires of the flesh was one of the first principles of the Brotherhood of the Rosy Cross, then this was how I might have imagined a Rosicrucian would live.

The walls were painted a pale yellow. Almost primrose colour. In contrast with the dirty, distempered walls of the kitchen entrance, it had an effect of sunlit cleanliness. But it was the ceiling that first arrested my attention. Whether for a modern effect—which seemed doubtful to me—it was painted a midnight blue. The modern touch I doubted because, in the centre of this expanse of colour was painted, like one of the illuminations in Simon Studion's manuscript, a symbolical rose in scarlet and gold. The sacred rose of the alchemists. Scarcely a figure to be used for the mere fanciful purposes of decoration.

That room was not designed to please Gollancz's artistic eye. I was quite certain of that. Beyond the dark purple curtains hanging against the windows, there was nothing about it to suggest he was one of those who talk fatuously about the—*décor*—of his surroundings. What reason had he to care anything about—*décor*? That at least was not the kind of individual I conceived him to be. The remaining effects of the room justified this. Had there been any intentional scheme about it I should have described it as monastic in its severity. But it was not even that. The ecclesiastical feeling was not to be imagined in the plain deal table without a cloth. This piece of furniture might have been more suited to the kitchen had there been room. There were two or three plain wooden chairs and a wicker arm-chair, sagging down a little on one side, as from days in medical students' lodging-houses I seem to remember is the habit of wicker-work when it is put to prolonged use.

Beyond these simple things and an old threadbare Eastern rug on the floor, there was nothing but a bookcase, running down the entire length of one wall. But no pictures, no ornaments. Nothing to distract the wandering eye of the mind. I looked for the candlesticks in which his candles had been burning the night before. There were none. This was how he lived, surrounded by an impecunious austerity and brooded over by that scarlet rose in its firmament of blue.

I stood for a few moments gazing up at it, and gradually it appeared as though that ceiling of blue and scarlet and gold were descending upon me, obsessing all my perceptions and dominating the whole effect of the room. The yellow, undecorated walls seemed to disappear. The flaming petals of the rose enveloped everything with a sumptuous warmth. The lightning streaks of gold that shot in a sunburst from the rose's centre, appeared to pervade the room with a gorgeous splendour. Almost for those moments while I stood looking up at it, I could have believed myself in a side chapel, which the ecclesiastical skill of some Renaissance artist had decorated under the approving eye of Holy Mother Church.

Then again, but with a very different sense this time, all my impressions of the night before began to come back to me. The lighted candles, the burning incense. Beneath the oppressing blue and the penetrating gold and scarlet of that ecclesiastical rose, the existence of the world outside, the charwomen's laughter, the typist in the architect's office, the empty bottle of milk and the bucket of dirty water, all those things that had coloured my perception of the day lost their persuasive meaning. Only the cooing pigeons I could still hear on the roof outside seemed in the essence of the eternal laws of their mating to have any comparable relationship of being to these intangible sensations of which my mind had become possessed. It was quite probably due to the forced position in which I was standing, my head thrown back in an unnatural balance, because the sensation departed when I lowered my head again.

I was looking about me for the candlesticks, for the brazier in which the incense must have been burnt, for any of those ecclesiastical objects without which I should have imagined no celebration of a Mass, or whatever it was the Rosicrucians gave, could be held. It was then for the second time I observed the door of that cupboard at the farther end of the room. For a moment I stood staring at it. The curtain, shutting off that other portion of the room, was behind me. On the other side of that I assumed Gollancz must be sleeping. I imagined I could hear his breathing. Beyond that there was no sound. He had not wakened. The charwoman had said that some mornings he slept heavily. Those mornings, doubtless, after the celebration of his Mass. He was sleeping heavily, then. I had no immediate fear of his waking. And yet my mind was vacillating first one way, then another, before I crossed the room to that cupboard.

Because what was I doing? I was spying on the private life of a man who, I had every reason to know, would bitterly resent my intrusion. It was unpardonable. It was caddish, if you like. As inexcusable as reading a letter that didn't belong to one. I don't attempt to mitigate what I did that morning. I hardly knew I had done it. I could see the key left there in that cupboard door and I found myself opening it and looking in.

And there was the answer to all my speculations.

It was an unusually large cupboard space. Almost a little room. What, in the days of wigs and patches, they would have called a powder-closet. There was, of course, no window, yet as I opened the door, I found it filled with a warm, rosy light that penetrated every corner of the cupboard and seemed, notwithstanding its faintness, too sufficient for the space it filled. It was like a perfume that escaped into the room as it found its freedom through the open door. At the same time it would have been impossible to describe it as an illumination. For the first few moments I could not even discover the point of flame from which it derived its light. The glow was everywhere. And then, as I looked about me, I saw a lamp, one of those boat-shaped lamps as were designed in bronze in the Roman period, standing on the floor at the far end of the cupboard.

The string of its wick, passing through the oil in the belly of the lamp, was alight. A tiny tongue of flame, less than a flickering match. Nothing in substance to provide that glow of light that filled the cupboard and passed over me like a mist into the room. Yet there was no other source from which it could have emanated. And as I looked at it, I had the impression of something emitting its waves of light as an organ emits its waves of sound. One presses a little key upon the keyboard and far away in vaulted spaces of a cathedral the volume of a single note fills the vast, silent emptiness. In the same kind of way that tiny flame was giving out its waves of light.

Somewhere I had read of the Rosicrucian lamps. Flames that had burnt for unconscionable time; that could not be extinguished. Perpetual lamps, the light of which was one of the hidden secrets of the Brotherhood of the Rosy Cross.

An insane and impudent impulse came over me to step into that cupboard and, with my own breath, blow the flame out. Why didn't I? Put an end to that humbug so far as Gollancz was concerned? The only explanation I can give of my resistance to that impulse, was that already I was an unpardonable intruder. These were not my rooms. I had no right there. Extraordinary as the light of that lamp was, I felt I had no justification to investigate any farther.

Obviously that cupboard concealed all the paraphernalia of their mystical services. There on a shelf was a seven-branch candle-stick, a lot of other single ones beside, with the almost-gutted candles still left in them. Close to these I could see the brazier in which the incense had been burnt, and beyond it a silver chalice of some old and remarkable design and workmanship. And this was not all. For beneath the shelf were pegs upon which hung a variety of garments I could only suppose to be vestments.

I refuse to admit I was impressed by all this. That, I would swear, was not the reason why I refrained from performing what no doubt would be an act of desecration to them, but which in my mind, as the impulse came to me, was merely one of practical investigation.

Here in the heart of London, surrounded by all the evidences of our material civilization, I had discovered a nest, as it were, of mediæval magic. But if it had been unpardonable and inconsiderate of me to pull aside so far the branches and expose it to my sight, I felt myself compelled by some sense of vague respect to stop at stealing the eggs. There is, I suppose, a certain sense of sacrilege which restrains one from interfering with the religious beliefs of others. After all, what was it to do with me? I lived in a country of religious liberty. If Gollancz and such a company of worshippers as he may have gathered about him believed in this kind of communication with the unseen world, they were at liberty to pursue it. Hearing the steps of the charwoman mounting the bare wooden stairs, I closed and locked the cupboard door.

I had turned away and was looking out of one of the windows when she entered.

"'Asn't 'e waked 'isself yet?" she asked.

"Apparently not," I replied.

"'Aven't yer tried ter wake 'im yerself?"

"No," said I. "I don't know that I quite like to. Sleep is somewhat of a personal belonging. I'm not sure that anyone has the right to take it away from you."

"Well, 'e won't wake 'less you don't go and shake 'im," she said. My nice distinctions about sleep were obviously lost upon her. "Most mornin's when I come, 'e's up, writin' or readin' at the table with 'is breakfast ate an' everythin'. But when 'e's asleep like 'e is this mornin', nothin' can stir 'im. I gets 'is fruit an' 'is glass of water. 'Breakfast's ready,' I says to 'im, pullin' the curtain—but 'e never moves a heyelash. Never turns a 'air."

With a callousness that surprised me, she pulled aside the curtain then.

"'Ere's a gentleman called to see yer," she said.

There was no sound. No response.

I crossed over to her from the window, so as to be able to see into that L-shaped portion of the room. I stood beside her at the drawn curtain, looking in.

There was no window there. Being narrower than the rest of the room, and without illumination, it was not quite easy to see at first. In the semi-light, I could make out a construction of boards, a plank bed, no more than wide enough for a man's body to lie on. But there were no bedclothes. The boards were bare. And there, in a white garment, hardly to be called a night-shirt, though I could see his feet and legs were bare, lay Gollancz. He was lying on his back. His eyes were closed. His hands, in some extraordinary and uncomfortable position, were folded beneath his body. He was lying on them.

But it was the face most of all I noticed. It was the grey colour of clay. The eyelids closed over the eyes as though they were sealed. The lips appeared to be locked. I had never seen a face so far removed from consciousness. And the whole of his body was as still as though it were carved out of granite stone.

"That's the way 'e sleeps," said the charwoman. "Queer, ain't it. Blessed if I could sleep on 'ard boards like that. No bed to make, I will say. But I likes my bit o' stuffin' under me. Still, 'e sleeps 'eavy enough. Talk to 'im an' 'e won't 'ear a word. You go an' give 'im a shake. P'raps that'll stir 'im."

And all that time, while she was gabbling on like this, I was standing there at the drawn curtain, staring, as my eyes grew accustomed to the light, at the ashen face of Gollancz.

The way he slept?

"That body's not asleep," said I.

But she had turned away to go on with her work in the room. She had not heard me.

CHAPTER IX

I shall never rely upon a charwoman to preserve the privacy of my domestic life. Presumably they have no sense of belongings. In their transient and casual relations with other people's houses perhaps that is understandable, though it must be supposed they have homes of their own where they hang up their masculine cloth caps and assume a more sensitive attitude towards domesticity.

At twelve o'clock, this female informed me, she had another job in an office of accountants in Chancery Lane. In the process of dusting the other portion of the room, she was telling me all about them. The partners in the firm and the pretty typists they employed. With a leering note in her voice, she suggested that since young women had come into business, morality was not what it used to be in her maiden days. But could her days ever have been maiden? To look at that cap of hers it seemed impossible.

And all this time, taking no notice of what I was doing, she left me there beyond the half-drawn curtain alone with Gollancz. One of the most extraordinary situations in which I have ever found myself. I, standing by the bedside of that unconscious figure, and this old woman in the room beyond, gossiping away without a pause, as though I were one of her cronies upon whom in my ignorance she was eager to unburden the whole of her life's history.

"Fair fright it gave me, I can tell you," I heard her saying between whipping flicks of her duster, "first time I found 'im there like that. Dead, I thought 'e was. A real stiff 'un. Ran out for the doctor. That's what I did. Fetter Lane, there's one. Red pane o' glass in the lamp outside 'is door. That's 'ow you know it's a doctor. 'Arf an hour I was, goin' an' comin' back. You know what I mean. Fetchin' 'im an' bringin' 'im 'ere. ''E's a corpse, right enough,' I told 'im—'as cold as a joint o' meat.' 'Cos I'd tried to shake 'im by the shoulder, yer see, an' I'd felt 'im, an' it sent a shiver all through me. I've seen dead people, of course, stretched out, same as what you 'ave, I've no doubt. But I've seen 'em die, proper. I've never come in, thinkin' they was alive and found 'em dead. Different thing, that. Ain't it? Any'ow I was all of a doo-da that mornin'. What with findin' 'im an' bringin' the doctor up 'ere. Felt as if I was chewin' me 'eart in me mouth, if yer know what I mean, when I opened the door. But when we come into this room, there 'e was, sittin' at this table I'm dustin' now. Eatin' 'is apple, that's what 'e was doin', eatin' 'is apple an' drinkin' 'is glass o' water. Same as what you an' I might 'a' been doin' if we eat apples for breakfast. Which I never does. 'Tain't more'n a couple of apples I eats, if I eats an apple at all from one year's end to another. Bit o' meat I 'as to 'ave for my breakfast. Somethin' substantial as'll take the taste out o' yer mouth."

She was going on like this. A ceaseless stream of words accompanying the occupation of her work. Much the same as an ostler hisses through his teeth while he is brushing down a horse. How she worked at all when there was no one to talk to, I could not imagine.

And this sort of thing, so I gathered from her incessant gossip, happened sometimes as many as two or three times a week. Working there for the last six months and being paid regularly—not usual, she gave me to understand, in these casual occupations—she had grown accustomed to it. Finding him like that, she just put out his apple on a plate with the glass of water, dusted the room, opened the windows, and left him, still lying there on his wooden bed. And the next morning when she came, he would be reading or writing, as she had already told me downstairs.

I asked her no questions all this time. She volunteered this information. In fact, it was not even volunteered, for it was quite involuntary. She could not, I felt, have stopped talking. And there was I, standing by the side of the rigid and recumbent figure of Gollancz, stretched out in that white robe on those bare, wooden planks of his bed.

A crucifix was nailed to the wall above him. The figure of the Christ was exquisitely carved in ivory. I reckoned it to be a fifteenth-century piece of work. The cross itself was of some kind of fruit wood, delicately inlaid with mother-of-pearl.

That was the only decoration there was on the walls of that

part of the room. And beneath it, lying there with his clay-like face on those naked boards, in that white garment, made of a coarse, flannel cloth, he looked like a Trappist monk who has slept so long in his coffin bed that death at last has intervened between slumber and waking.

No wonder the charwoman had thought him dead that first morning when she tried to wake him. With all my experience, just standing there, looking down at him, I should have declared him to be dead myself. There was no sign of his breathing. Not the faintest rise and fall of his breast. It was only when I stooped down and laid my hand on his heart that I could feel the weak pulse of that organ maintaining the faint persistence of life in his body.

But this I knew was not sleep, as she supposed it to be. Waiting all that time, while she was gabbling away beyond the curtain, for any sign of returning consciousness, and seeing none, I took one of his arms and slowly drew the hand out from beneath the body where he was lying on it. It was milk white. The pressure of his weight had excluded from it all circulation of the blood.

Again I waited for some signs of life. There were none. The charwoman was still talking in the other room, but I was not even listening to her now. She asked questions, but needed no answers. Her volubility was a purely automatic function. The presence of another human being, even if they were removed from her sight, was quite sufficient stimulation. She went on and on, flicking her duster, shaking it out of the window, retiring to the kitchen to get water out of the tap, and coming back again, talking all the time, and I paid no heed.

I was taking that hand of Gollancz's, and with a trocar I always carry with the canula like a fountain pen in my pocket, I was slowly inserting the steel point under one of his finger nails. Only so far as would draw a small drop of blood, but far enough, if that were sleep, to wake him with a start from the pain of it.

He never moved.

It was not sleep. I knew that. It was a trance. That body lying on its bed of boards was incapable of sensation. It was not merely in a subconscious state. The subconsciousness had passed out of it. It was in that condition between life and death when, as the clerics would say, the spirit has already left it for another world. In medical terms it was comatose. Psychologically I do not know how this condition would be defined. It is scarcely life.

This sentient essence known as Gollancz, the person I had spoken to at the "Scarlett Arms," the man I had seen that morning in the Haymarket with my friend Crawshay-Martin, three years ago, was not there. There was just a body, bereft of all the articulations of being except that faintly beating heart which alone sustained its claim to existence.

Then where was he? Where was Gollancz, then?

I had seen people in that condition before, but, like the charwoman, Mrs. whatever her name was, I had observed the natural steps of disease by which they had become comatose. Just as she had seen others die. But this, from all she had told me, I gathered to be a voluntary state of trance. The way he was lying, with his hands under his body. I knew the Mahatmas, when they set free their astral bodies, so contrived their physical that any movement disturbing them from their trance was almost impossible.

Gollancz, of his own free will, had suspended his animation. Of his own free will he could restore it at any moment that he chose. In half an hour after the charwoman had left him, that morning she told me of, he had returned to the normal conditions of articulation. This was not the recognised coma of disease. It was something outside the knowledge and practice of medical skill; something beyond the experience of exact science.

And so, as I stood there that morning beside his bed, the unwilling function of my mind came surging back to those suspicions I had felt about the death of my friend, Crawshay-Martin, about the origin of Juniper's dreams which had led her, in complete ignorance, to the actual place where this man Gollancz lived.

Had it been the essence of him, transported from this almost lifeless body, that had visited my friend that night at the "Scarlett Arms"? Was it to a transmitted vision of Gollancz that Crawshay-Martin had spoken in those few minutes before he took his own life? In obedience to the silent but expressed demands of that vision, had he hidden that book beneath the loose board in the panelled room where, with the material body, its material substance could be recovered the next day? Was that why Gollancz had returned so soon? Was that why I had seen him coming out of the panelled room? And during the time while Crawshay-Martin was confronted with his vision, was that body of Gollancz lying here in this room in Clifford's Inn, rigid and lifeless as I saw it then?

How was it possible to believe a word of this? And yet this was the form of those questions my mind was heaping upon itself.

It is a very comfortable process to go through life laughing at and contemptuous of what is generally termed the miraculous. Science provides us with reasons enough to solve all the common and average problems of existence. In the ordinary way of things, it has proved quite sufficient for our needs. So much so that whenever we come upon something—like, for instance, relativity—entirely beyond our comprehension, we are content to let it pass with the placid assumption that science, of course, has some explanation, if only we took the trouble to seek it out.

It is this condition of modern civilization that has made us the materialists we are. Mystery in life there still is, as much as ever, but the scientific habit of thought causes us to ignore it. The religious sense undoubtedly is disappearing with it, and the futile arguments of the Church about orthodoxy, in which are to be found none of the white-hot temper of urgent faith, only make us the more convinced that science is the sole panacea for all our doubts of the mind.

But when one comes up against an inexplicable fact, as I found myself that morning in Clifford's Inn—as anyone may find themselves when met with the simple mysteries of birth and death—science becomes pathetically unavailing.

How else could I explain to myself those dreams of Juniper's, when the spirit of Gollancz had been so plainly traceable in her mind, than by the actual presence of that spirit while she slept?

It is all very well to call it telepathy, thought-transference. Ostensibly a thought is transferred. But what is a thought? It must have being. And how can it be transmitted while the mind that thinks it is conscious and thinking other thoughts at the same time?

A message that is sent by wireless is lent the substance of the electric wave. It is a thought expressed in terms of electricity. It is consciously dispatched. The instrument that sends it forth, at the moment of sending is not occupied in other functions.

Thought, according to Descartes, was the essence of being. "I think—therefore I am." To call it telepathy and let it go at that may satisfy the scientific mind, but even with such training as I had had myself, telepathy was not a sufficient answer for me then, seeing that silent body of Gollancz lying there. There, without doubt, was his material substance. But without consciousness, without thought—because the mind does not dream, it is not even subconscious in the condition of trance—what was it? Nothing. A clod of unanimated earth. Then where, at the moment, was Gollancz himself?

My mind involuntarily and inevitably sought out Juniper. Had I the power of a Rosicrucian, an adept such as Gollancz, could I then have transported myself at will to find and guard her?

All I was aware of—as must be the common experience of any who choose to examine their sensations concerning those they love—was an inordinate desire to be near, to protect her.

Was this desire the nucleus of that power that Gollancz possessed? Could the human mind conceive anything—even in the form of a transient wish—which it was unable to perform? I think—therefore I am. I conceive—therefore I can do.

None of this, I admit, in these so-called enlightened days, sounds like the reasonable considerations of the mind of a man of science. Yet there in that room, beside that lifeless though still living body, nothing seemed impossible to me. I accepted the unseen world as one accepts the unknown composition of electricity. It was there before me, as the electric apparatus is before the wireless operator, who can use it at his will without knowing what is the substance of the force he is using.

But there was nothing more to be done, nothing further that I could investigate. So far as the private life of Gollancz was concerned, I had seen all that was to be seen. In so far as anything possessed of power is dangerous that we do not understand, I could warn Juniper of her danger in having anything to do with the Brotherhood of the Rosy Cross. I should have warned her of Spiritualism in the same way. Not that I do not believe in its contentions, or the sincerity of its purpose, but because I have seen those who, becoming obsessed by it, have lost the true function of their reason. I have seen sane people come to a kind of madness, losing utterly their grip upon the practical necessities of life, from dealing with the forces over which they have no control. Just as I have seen a man struck dead from the very electricity which he himself has generated.

One thing at least I was determined upon. There should be as little delay as possible before I saw Juniper again. No time I felt should be lost before I administered my warning. She had experienced the sensation of his presence in her room that night when she had wakened from her dream. In her dream he had kissed her. In her dreams he was exercising that same influence as drove Crawshay-Martin to his suicide. To what might he not persuade her? I confess to a definite sense of terror for her safety and, once conscious of that, I turned away to leave that room, to get back again into the normal atmosphere of my life where I could think again like an ordinary common man.

"'As 'e waked 'isself up yet?" inquired the charwoman.

She thrust her cloth-capped head round the edge of the curtain to put her question.

"No," said I. "He's still—asleep."

What was the good of calling it anything else but sleep to her?

"Well, yer'd better leave 'im there an' come along with me. 'Cos I'm supposed to lock up when I've done my bit o' work. 'Course, I suppose you're all right, but I've got to lock up an' take me key, an' if I don't lock up, I ain't done me job—'ave I?"

"I'm just coming," I replied. "Obviously there's no sense in waiting. I shan't wake him up out of that."

"No—nothin' won't wake 'im, 'cept 'imself."

What did she mean by that? Did she realise it was a self-imposed trance? I asked her what she meant.

"Why, there 'e lies," she said, gathering her belongings together, "an' lies an' lies an' nothin' I can do won't stir 'im. But when 'e does wake up—I seen 'im once or twice—'e takes one of 'is 'ands from under 'is back—what 'e's lyin' on. Slowly 'e takes it out. See. Like 's if 'e was doin' it 'isself to wake 'isself up."

So that was all she meant. How could I have supposed she had any clearer conception of it than that? From a constant experience, she had grown accustomed to the sight of that death-like sleep, as in the habit of life we become accustomed to the mysteriousness of birth and even of death itself.

I moved away from his side and passed out of that curtained recess into the room beyond. She had gone into the kitchen and was, so to speak, tidying herself up for the inspecting and critical world outside. A broken piece of mirror was standing on the shelf over the gas-cooker, and with equanimity, almost one could have supposed with satisfaction, she was regarding in it the reflection of her unpleasant face and settling the wisps of colourless hair under her check-cloth cap.

"Can't go up to Chancery Lane," she explained, as though to one of her own sex, "not 'nless I makes meself a bit presentable. Those young typist girls, yer know, they do look at yer, straight. Sharp, yer know what I mean?"

She assumed I did, anyhow, for as I stood at the door leading from the sitting-room into the kitchen, she continued with her titivations as though it were a ladies' dressing-room and I were no more to be regarded than the female attendant.

"You ladies have a lot to compete with these days," I said, endeavouring to regain my own sense of humour.

"You're right there," she retorted, with an emphatic nod of her head. "Little chits o' things, settin' themselves up to take any man away from 'is wife with a bit o' lipstick and showin' their legs. Disgustin', I calls it. An' not even drawers, mind ye, but them tight-fittin' knickers, might as well 'ave nothin' on at all. Excuse me talkin' like this"—for the moment she appeared conscious of my sex—"but you know what I mean? You're a married man, aren't yer?"

"I have been married," said I. I don't know why I added that my wife had been dead some years. Her loquaciousness was infectious, I suppose. The fund of her information induced one to draw upon one's own fund in self-defence. Anyhow, at that, she looked at me with the first sympathetic and human expression I had seen in her face.

"Ah," she said deeply, "I know what that's like. I lost me first 'usbingd twenty-three years ago. An' can I forget 'im when I'm goin' to sleep with me 'usbingd as is now?"

She asked me that piercing question with a frank elevation of her eyebrows and waited for my answer. Then, seeing that I was quite unable to tell her, she was beginning to describe to me all the intimate details of her first husband's love and life and death, when I suddenly remembered I had left the trocar and canula behind me by the side of Gollancz's bed.

"Excuse me a minute," I said, "I've left something behind me," and I hurried back into the room.

It was there on the floor. I picked it up, put it into its case, and thrust it into my breast-pocket. With another glance at that grey face, those sealed eyelids and locked lips, I was turning to go when the arm, the arm that I had placed beneath his body, twitched. Slowly it began to move. Slowly it began to extricate itself from the pressure of the weight that imprisoned it. I did not wait to see any more. I hurried out between the curtains and pulled them together behind me. I had reached the door into the kitchen. I was just going to tell the charwoman I was ready to accompany her downstairs, when I heard a voice. We both heard it.

"You can stay," it said, and the words were repeated.

"There! 'E's woke 'isself up," said the charwoman, and gathering up the bundle of her belongings from the top of the gas-cooker, she bent it under the grip of her arm, nodded familiarly with her head at me, and departed. The door closed, and I was left there in Gollancz's chambers in Clifford's Inn.

I was standing in the kitchen, at the door into the living-room, the room with the painted ceiling where he held his Mass. Beyond those drawn curtains in that L-shaped recess, I could hear the slow movements of his body as it returned to animation.

I am not one who ordinarily is given to the uncomfortable sensations of terror. The imperative fear in the common affairs of life does not attack me. What I mean is that I am not of a neurotic or imaginative disposition. But then, at the sounds of his stirring and hearing that voice—hollow, like a voice in sleep—I admit I felt far from being at my ease. The sense of my intrusion came back upon me, accusingly. I was quite aware that any umbrage he might take at finding me there was perfectly justified. But more profound than any discomfort like that was the feeling that my mind was utterly incapable of gripping the facts of the situation.

Death, to those who have seen it often, is not terrifying in itself, in so far as it is possible to understand its causes. But I take it that even one of the strongest nerves would be awed by the sight of a body risen from the dead. Not so much because he was amazed as because his mind was incapable of explaining it.

A few moments before I had seen that body of Gollancz, lifeless, like a piece of clay on his bed of boards. Something, that had been invisible, perhaps in the very air about me, had returned to it, and now I knew I must face that re-animated body. The inclination to leave the place, get away, having nothing more to do with the whole business, was as strong as at the same time it was unthinkable. I had undertaken this job. I must go through with it.

I stood just inside the room under that painted ceiling in a kind of passive obedience to the summons of his voice. I could hear him rising from the bed. The faint sound of his voice, muttering, just reached me, beneath his breath. As though he were intoning some form of prayer. I can't tell how I obtained the impression, but I felt it to be some kind of thanksgiving, as of one who has returned from a perilous journey.

At last the curtains parted and he came out. He was still wearing the robe of flannel cloth that made him look like a Trappist monk. But his feet were no longer bare. There were sandals on them. A drawn pallor was still about his face. The pallor of one who denies himself the strong meat and invigorating foods of nourishment. But now at least there was life in it. It was not the clay-like pallor of death. Only his eyes, which at other times as I had seen them, burnt in the hollows above his cheek-bones, were dull, as though the full fire of his mind was not yet kindled behind them. It was not exactly a stupor. They were more like the eyes of some hibernating animal that wakes slowly after its winter sleep. And as slowly, I could see, they were waking to a dull anger, of which, even in that condition, he had more than ordinary control.

For a moment he stood there at the curtains, regarding me. Then he moved to one of the wooden chairs at the table and sat down.

"Are you satisfied?" he said, and he looked up at me again.

There was nothing to do but hold to the intention of my visit as I had planned it out in the taxi coming down to Fleet Street. I assumed a tone of surprise as I repeated his word:

"Satisfied? I don't understand."

"Satisfied with what you have seen? Satisfied with all that you now presume to understand? Satisfied with what you are taking away with you?"

This last sentence of his took me unawares. Involuntarily I bridled at it. He was obviously guessing at the reason of my visit to Clifford's Inn, and there he had guessed wrong. My conscience might be smiting me for that unpardonable intrusion into his private life, but at least I could exonerate myself of the charge of taking anything away that did not belong to me.

"I don't understand what you mean!" I said hotly. "I came here to give you a piece of information about something I knew to be of interest to you. Your charwoman let me in. I found you asleep. I was just going away, but certainly not with anything I had no right to."

He smiled. At my temper, perhaps. But if he could control his feelings in making a charge like that, I certainly could not in hearing it. I made no attempt to.

Still he continued to smile. That same light about his face, rather than a parting of his lips. The light was still there as he said:

"In your profession as a doctor, performing surgical operations, it does come to seem, I suppose, that a man's blood scarcely belongs to him?"

I thought his senses could not properly have returned to him. I did not know what he was talking about. I stood there, in the doorway, staring at him.

"I don't know what you're talking about," I said. "I haven't come here professionally. I told you why I came. What my work as a surgeon has to do with it, I don't understand."

"If you examine the point of the probe in your pocket," he said quietly, "I think it'll be quite clear to you. There's a stain of blood on it. I presume you were taking the instrument away with you?"

I was at a loss to know what to say. In all probability I stood there looking like a fool. I felt like one. His eyes regarded me coldly, without any pity. For the matter of that, he did not seem even to enjoy the point he had scored. He just looked at me with a supreme indifference, waiting, without interest, to see what I had to say.

But how had he known? That, in a swift thought, I asked myself, and could not answer. Unless it was a fact that his astral body had been present all that time while I had been by his side. Obviously he had been about to reimpose the consciousness of his will upon that inanimate flesh into which I had thrust my instrument. In spirit, then, had he been standing beside me? Had he seen what I had done? How else did he know that trocar was in my pocket? Any other man than Gollancz would have enjoyed my confusion.

"You—you were asleep," I stammered. "It—it was more than sleep. As a medical man, I could see that. Your—your body was cold. I felt it. Your heart was scarcely beating. I was—I was alarmed at the condition I found you in. I did what any other doctor in my position would have done. I inserted that probe under your finger nail to see if your body would respond to any sensation. It was then your charwoman informed me that she frequently found you like that. On the first occasion she had called a doctor herself. But she assured me it was nothing to worry about. That you always regained consciousness. And so, not being able to wait for that, I was coming away."

He listened to all this with the increasing light in his eyes, but without interruption. When I had finished, he said ironically:

"It must have reassured you, as a scientist, to have been able to accept the experience of my charwoman!"

I didn't answer that. His whole attitude and the implication of what he said was stinging me to an anger to which I knew I was not entitled, and which I had no desire to show to him.

He gave me the opportunity of a silence to reply, but I did not take it, and then he said:

"Dr. Hawke—we have met two or three times before, and always I have known the antagonism of your mind to mine. You are a scientist. Without the facts of life your mind refuses to respond to the thousand thoughts and impressions which experience is constantly presenting to it. Besides being a scientist, you would call yourself a Christian. There are occasions, such as the death and the marriage of your friends, when you go to church and say prayers which have lost all meaning for you, and of which you are even unconscious as you say them, of the desecration of your tongue. Of all that lies beyond your world of accepted fact, you know nothing. And stoutly you refuse to know anything. Though it constantly occurs that the facts you have rigidly adhered to one day, you find yourself having to discard the next, you are still convinced that the line of progress you have adopted is leading you to the truth. I admire you for that, as much as I pity. And that is a great deal. Because I think, in your way, you are an honest man. And honesty is something, even though it be misapplied."

He looked up at me again with the same light over his face. It may have been a smile of contempt. I couldn't tell what it was.

"As you know quite well," he went on, "I am a member of the Brotherhood of the Rosy Cross. What you think that means to you or to me, is not what it means at all. It would be futile for me to explain its meaning. You would not understand. Except, I will say this. Neither death nor birth are the conditions you suppose them to be. The gestation of life in a woman's womb is only the process of fact about which it is possible for you to ascertain every detail without coming into touch with the spiritual reality. The disintegration of the body in death is merely a superficial process of the separation of those facts you have watched being built up. Birth and death, these are not life or the cessation of it. You are all looking for life in the dust, Dr. Hawke. And it is not there. I will not say any more. But let me warn you that these things you are endeavouring to investigate with steel probes and curious eyes, are not to be found that way."

Suddenly he stood up to his feet.

"Go away from here," he said firmly. "It is not so much this room in Clifford's Inn I warn you not to return to. Where he sleeps and eats is no more than the perishable shell around the body of the man as he lives. It is me and my way of life I warn you to leave alone. You are not prepared to understand it."

These were the last words he said. Passing by me as I stood there, he went into the kitchen and opened the door on to the landing. There were no amenities of parting between us. He did not offer me his hand. I had no alternative but to go.

As I descended the stairs, I heard him shut his door. The same soft sound I had heard the night before. I passed out of the building into the sunshine. I made my way under the arch of the porter's lodge into Fleet Street. The buses were tearing by in the crush hour of the day. I was there in the midst of the swarming facts of life. But all I could think of, and all I could see in my mind, was that man in his flannel cloth robe, sitting in that room under the blue ceiling with its scarlet alchemical rose, and the streaks of gold that shot in a sunburst from the midst of its petals.

CHAPTER X

So far as Gollancz and the practice of his life was concerned, I had now definitely closed the door against myself by which any further investigation could be made in that quarter. It was not to be denied he was entitled to the liberty of his own religious beliefs. Once and for all he had told me he resented my interference. He had warned me, as he was justified in doing, against thrusting my way again into Clifford's Inn. However peculiar it might be, it was his own private life, and I was compelled to respect it as such.

But by what means he had known of my use of that probe; how he had induced in himself that state of trance from which I should have supposed there was no immediate recovery; and how, within that short time, he had recovered consciousness—of that I was still ignorant and likely to remain so. In every way it was similar to the state of unconsciousness in which I had seen the Mahatma in India. But in that case I had not witnessed his recovery. Nor had I been able to ascertain his knowledge of things that were happening while his body was lying in that condition.

But here it was obvious Gollancz had known. The insertion of that probe under the finger nail, the pain of which, even in a state of the deepest sleep, no one could have borne without waking, had not been hidden from him. And if he had known of that, what was to prevent him from knowing everything else? My examination of the contents of his cupboard—everything, indeed, that

I had done and thought while I was there in his rooms. And if there, why not anywhere? In any place where he might choose to project the susceptibility of his subconscious mind?

The farther in time and space that I found myself removed from the influence of his surroundings, the more protectively my mind adopted an attitude of ridicule and incredulity to the belief of these fantastic possibilities. But in one conviction I was unshaken. Gollancz was not a safe man to have anything to do with. All that he had said about science, of course, was the mere talk of a crank and fanatic. I had heard it before from fatuous idealists and footling divines. I was paying no attention to all he had said about birth and death. What did he, an ordinary layman, know about the processes of gestation? And yet I was convinced that the sooner Juniper was warned against him, the better.

Sitting down at my desk as soon as I got home, I wrote her a letter saying I was coming down into Hampshire for the week-end. Would it be convenient for me to drop in at the Court House, Stoke Charity, and see her? The following evening I received her answer. Less laconical from her than I should have imagined. She would be very glad to see me. Indeed, she wanted to see me.

I had no friends in Hampshire. I had no business there. Ostensibly, I told myself, my reason for going to see Juniper was to warn her against Gollancz. But well within myself I knew it to be something other than that. At haphazard I telephoned to an hotel in Winchester for a room, and on the Saturday, early, having no hospital that morning, I motored down. At about lunch-time I drove over to Stoke Charity.

The Court House was an old Tudor building that had, in fact, been a court-house in the days of the Star Chamber. In the big hall, used by them as a sitting-room, out of which the main staircase led to a landing above, Judge Jeffries had conducted his infamous trials of the Bloody Assize.

As I drove up in front of the house, Juniper came to the door to meet me. Seeing her again, it was difficult to conceive of there being anything that could relate her in thought or fact to that man in his monastic cloth garment and his sandal shoes in Clifford's Inn.

Even there, in those country surroundings, she was essentially the modern young woman. A designed and effective carelessness about her dress. A freedom of limb in the short skirt and sleeveless jumper. Almost a suggestion of untidiness about her loose but well-coiffeured hair, and yet that same unsatisfied disillusionment at the back of her eyes as though life had little more meaning left for her than to be got through with as callously and effectively as possible.

The insolent indifference had certainly more or less disappeared with our acquaintance—brief though it was. These young women are not slow to adopt a kind of superficial familiarity. In place of it, she had assumed that cynical air of disillusionment which I had noticed when she dined with me at the Bath Club. Her smile, as she gave me her hand at the door, was ironic rather than openly good-natured, and yet it did not lack a certain air of friendliness. I felt she was glad to see me; was not indifferent to my having come all that way to see her.

It was about half an hour before lunch. She told me to leave my car there in the drive and walk round the garden with her.

I am a town bird. I have lived in London all my life. I don't know much about gardens. For that half-hour, in a dim sense beyond my consciousness of being with her, I was aware of being surrounded by the masses of colour and the scent of flowers. There was only one I took notice of by name. A huge clump of delphiniums in the herbaceous border, with spikes of bloom that were high above her head.

That I was made acquainted with because, stepping off the grass path on to the bed, she picked a single blossom from the spike. I was wearing a blue shirt, a fact I had forgotten and she had noticed. Inserting the flower in my buttonhole, with the matter-of-fact air of a girl in a florist's shop, she said:

"May as well seize a note of harmony when we can. Did you anticipate the delphinium when you put on that shirt? Or do you imagine God just made delphiniums anyhow?"

She was talking sheer nonsense. In that preliminary mood, I doubt if she wanted to talk anything else. And yet, as the nonsense of a dream is indicative of the sleeper's mind, so this talk of hers was expressive of all that was away there behind her thoughts. "May as well seize a note of harmony while we can." That was her mood. There was nothing more harmonious to her in life, just then, than my blue shirt and her delphinium.

I could do nothing while she was in that humour but accept her at her own valuation.

"Why drag God into it?" I said.

"Yes, why," she replied. "Except that He's a figure of speech one finds it difficult to avoid in ordinary conversation."

"That's your mood to-day, is it?"

"Don't know why you should call a conviction a mood. I am in a mood, I suppose. One always is. Some kind or another. But the Gentleman of the Old Testament hasn't got anything to do with it."

She stopped abruptly on the grass path between the borders of flowers and looked at me.

"You remember that night I dined with you at the Bath Club?" she said.

I restrained myself from anything sentimental.

"Now you mention it," I said. But I smiled as well.

"Something happened here—in the house—that night."

"What?"

"My husband. Something about his drug."

"Well, what about it?"

She was hesitating. That same reluctance she had shown when she told me about her dreams.

"I told you he took heroin. That I kept a supply of it in the house. Locked up. I have the key. We have to do that. Sometimes he gets absolutely out of hand with his craving for it. A maniac. There's no curing him. He's been under the doctors. He's been to a home. They tried starving him out of it. He became an absolute physical wreck. All the same, they said they'd cured him of the habit. He came home. For a time we did think he was cured. But somehow or other he got hold of it again. We traced the source of it. A black man—a nigger—living in Cleveland Street. Somewhere off Soho. One of those brutes who trafficks in drugs. He was arrested. You may never have heard of the case. They made me give evidence. Thank God, they had the decency to keep our name out of the papers."

Suddenly in the midst of that she smiled. The same ironical smile.

"The Gentleman of the Old Testament, again," she said. "He's a sort of a cliché."

"Never mind the Old Testament," I said. "Tell me what happened that night."

It was impossible not to remember what had happened to me. That night up those stairs in Clifford's Inn. The smell of incense. The light of the candles between that slit in the curtain. And the next morning. In that room.

"I got a telephone message the next morning at my club," she went on, "asking me to come back at once."

"Yes. I know that."

"How did you know?"

"I rang you up the next morning. I wanted to take you out to lunch. The hall porter told me."

Receiving that information, her eyes appeared to dwell upon mine for a moment. But whatever it was she thought, she did not say. Yet, somehow, I felt she knew then. Nothing, of course, to hear that a man had wanted her to come out to lunch with him after their second meeting. But the intuition of women is not to be measured by the insignificance of the facts that rouse their instincts. She knew then that, as far as I was concerned, our acquaintance was more than casual. I was quite sure of that. She knew this visit into Hampshire was solely on her account. But whether she cared, whether it meant anything to her, whether it even flattered her vanity, of that I could see nothing. After that one glance at me, she went straight on:

"Then you heard that I came back here?" she said. "He'd got hold of my key that locked up the heroin. It was on a big bunch of keys belonging to the house. I suppose I ought to have taken it off the ring and brought it away with me. That didn't occur to me. It was a fat bunch. But I'd hidden it. He couldn't have known where it was. He didn't even know where I kept the bottle. Often he'd tried to find out. It was in a locked drawer of a locked cupboard in an old room where the servants keep their brooms and things. A room that used to be used for the household washing in the days before they had laundries and everything like that was done at home. He couldn't possibly have known where it was. All the same, he'd got it and taken a dose that nearly killed him. When I came back, that poor, blind angel—his mother—was nearly at her wits' end. They brought him round. But only just. For two days he was incapable of doing or saying anything. Even now he's a wreck. But he's told me how he found out where it was."

"How?"

I expect I asked that question over-sharply. The tone of my voice broke the thread of her information.

"Why? Do you know how he found out?" she asked.

"No," said I. "How should I know? Sorry if I sounded abrupt. It was only that I was eager to know. How did he find out?"

"He dreamt it," she said.

There we were in that garden between the herbaceous borders of flowers, and somehow or other there returned to me at that moment the same impression of unreality, of incongruousness, as when I had seen Gollancz in that garden at Malquoits. As again as when I and the sergeant had found him seated at the end of the bowling green in the garden at the "Scarlett Arms."

"He told you that? He dreamt of the place?"

I suppose when a thing is difficult to believe, one discredits one's actual hearing of the words.

"More than that."

"How do you mean—more?"

"He went there in his sleep. To that cupboard. Walked. In the middle of the night. He told me. Woke up and found himself in that room with the cupboard door opened and my bunch of keys and that bottle of heroin in his hand. As if someone had led him there. That was what he actually said. As if someone had led him there."

There was a stone seat at the end of the herbaceous border. We had reached it. I suppose we hardly knew it, but we both sat down.

"Have you dreamt of—of that man since?" I asked her.

"No."

"Have you thought about him?"

There was a piece of moss growing on the side of the stone seat. As though it were something that disfigured the look of it and had to be removed at once, she pulled it off before she answered.

"Oh, yes. I suppose I have. Not the kind of person you can forget very easily."

That was candid. Up to a point. But in the very admission of it and the callous way in which it was made, I felt she was concealing rather than confessing the truth. "Not the kind of person you forget very easily." And I was to suppose from that that on occasions he had crossed her mind. But this was very different from the impression I received.

She was obsessed by her thoughts of Gollancz. That was what I felt to be the state of her mind. And she possessed that capacity—a finer art in women than in men—of telling half the truth to hide the whole.

For a while after her answer, I sat there on the stone seat wondering what line I should adopt. I will confess the degree of my own emotions was not lessened by what I thought. Everything I did and said was now coloured by this.

The ardour of a man of forty-five is none the less intense because his mind is tempered with considerations of expediency. It occurred to me that if I told her my experience of that night and morning in Clifford's Inn, she might be only the more intrigued by the mysterious character of Gollancz. There was only one thing about this man I wanted her to know. He was dangerous. It could do me no harm to warn her of that, unless, as is possible with her sex, the very danger to themselves is the essence of a man's fascination. I took my chance of that. What I was determined to say was not going to represent him as dangerous in that kind of moral sense that makes men attractive to women.

"Has your husband still got that book?" I asked her presently.

"Yes."

"Has Mr. Holt, the American, made any further offer?"

"Not an offer. He's written. Said he'd like to come down and see it again. Claude has got so interested in the wretched book now that he can't put it out of his sight. He's a bit of a Latin scholar. He's begun to translate it into English. It's most extraordinary. Symbols. Incantations. He's shown me some of it. It sounds like the purest nonsense. Chemical nuptials. What on earth does that mean?"

"Chemistry is only in its infancy," said I. "We're only just beginning to discover the relation between chemistry and psychology. Actually, the mind is capable of affecting chemical changes in the body. Anger, for instance, converts harmless salts into poisons. It's conceivable that in the ages before Simon Studion wrote that book, the alchemists knew secrets about chemistry we're only on the verge of discovering now. Look at ectogenesis. A few years ago, who'd have thought of the possibility of developing human life in the laboratory! There are men now spending all their time in research upon that subject alone. One of these days, human life will be able to be generated without the need of maternity. There's no end to the secrets that are still hidden in the vaults of chemistry. Chemical nuptials isn't so nonsensical as it may sound. One has to remember that practically all the accumulated knowledge of the astrologers was destroyed in the great library at Alexandria. Destroyed because it was feared to be too powerful for the safety of man. A book like Simon Studion's, describing the mysteries and rites of the Brotherhood of the Rosy Cross, is unique. There can scarcely be any other in existence like it."

She was listening intently to all I was saying, and as I expressed this last opinion about the Rosicrucian manuscript, it occurred to me. A unique book, revealing the secret mysteries and rites of the Rosicrucians to those who could read its archaic language. And Claude Weaver was translating it.

Involuntarily with this thought, my mind took up the memory of Crawshay-Martin's story of the day in the library at Malquoits when, as a student, he had set to work on the translation of that very book and had been found engaged upon it. The sudden anger of his father. The snatching away of the volume. The threat to burn it and the ultimate precaution of hiding it in another binding.

To what lengths would an acknowledged Rosicrucian not go to preserve the secrets of his faith. And here, again, was another attempting to disclose them. I asked myself that question, and then sharply I turned to Juniper sitting there beside me.

"Gollancz means to bring about your husband's death," I said.

Would that convince her of the kind of man he was? Because, without any stretching of my imagination, I did believe it to be true. I did believe then and after what I had seen in Clifford's Inn that, by some telepathic means beyond my comprehension, he had brought about that self-inflicted death of my friend, Crawshay-Martin. He had not recovered the book then, but surely he would do so in the end. How, I could not conceive. But he would do it. To buy it at its market value was not in the realm of his transactions. He had tried that through one of his disciples—Mr. Bannerjee—at the auction at Malquoits. He had tried to steal it—not that he would call it stealing—from beneath the loose board in the panelled room at the "Scarlett Arms." Again it had eluded him there. But he would get it in the end.

Obviously his powers were not supernatural. I had never for one mad moment supposed that they were. They were natural enough, if one had his supreme knowledge of psychology, self-hypnosis and auto-suggestion to understand them. And it was by these powers, as dangerous as the accumulated forces of electricity would be in the hands of a child, that he was dangerous to the woman I loved.

"He means to kill him," I repeated firmly. And to that, with her eyes set in front of her and her voice so quiet that I could scarcely hear the words, she said:

"Does he?"

It was not even a question. It was an acceptance of fact. As though I had told her it was fate. That nothing she might do could alter it, and she was content. God knows she might well have been glad that it should be so. Her life was hell. There was no need for her to tell me that.

What prevented me then in that moment from putting my arms about her, from telling her that I could bring back the sense of joy into her life, I don't know. But she sat there staring in front of her. And I sat there staring at her. And I said nothing, because an instinct in me was warning me that Gollancz, and not I, still had the first place in her thoughts.

"If you felt," I continued, "that Gollancz was there in your room that night when you woke up out of your nightmare, then can't you suppose it was he who led your husband down to that cupboard the other night?"

"Do you mean Gollancz, himself?"

"Why not?"

"But do you believe that? Do you believe it's possible?"

She turned round eagerly to look at me as she put this question. And, with the picture of that clay-like, rigid figure on its bed of boards in my mind, I tried as truthfully as I could to answer her.

"I don't know what's possible and what's not," said I. "Who does? Gollancz isn't an ordinary sort of man. You can see that for yourself. I can assure you the less you have to do with him, the better. He's dangerous."

"Why?" she asked quickly. "Because he's a Rosicrucian? At any rate, my God, there must be something in being one, if it can do things like that."

And when she said that, I felt the disillusionment of her spirit leaning out—not, like the Blessed Damozel, from the golden bars of heaven, but from the iron bars of the hellishness of life that imprisoned her.

"Oh, come on! Let's go into lunch," she said, and she stood up with a forced impulse to her feet. "I suppose something's left for everybody to hang on to. At least, there are cocktails. And one can eat."

"Gone back to cocktails?" I asked, as I walked with her down the grass path.

"Yes. What does it matter whether I sleep well or not. Doesn't seem to make any difference."

I said nothing. So she was still dreaming of him. But how could one blame her for telling lies? If she knew what was in my mind about her, it might even be some sense of pity in her that made her withhold the truth. A damned poor consolation. But with what I felt, I was eager for anything.

"You won't see him," she said as we entered the house by a door that opened from the garden into a spacious drawing-room. "Not unless you'd like to go up to his room. He's still in bed."

She was saying this as she moved across the room, and, as I followed her, I became aware of an old lady sitting in a window at the farther end, as though to catch the light for her knitting, the ivory needles of which were clicking in and out in her fingers with industrious precision.

She looked up as she heard our voices, and then I realized, from the peculiar searching of her eyes, that she was blind.

"Mother," said Juniper. "This is Dr. Hawke. He's staying to lunch. I'm going to see about the cocktails."

With that she left us. I took hold of Mrs. Weaver's outstretched hand to shake it and was conscious of a lingering hold in the fingers before I could let it go.

"You knew my brother," she said. "Please sit down."

I took a chair, telling her as I did so that Crawshay-Martin and I had been friends—though not seeing a great deal of each other—for a good many years before his death.

"And you were there when he died, Juniper told me."

"Yes."

"One of these days," she said, with an emotion that was possessed with calm, "I want you to tell me about that. There's plenty of time. At least, I mean there'll be plenty of opportunity."

I reminded her I was only staying to lunch and that I had to return soon afterwards to Winchester, and then to town first thing on Monday morning.

"Yes—but you'll come again," she said.

"I shall be delighted," I replied, "if you'll ask me."

She made a movement of her hands on her lap—a half-completed gesture that seemed to inform me that the act of asking was not in her province, but it was all the same. I should come. And then, leaning a little nearer to me, she said what sounded to me an extraordinary thing:

"Take care of Juniper," she said. "I feel sorry for the young women these days."

"How do you mean—take care?"

"Well, you're a doctor. She's been to see you, hasn't she?"

It was a reasonable enough answer to my question. And yet it was not that I felt she meant.

At that moment Juniper came in with the cocktails on a tray and I did not feel I could say any more.

CHAPTER XI

We had lunch together alone—the three of us. I gathered that people had been asked down for the week-end, but had been put off because of Claude Weaver's condition. Nothing was said about him during the meal.

The principal thing I noticed while we were there together in the dining-room was the sympathetic understanding that seemed to exist between Juniper and her mother-in-law. She sat near her at the table, anticipating the tentative movements of those expressive hands with which she had conveyed a delicate meaning to me in the other room.

It is not usual to find an intimate relationship between mother- and daughter-in-law. It seemed to me I discovered the clue to it, in a remark made by Mrs. Aubrey Weaver in the course of the meal.

We were talking about some daring aeronautical exploit that had recently been performed by a young woman.

"Young women nowadays," she said, "find it less painful to break their necks than their hearts. I don't blame 'em."

"Why not?" I asked.

She smiled into a space which blind people see.

"Why not?" I repeated.

"Not an easy thing to be a woman," she said. "The prejudices of life are all against her. Juniper's just been reading me Lord Birkenhead's new book on what is likely to be our fate in two thousand and thirty. Not a particularly pretty picture. He points out how false an argument it is to say that women have not created nearly so many works of genius as man because they have not had the same opportunities and education. In support of his contention that education has nothing to do with it, he names many of the men who, from quite humble beginnings, have achieved great things. That is one of the prejudices, I mean."

I asked her to explain a little more.

"Well, you see, he quotes individual men who have achieved without education, and compares them in numbers with individual women. That, to me, is even more false than the argument he complains of. Perhaps because it has the element of self-deceit. It's not the individual woman who lacks education and tradition. It's the whole sex. Women, besides being individuals, are members of their sex. So are men. There is something of assurance in being a man. There is something inherently inferior in being a woman. That is their real disadvantage. Lord Birkenhead is very much a man and he doesn't know that."

So she was a feminist—which by no means every woman is—and that explained it. Even from that little she said, I received the impression that her own marriage had been an unhappy one. But that I had had reason to suppose already. Crawshay-Martin's opinion of the man who had married his sister, reserved though it was, had not led me to imagine a happy marriage. And in marrying him she had paid the price of losing her brother's affection. Probably, as Juniper had said, Crawshay-Martin had not treated her very considerately over the matter. But he was a man of strong likes and dislikes, successfully though he concealed them. His sister had abided by the choice she had made, and she had lost her brother by doing so. It had not, however, impaired her love for him. If in no more than the tone of her voice, as she spoke before lunch about his death, it was not difficult to see how deeply she had felt it.

After the meal, when Juniper left us alone again in the drawing-room to go and see her husband, Mrs. Weaver listened with a calm expression on her face, but I am sure a depth of emotion, to my account of that last day I spent with Crawshay-Martin.

"He felt things much more poignantly than one supposed," she said. "Selling Malquoits and all the furniture must have hurt him to the quick. Well—one realizes now how much it hurt him."

"You believe it was an ordinary suicide?" I asked her.

The eyes of blind people can be strangely expressive at moments. Without sight they can still display the quality of inward vision. As she looked at me then, I felt she was seeing something through her mind more clearly than anything I could have presented to her physical sight. And her hands that had been lying quietly clasped in her lap, just separated and lifted a little in the air. It was a slight movement, but more effective than any exclamation in her voice. Then, after I had waited a moment, she said just two words. Almost under her breath she said them.

"The book," she whispered.

"What do you know about the book?" I asked.

She told me then something that Crawshay-Martin had never spoken of to me. Their father had died under peculiar circumstances. He had been found unconscious in the street early one morning by one of the Corporation men who work most of the night with hoses and carts washing and cleaning away the accumulated rubbish and dirt from the public highways.

"There were no signs of foul play," she said. "He was just unconscious. A heart failure, the doctor said. But he never came to. He never spoke again to say how he had come to be there at that hour of the night. Of course, he was rather a strange man, my father. I don't think we ever understood him. Certainly John didn't. They were always at loggerheads. I suppose I was his favourite. He used to talk more to me. Besides living at Malquoits, he had bachelor's rooms in Jermyn Street. Ever since my mother died. Sometimes he would go up there for three or four weeks at a time. When he came back to Malquoits again he was always very strange for a while. Shutting himself up in his room. Going for long walks by himself. Though sometimes, indeed, he did take me with him. But he always talked about queer things."

"What sort of things?" I asked, because she had paused, as though her memory were accompanying him on one of those walks and she had forgotten my existence.

"Oh—things like the influence of the stars. He had read a great deal. You know there was an exceptional library at Malquoits."

I nodded my head. That becomes one's habit with blind people. As you talk to them you come to think they can see.

"He used to quote the writings of Placidus de Titus and Justin de Florence to me. The old astrological writers. He was keenly interested in astrology. Every sign of the zodiac, I believe, occupies a place which is called the Celestial House or the House of the Sun. The House of Aries is called the Orient Angle. The House of Taurus is called the Inferior Gate. Gemini, the Abode of the Brethren. And so on. I can remember a few of the things, even now, but I didn't understand much. Still, I used to listen.

Sympathetically, I suppose, as women must. And do. I think, perhaps, he liked the sound of his own voice against the congenial silence of mine."

She smiled as she said that. A smile, I felt, Lord Birkenhead might not quite have understood.

"I suppose it was John told you about the book," she continued. "As you seem to have heard of it. John was translating it one time during the vacation."

"Yes—he told me that. And his father took it away."

"That is so," she agreed. "But I heard nothing about it at the time. Apparently, father took it away up to London with him and kept it there in his rooms in Jermyn Street for some years. Well, in fact, until the very day before he died. The day before he died, he brought it back to Malquoits. I remember his calling me into the library and showing it to me. John was out shooting. There was a party at the house. My husband was amongst them. It was some time in October. Father wasn't with them. He used to shoot, but had given it up. Suddenly. He refused to touch a gun. So he and I were alone in the house. He brought me into the library that day and showed me the book, telling me how he had taken it away from John, and then I remember so well his saying:

"'Nothing's safe in the hands of women.'

"Which was not a particularly good way to begin, was it?" she interposed with a smile. "Still it was very like him.

"'However,' he went on, 'I trust the negativity of your nature more than I trust the positivity of John's. I'm bringing this book back here again. It's not safe in London. I've concealed it in another cover. John won't recognize it. And I'm going to put it on this top shelf where there are only old books of history and no one will think of taking it out. But if any stranger ever comes into the library while I'm not here, I want you to keep your eye on it.'

"I suggested it would be better if he locked it up right away. But in a sort of obstinate way, he said that locking it up made no difference. That, in fact, it was better hidden in that false cover amongst those old history books than in any place under lock and key. And then he said the thing that has always remained in my memory.

"'That book,' he said, 'has life and death in it. P'raps my life. You don't know.'

"He had come down to Malquoits that day, specially to bring the book, and in a great hurry he returned that same evening to town. He didn't care for John's shooting parties.

"'I must go back,' I remember his saying. And then he kissed me—a thing he very seldom did—in a peculiarly tender way. That was the last I ever saw of him—alive. He was found the next day at about three o'clock in the morning, unconscious on the pavement in London."

"In Jermyn Street?" I asked.

"No. Not in Jermyn Street. Nowhere near where he lived."

"Where, then?"

"In a little passage that leads out of Fleet Street into one of those lawyer's quarters they call Clifford's Inn."

I knew she could not see the expression on my face. But by some instinct, peculiarly developed in blind people, she had realized the sudden arrest of my mind.

"What is it?" she asked.

I tried to assume an ordinary tone in my voice as I asked her how long ago that was.

She said her father had been dead nearly twenty years. Her son, Claude, at that time was a young boy.

Had Gollancz, then, been in occupation of those rooms all that time? I didn't know. It was not impossible. Tenancies of chambers like that in those inns of court are often of long duration. I was speculating on the probability of this and for the moment had forgotten her. She reminded me of her presence by asking what was the meaning of that sound in my voice. I paused another moment, and then I said:

"Have you ever heard of a man called Gollancz?"

She looked in front of her for a little while. I can't avoid that word—looked. Her eyes had the expression of inward sight. I knew directly that she had heard of him. And still I was not prepared for her answer.

"I knew a man called Gollancz," she said.

"Knew him? When?"

"He was at college with John."

"Yes."

"He came to Malquoits one vacation to stay for a few days."

"Your brother never told me that."

"That's quite probable. Something happened, I believe, at Corpus. That was their college. Something peculiar and rather terrible, I imagine. I wasn't told what it was. I don't know why. But John who, as you know, was a very matter-of-fact sort of person, never spoke of it. He never even spoke of Mr. Gollancz again. I sort of felt at the time he was not particularly proud of having had him as a friend."

"And you met him when he came to Malquoits?"

"Yes."

"What was he like?"

Allowing for the way that women appreciate different qualities and peculiarities in men, she described to me, with quite extraordinary vividness the man I had seen that day in the Haymarket, the man who, only a few days before, had warned me of my interference with the privacy of his life in Clifford's Inn.

"And how long ago is that?" I asked.

She reckoned a moment. Informed me of her own age, and then calculated it to be about forty-five years ago.

"John must have been twenty then. I was two years older than he. Oh, yes. I haven't forgotten Mr. Gollancz. But why have you asked me about him? What has that got to do with Clifford's Inn? It was when I said my father was found dead there that you—well, I felt something."

I cannot exactly explain why but, just as with Juniper, I felt a strong reluctance to tell her all I knew. What good would it do? It could only disquiet her mind. She couldn't understand it any more than I could. With that inferiority of her sex she had talked about, she might imagine possibilities which, with the assurance of my sex, I should scoff at. There was a lot in what she had said.

Anyhow, on the spur of that moment I made up my mind not to distress her.

"Only," said I, "that I know a man named Gollancz, who lived in Clifford's Inn."

I hardly thought the meagre association of that fact would satisfy her, but as is characteristic of old people who live nearly altogether in their memories, that name of Gollancz had carried her back those forty-five years. From the remote expression that had settled about her lips, I could see she was thinking of those days when she was a girl at Malquoits, and with an instinct I seized upon that.

"What sort of a young man was this Gollancz then?" I asked.

Her hands folded and unfolded upon her lap before she answered. I watched them. With their peculiar expressiveness they were conveying to me a kind of shyness. The sort of modesty of a young girl, confessing her first love affair. I knew by those hands, before she had said anything, that forty-five years ago she had been infatuated by the young undergraduate her brother had brought back with him from the 'Varsity. She may only have seen him those few days. There may never have been any love passage between them, but she had not forgotten her emotions.

For all I could tell, it was one of those little tragedies that must be a common occurrence in a young woman's life. An infatuation which, being a woman, she had been unable to disclose. Especially in those latter Victorian days. The man had passed across her life and probably he had never known.

"He was the most attractive man I think I've ever met," she said slowly. "Though attractive isn't really the word. It's a silly word. Or it's become so. Young women use it so easily nowadays. But if you can understand he had a personality that stirred a woman to the depths of herself."

"He stirred you?" I said quietly.

"Yes. But I don't think women meant anything to him. He scarcely noticed me."

Forty-five years before. The incongruousness of that suddenly amazed me. Forty-five years ago, when that old lady was a young girl, Gollancz had imposed upon her the fascinations of his personality. Now still he was able to influence her daughter-in-law in the same way. It was incredible. But how could I escape the facts of it? Here were two people I knew of, this old lady and her brother, my friend, who had informed me, convincingly, that in so many years this man Gollancz had not changed in outward appearance.

"How old do you think he was then?" I ventured.

"Oh—he was not young for an undergraduate. Thinking back, it's almost impossible to place his age. He might have been as much as twenty-eight. Or even thirty. I can't remember that I ever considered what his age was. His visit was very brief. Only a few days. I don't imagine John found him so companionable as he had supposed. John was a very out-of-door young man in those days. He was fond of his shooting. And Mr. Gollancz wouldn't shoot. I remember him saying life was not as valuable as we made it out to be, but at least it belonged to the creatures that owned it and should never be taken from them unless it was manifest that they were misusing it. A peculiar fancy. But I've always felt there was something in it. No—all Mr. Gollancz was interested in was the library at Malquoits. Apparently he had heard about that. In fact, so John told me after he had gone, he had really invited himself for those few days. Certainly he spent all his time with the books. In those few days he must have gone through nearly all of them. I used to sit with him there in the library and watch him climbing up and down the steps, taking one volume out after another; glancing through it and then putting it back again. In the evenings he talked a great deal with my father—alone in his study. Then one day, I think it was the fourth he'd been at Malquoits, they suddenly went up to London together. And Mr. Gollancz didn't come back. John wasn't sorry."

Her voice dropped a little.

"That was the last I saw of him," she said.

It was her picture of him climbing up and down those library steps that flashed itself into my mind. He was looking then for that manuscript of Simon Studion's. How could I escape that conviction? But how far had he become then the adept he was now in the degrees of his Brotherhood? Surely, if he had been able in those days to practise a transportation of his subconscious, as it seemed he could now, that volume would not have escaped him.

He and my friend's father had talked a lot alone together at night. Could that have been the beginning of the elder Crawshay-Martin's acquaintance with the Brotherhood of the Rosy Cross? Did Gollancz himself reveal to him his possession of that invaluable book? Was that the meaning of his taking it away from his son? Was that why he had taken it up to London and then, the Brotherhood demanding it of him, he had brought it back again to Malquoits? It was not safe in London, he had told his daughter. "That book has life and death in it. Perhaps my life." And then, surely enough, within a few hours from saying that, he had been found, on the verge of death, in the passage leading to Clifford's Inn.

It was all too bewildering to tell her what I knew and what I thought then. Again I was conscious, and more than ever now, that Juniper was in danger.

"And haven't you heard the name of Gollancz mentioned since?" I asked. "Hasn't your son said anything about him, or Mrs. Claude?"

"No," she said. "Why should they?"

"Because that day when they went to Bedinghurst and stopped at the inn there, they met a man named Gollancz. He told your son the value of the book."

"I've heard Claude speak of a man," she replied, "who told them what that wretched book was worth. I wish to goodness he hadn't. I'm afraid Claude is rather avaricious. It's made him expect so much of the value of it. There was an American offered him two thousand pounds for it. I begged him to take it. Somehow I always associate that book with my father's death in some way. But he held out. This man at Bedinghurst apparently had told him it might be worth fifty thousand pounds. But do you think that was the same Mr. Gollancz who came to Malquoits with John?"

"I fancy it's the same," said I. "I was there. That was where I first met your son and——" I had the inclination to say Juniper. Did she guess that? She turned her eyes to me. "And his wife," I added. "I understood from what this Mr. Gollancz said then, that he knew all about the book. In fact, a friend of his had tried to buy it at the sale."

More than this I somehow felt it unwise to say. The fact that Juniper had said nothing to her mother-in-law about Gollancz, notwithstanding the sympathy that existed between them, made me feel that a certain degree of caution was necessary, if only out of respect for her. But I did not like that silence of hers. It seemed to mean something. And her perversion of the truth to me before lunch. Of course she had dreamt of him again. How could I like it? But I could not give her away, and so I turned the conversation to the condition of Claude Weaver's health.

"There is no need to hide from you that I know he takes drugs," I added to my inquiry. "Mrs. Claude knows that I know. You must have had a terrible shock the other night."

She looked up at me with the pathos of the physical impotence of blind people in her face.

"There's no cure," she said. "I've reconciled myself to that now. His father was a prey to alcoholism. I didn't know that when I was married. It's descended from father to son. There's no need to tell you what a horror it is. Sometimes I wish it was all over. For his sake, as well as for hers. His life belongs to him, I know. But he's misusing it—isn't he?"

Had she known she had used Gollancz's own words? Or had they just come back involuntarily out of her memory?

There was a long silence between us after she said that. Her hands were lying in her lap, and as I looked at them I saw the fingers of her right hand turning round and round the wedding ring on her left. Round and round she was twisting it, as a squirrel might spin itself in its revolving cage. And that, I felt, had been her life—the life of a woman conscious of the imprisoning inferiority of her sex.

CHAPTER XII

We had talked a little while longer about ordinary things, and then Juniper had come back into the room, standing at the door, half apologetically and without any tone of persuasion asking me if I would like to come up for a moment and see her husband.

I felt she did not particularly want me to come. I didn't want to go either. But in deference to that old lady—the blind angel, as Juniper truly called her—I went.

He was still in an exhausted condition. I gathered from Juniper he had reached the stage of coma consistent with morphia poisoning, and had only just been revived. But nothing was said then about the drug. With the convincing assurance of the morphia-maniac, he talked about his health as though it had been a normal illness. Juniper stood by, listening, with an inscrutable expression on her face.

Associating me with my interest in the Rosicrucian manuscript, he talked mostly of that.

"Has Juniper told you I'm translating it?" he asked.

I said she had.

"Most interesting, really, though I can't understand a word of it yet. May explain itself a bit when I get more done. Funny thing, I dreamt about that man the other night—forget his name—the chap you brought into the inn at Bedinghurst."

"What did you dream?" I inquired. Not that I supposed he would tell me.

"Oh, in the dream he warned me not to go on with it. 'Stop,' he said. 'Stop.' He didn't say what. But in the dream I knew what he meant."

"Well, aren't you going to take his advice?" I suggested.

"Huh!" It was a kind of laugh. "A dream! Not suggesting I should take any notice of a dream—are you?"

"The importance of dreams is more realized than it used to be a few years ago," I remarked. "The modern interpreter is becoming as important a gentleman as he was in the days of Pharaoh. He sets up in Harley Street now, and does no end of a trade."

I didn't want to make too much of it to him, but there was the suggestion if his mind liked to take hold of it. Seeing the fractious condition of that mind, I hardly supposed it would.

Soon after that, I left him. If it was a duty to have come to see the man whose wife I loved, I had done it, unpleasant as it was. Life provides one with queer situations. The problems presented by modern civilization are delicately ironical. It must have been considerably easier to know what to do in the days when, to see a woman suffering as Juniper was from a worthless husband, it was only necessary to pick a quarrel with him and run him through.

She came downstairs with me and we went out again into the garden. For the remaining hours that I stayed there, we talked of nothing that concerned Gollancz, or her husband, or any of the things that were really occupying her mind. She was not well read. She was not even what you would call well educated. I don't know what they teach the young girls at their schools nowadays. But there was a freshness and originality about her vein of thought, cynical though it may have been. I know it only made me the more in love with her.

If she was at all like the rest of the young women one meets, then there is a pathetic sense of loneliness, of isolation about them. As though, suddenly discovering themselves in a new world of thought, they could find no men of their own age to share the peculiar sensitive quality of their youth.

I can't say that I pitied—she made me laugh too often—but I felt damned sorry for her. She was worth so much more than she ever valued herself. Again and again I remembered those lines of Browning as I listened to her cynicism or watched the expression of indifference in her eyes. She talked about love as though it were the last, fatuous resource of futile minds. She spoke of religion as if it might have been a kind of fortune-telling by gipsies with a dirty pack of cards. But none of this destroyed my conviction that a deep emotion would discover her, not only for herself, but for the man who loved her.

An hour later I motored back to Winchester, promising to come over the next day, Sunday, and have tea with them in the garden, if it were fine.

Had there been any doubt in my mind before as to the issue of all this business, I was quite certain about it then. Not all the powers of darkness or the conventions of an artificial society should keep her from me. The only question upon which I could not satisfy myself was whether it were the moment then to tell her what I felt.

Sitting alone at my dinner in the Winchester hotel, I argued it out this way and that. Sometimes, when I felt she knew already that my interest in her was not merely of a platonic nature, it seemed a confession of indecision to delay it any longer. She must have known my coming down there for that week-end, apparently with no purpose other than to see her, was not the action of a disinterested man. Unmistakably I had seen that knowledge in her eyes. Then why keep silent about it any longer? Would she believe in the force of an emotion that could contain itself in silence like that?

But then, on the other hand, there was her deception to me about her dreams. A thousand times if she had denied it, I should have still been convinced she had dreamed of Gollancz again, that she was still feeling the power of his influence, that the same infatuation her mother-in-law had felt when she was a girl, was occupying every thought in her mind, every impulse in her nature. And these were not late Victorian days now. I had not forgotten her first questions to me about the celibacy of the Brotherhood of the Rosy Cross, or her frank statement that there were other relationships than that of marriage between men and women.

If this actually were the condition of her mind, it would still be premature to the point of destroying all my hopes, if I tried to sway her with my own emotion then. An infatuation like that—if it were as I feared—had to burn itself out. I forced myself to recognize that. At least I had no fear that Gollancz would reciprocate it. From what I had seen in Clifford's Inn, that bed of naked boards, the austerity of his room, cleared, all but for that ceiling, of its religious purposes, I knew there was no weakness of the flesh about him. The power of women did not exist in his life. He was beyond the human passion of a man. She would find that out. He would pass across her life, not so faintly as he had passed across the life of that old lady when she was a girl, but inevitably her nature could not be satisfied with that and Gollancz would go. As suddenly and strangely as he had come that day at the "Scarlett Arms," when she had passed him on the stairs and later seen him walking by the window.

It was not the moment to speak. I was finally convinced of that. I went to bed and slept, fretfully, as one whose whole nature is being thwarted of its most eager intentions, until the morning of Sunday roused me with the thought of how soon I was going to see her again.

We had tea in the garden, under an old elder tree that had been left standing, because of the quaint formation of its trunk, probably since the days when the Bloody Judge stretched his legs outside the Court House between the lives of his victims. Mrs.

Weaver was with us. She wanted to have tea indoors, alone, but Juniper insisted upon her coming out. She took her by the arm and led her to a chair under the elder tree.

I had the impression in this determination of hers that she wanted to avoid being left alone with me. She did know, then. Once a man is aware of being in love with a woman, presumably he gives it away at every turn. Any woman with half her instinct can detect it. Juniper knew, but did that avoidance necessarily mean I was unwanted?

Probably the conceit of a man in this state of mind is only equalled by the preposterous pride of the male animal in the mating season. A peacock struts about wholly convinced of his superiority in the beauty of his tail-feathers. It is wellnigh impossible for a man really to believe he is not wanted. Would he ever win a mate if he did?

Distressing to me though it was, I did not regard her evidence as being wholly unfavourable to myself. Her manner, I argued, once she knew, would have changed if she had really disliked me. Apart from being alone with her, she would have shown me she did not want me there at all.

But it was far from anything like that she did. There, under that elder during tea, she was more lively, amusing—though still cynically—than I had yet seen her. As though there were something she had found to be a stimulation, lifting her out of her usual indifference. Was it a woman's knowledge that she was desirable? The most effective stimulant she knows. It may, after all, have been, not conceit, but a kind of determination of despair that made me force myself to read it like that. I could not believe that I should not win her in the end. I would not believe it. Every moment I saw some fresh trait of hers, I felt myself to be the more in love.

It is impossible to give a true account of all that happened without confessing at moments to my own sensations. I am not concerned with telling a romantic love story. I have no desire to represent myself as an ardent young lover, carrying away his mistress with the torrential stream of his passion. I was a man of forty-five and she a married woman. There are not a few people who will say, as they read these pages, that at my age there was no excuse for me to involve myself in an affair of that nature.

But if I had felt that, this story would have ended where I began it, with the death of my friend Crawshay-Martin in the "Scarlett Arms." It is because of what I felt for Juniper that I learnt what I did. And therefore it is necessary for me on occasion to describe those feelings. It was because of them that I was drawn on into the business. It was because I hoped for the ultimate success of my love for her that I persisted.

Though I did not see her alone again, though successfully for the rest of that afternoon she used her mother-in-law to prevent any intimate conversation between us, that visit into Hampshire finally sealed my determination to win her love; to give her all the happiness I could. I knew enough of the horror of a drug-taker's life, to realize from Claude Weaver the miserable conditions of her existence. Not only must she have grown to hate him, but there was no escape for her hatred. There she was in that place, cooped up with it. Her life strangled by it. Even on the few occasions when she came to town, she was not to know what would happen in her absence. Rightly or not, the doctor had entrusted the care of his drug to her. In Stoke Charity there was little chance of his getting it through any other means. And always it was up to her discretion and her courage to keep it from him as long as possible, until, as she said, he became maniacal in his craving for it.

From the horror of a life like that, I was determined to save her. At the rate that he was going, I could see Claude Weaver would not last so very long. If I could not persuade her to take the plunge and leave him to his own devices, it was only a question of waiting. Even his mother had said she wished it was all over.

As I remembered that, I realized, of course, that they could not leave him. With a man like that it would amount to being criminal. He would be dead in a month. It was not so easy as it might seem. But once I could tell her all that was in my mind, we could wait. It could not be long. But at that point of my thoughts, I found myself again face to face with Gollancz.

He was the real crux of it all. Not Claude Weaver. She was avoiding me that afternoon, not because of any actual dislike of my company. Indeed, I believed she liked our conversations. She was avoiding me because some other consideration was taking up the occupation of her mind. She was not free in herself to wish to be alone with me.

Then what was it, if it were not Gollancz? The day before, Mrs. Weaver had asked me to take care of her. What had she meant by that? At the end of tea, when Juniper had gone into the house to get her objectionable Virginia cigarettes, I asked her.

"I felt you were interested in her," she said evasively. "With the life she has to lead—and what's the good of trying to conceal that from you, you're a doctor—you can see she has a good deal of loneliness to contend with. I don't think loneliness is good for young people. The idle hands that Satan finds mischief for," she added with a kind of smile, "must be all young ones, I think. When life's in front of us, we don't want to be alone with it. We want others to share in what we're doing. It's only when life's behind us that we want to sit alone and look back on what we've done."

All that was true enough, but I felt it to be rather in the nature of dust in my eyes. She was not really telling me what she had meant. I pressed my question again from another angle.

"But *how* take care of her?" I repeated. "What's she in danger of?"

"Herself."

"But how?"

Again I was watching the play of her hands. A kind of elusive restlessness in her lap.

"I know Juniper very well," she said presently. "Tell me when she comes out of the house, because I don't want to have to stop awkwardly in what I'm saying. Her instincts are very quick."

I promised I would tell her at once.

"I know her so well," she continued, "that although I can't see—perhaps because of that—I can feel her moods more plainly than if I saw the expression of them in her face. She's had something on her mind these last few months. She's always wanting to get away to London. To stay at her club. I do my best to dissuade her."

"Why?"

She frowned a little, as though I were forcing her by my questions farther than she wanted to go. Then as suddenly the frown left her face. She appeared to have found a sudden acquisition of confidence in me. As though in that moment she had lost all doubt about the wisdom of what she was saying.

"You were a friend of my brother's," she said, "and it's impossible for me to tell you how much I loved and admired John. As soon as I heard you were a friend of his, I felt a deal of confidence in you. That was why, at our first meeting, I said—take care of Juniper. Because I care very much for her. I'm very sorry for her. And why I meant—take care—I don't see why I shouldn't tell you as well. You're not a young man. I don't mean to say you're old. Indeed, I feel you're in the prime of your life. But you have experience of the world. You can understand that when a young woman is situated as Juniper is, she is liable to get herself into all sorts of difficulties."

"Do you mean another man?" I asked.

I don't know how I made my voice as casual as it was. Perhaps it wasn't. Perhaps, despite all my intentions, it had in it the note of my fears and apprehensions.

She looked up at me as I said it. With her blind eyes. And then she did an unexpected thing. At least, it surprised me. She felt out with one of her hands and laid it a moment on my arm, almost as though to reassure me.

"I don't think Juniper would do anything foolish," she said. "At least, I hope not. Young women, as you heard me say yesterday, are more ready to break their necks than their hearts. But I think there is a man somewhere who has some influence over her. Somewhere. Probably in London, because I feel her being drawn there. It's not only that she wants to get away from Stoke Charity, which, God knows, I can understand. It is that she wants to go there. And yet, perhaps, that's only natural. There's more life in London than anywhere else."

"And do you feel this because she's always saying she wants to get away to London?" I asked.

"No. She's only said that once or twice."

"Then what?"

She smiled before she answered. Smiled to herself.

"You're a man," she said gently. "You won't credit the instinct of women and you wouldn't in any case have had any experience of the instinct of blind people. Juniper's restless. I don't see her wandering about the house or the garden. But I feel her wandering. I feel something I couldn't explain. When you're blind, senses are added to you, you know. I sometimes think that if we could suppress our five senses, reduce physical sensation, in fact, to a minimum, we should discover qualities in our minds that would astonish us."

At once I thought of Gollancz on his wooden bed. Every sense in him reduced to the lowest of its functions. His heart just beating and no more.

"You may not expect it of a man," said I, "but I accept all that. There is something influencing her mind. I'm sure you're right. But how can you know it is a man? Surely she has enough to make her mind restless here, in Stoke Charity?"

"Yes, yes, I know all that," she answered. "I can't expect you to allow me the peculiar instinct women have about other women when there is a man concerned. It is quite reasonless. Quite without any exact foundation. As a scientist, you couldn't possibly make allowance for it. And I shouldn't have expressed it in words, if something hadn't happened."

I asked her what.

"Juniper goes into the nearest town almost every other day for her shopping. She drives herself in in the car. Alone. She went last Thursday. I felt her to be very excited when she returned. That may be my imagination. I may have thought it since."

"Since what?"

"Since Friday, the day before you came, I was talking to a woman—a Mrs. Collins—who comes from Alton to do some sewing for me. Juniper was out in the garden. She happened to mention she had seen Juniper in the town. 'And what a strange-looking man she was talking to, Mrs. Weaver,' she said. She described his appearance, and I could realize it was not any of our acquaintances about here. So, you see, I suppose I put two and two together. A common mathematical weakness of women. All my apprehensions were materialized in that one fortuitous little piece of information."

"What did the woman say he was like?" I asked.

"Well, she didn't see his face."

"How did you know, then, it was not one of your acquaintances about here?"

"Because of the way he was dressed."

"How was he dressed?"

"Oh, he had on a big, black sombrero hat. Not the sort of headgear we country people wear."

I could have told her that myself. I could have shouted it out in that quiet garden. I was glad, with all her instincts, she could not see my face. I was staring in front of me across the lawn out of the shadows of that elder tree into the sunlight. And from the french windows of the drawing-room, I could see Juniper coming with her packet of Virginia cigarettes.

She smiled at me as she came up and joined us. An open smile. Cheerful and far less cynical than usual. And I could not help thinking what secrets there are lying behind the ordinary lives of men and women. And more particularly women, it seemed to me just then. How could I possibly hope to know what was in her mind!

CHAPTER XIII

I went back to town that night. There was nothing to keep me any longer in Winchester. I had to be at the hospital fairly early on Monday morning. For the next few days my time was so taken up with work that I had little opportunity to consider what could be done to dissuade Juniper from her acquaintance with Gollancz. Was there anything I could do?

No question of doubt remained in my mind that it was Gollancz she had met in their country town. But why there? And how there? Had he summoned her in her dreams again? Was this just a preliminary meeting for what was to follow? Whatever it was, I knew there could be nothing accidental about it.

In the evenings, when usually I go to a theatre or somewhere out to dine, I spent my time alone, obsessed by my own emotions, considering whether it would be wise at this stage to tell her what I knew. What did I know? I knew nothing. And so much as I had discovered of his celebrations in Clifford's Inn, was that the kind of thing that would put any woman off the natural curiosity of her inclinations? Wouldn't it only the more induce her to follow it up so long as the mystery of the man was still about him? Is not mystery itself one of the subtlest attractions to sex? Again and again I have seen that in the course of my practice. Something is elusive to a man about a woman, something about a woman to a man. And human nature being what it is, thirsting always for adventure, the pursuit is begun which seldom has more than one ending.

I had practically decided there was nothing to be done but watch what she did. Take care of her, as her mother-in-law had said, and, if she came up to London, occupy her time with all the amusements I could throw in her way.

It was not likely. I felt, after that last experience, that she would not come to town for a while at least, therefore I was not surprised one afternoon when I was in my consulting-room to hear that I was wanted on the telephone. A trunk call. Mrs. Weaver.

Ridiculous, that beating of the heart, when a man of forty-five, just because he is going to listen to the sound of a voice in a piece of vulcanite, can find that organ in his body suddenly palpitating with emotional anticipation. I tried to laugh at myself. Picking up the receiver, and with a friendly familiarity in my voice, I said:

"Hallo! How are you, my dear?"

It was the first advance I had made to a kind of intimacy, an intimacy, no doubt, she was accustomed to with even her merest acquaintances, but had not learnt till then to expect from me.

My heart fell as I heard the reply.

"It's not Juniper, Dr. Hawke. It's Mrs. Aubrey Weaver speaking."

I apologized. I don't know why. In a kind of confusion, I suppose. I fancied then that the old blind lady must realize what my feelings for Juniper were. She had never heard me address her daughter like that in her presence. Not that it mattered. I didn't really care if she did.

But she continued, apparently taking no notice, not even of my apology.

"I rang you up," she said, "to tell you that Juniper has gone to London. I expect, to stay at her club. I've only just found out that she's gone. She went out this morning in the car. I called out good-bye to her from the window of my bedroom. There are some disadvantages in being blind. I couldn't see she had her dressing-case with her."

"And she didn't tell you?"

"No."

"Isn't that unlike her?"

"Very. That's why I've rung you up."

"But how did you find out?"

"Oh, she couldn't conceal it from the maid. The girl knew she had packed her dressing-case. When Juniper didn't come in to lunch, she told me."

"How long will she have been in town by now?"

"I think she must have left by the eleven-thirty train. It gets in just before two. What time is it now?"

"About half-past four."

"Well, I think that must have been her train. And she will have left the car at a garage near the station. She often does that."

"What do you want me to do?" I asked.

I thought at first she hadn't heard. There was a pause in that piece of vulcanite. I was just about to repeat my question, when she said:

"What I told you. Take care of her. Somehow, I don't like it. She may, of course, have only gone to town for the day and is returning by an evening train. She does do that sometimes. But she's never done it before without telling me. Take care of her. That's all I want you to do. I can trust you, whatever may happen to Juniper—I don't feel I can trust that other man."

That was an extraordinary thing to say. I could hardly credit my ears. "Whatever may happen to Juniper." What did she mean by that? But it was the last thing she said that astonished me most of all.

"What do you know about the other man?" I exclaimed. "You can't possibly tell whether he is to be trusted or not. You've never seen him."

"Oh, yes—I've seen him," said she.

"When?"

"Years ago." This was her answer. "In the library at Malquoits."

For a moment there was nothing I could say. She had known all the time it was Gollancz. That was all I could realize. But how? And then, over the distance of those eighty or ninety miles, I heard her explaining. The black sombrero. Ridiculous to suppose it could have been the same, but evidently he had always worn that sort of hat. And on that alone, hearing that Juniper had met him at Bedinghurst, her instinct had leapt straight at the truth.

She might well say I could not allow for the instinct of women about their own sex where a man was concerned. And as for the intuitions of blind people, it certainly was beyond one's comprehension.

"But it's more than forty years since you met him at Malquoits," I said.

"I'm quite aware of that," she replied. "I'm not saying what his power over Juniper is. He would not have the same effect upon her as he did upon me when I was a young girl. But his voice can't be so different. He will say the kind of things I remember him saying when I used to sit with him in the library. The same insatiable curiosity of spirit would be roused in her now by what he says as it was in me. She's one of those present-day young women who have no religion. Women must have religion, Dr. Hawke. They come too near the chasm of the secret meanings of life, to find themselves without a guide rope to clutch on to. Juniper, with all her cynicism and apparent indifference, would seize upon some explanation of the meaning of her unhappy existence if it were presented to her."

So she had not guessed what I had every apparent reason to believe, that Gollancz, after those forty years, was still in appearance the young man of indeterminable age, who might be no more than twenty-eight or thirty. Her instinct had not led her so far as to suspect, what, with a secret fear, I imagined. That this with Juniper was an attraction of sex as well as spirit. Nothing could wholly eradicate from my memory those questions of hers about the Brotherhood of the Rosy Cross. I could not forget her saying that there were other relationships than marriage between men and women.

The whole of her nature there, in that unnatural house of hers at Stoke Charity, was thwarted and starved. If a normal life could not be given her, she would seize upon the first influence that roused and fed the hunger of her imagination.

I did not tell Mrs. Weaver all this. I simply said:

"Well, perhaps you're right. And if you are, then everything on earth must be done to save her from becoming mixed up in one of these fantastic religious cults that lead to God knows what."

She quickly agreed with that. "I'm sure it was that that had something to do with the death of my father," she said. "Sometimes I feel it had something to do with the death of John. But whether it did or it didn't, I beg you to try and save her from that man. I'm an old woman now and I realize things I didn't understand then. One of these days I'll tell you all I feel about Mr. Gollancz. I couldn't tell you here. All I can say now is, take care of her. Don't waste a moment. I feel so helpless myself, down here. I rely upon you."

I promised her I would do all I could and, directly she had rung off, I telephoned to Juniper's club. The hall porter answered.

"Is Mrs. Claude Weaver in the club?"

"No, sir. She's not."

"Has she taken a room?"

"Yes, sir."

I asked if she had left her luggage. She had. Did they know when she was coming in? They did not. Did she usually dine there when she was in town? Sometimes she did. Did she change for dinner? Nearly always. Did she say where she was going that afternoon? No, she had not.

I told him I would ring up again later or come round there and call myself, and I hung up the receiver.

It was more than likely that she had some shopping to do. For a woman who dressed as she did, their nearest town and even Winchester itself would be quite inadequate for her requirements. I had two patients to see and felt no immediate concern as to her whereabouts. It was nearly six o'clock when they were disposed of. Little did they know, as I questioned them about their condition, that it was with the utmost effort of concentration I could pay any attention to their replies. Honestly, their ailments meant nothing to me. I could not wholly release my mind from speculation as to what Juniper was doing and where she was as I sat there in my consulting-room talking to them.

It was just after six when I reached the club in Dover Street. Mrs. Claude Weaver had not returned. I sat in the hall and waited. Ladies came in and out of the swing door. The habits of women in their clubs might have been an interesting source of study to me for that next hour if I could have lent my observation to it. But I was thinking only of her. Looking sharply at every woman who entered until I felt beneath their gaze like a young man who has been cheated of his assignation at the appointed rendezvous. At last I could stand their commiserating glances no longer. I got up and told the hall porter I would call again later, and I went down to the Devonshire Club for a meal.

At eight o'clock, I told our hall porter to ring up Juniper's club and ask if she had come in. They had not seen her. At nine o'clock I went round there again myself. Still they had seen nothing of her. I walked down Dover Street at the pace of a man following a funeral, trying to decide what I should do.

She had not kept her promise and let me know she was in town. I don't know that that was more disturbing than the fact that she had left Stoke Charity without letting her mother-in-law know. But it added to my apprehensions. Despite all the excuses I invented for this sudden visit of hers to London, I could not drive the feeling out of my mind that there was something suspicious and unnatural about it. Again and again I threw away the thought that she had come to meet Gollancz, but irresistibly it returned to me.

I went back to the Devonshire Club, smoked a cigarette, and had a drink. Anybody who has known the sensation of losing someone in London will realize the helplessness I felt. Where was I to search? In which direction could I hope to find her? There was only one place. Back again and again it came inevitably into my mind. Clifford's Inn. The fact that he had warned me not to go there again was of little consequence beside my determination to find Juniper. What could he do? I didn't care what he could do. Once having made up my mind, his warning was no more than a trespasser's notice in a field. I was going that way and nothing could stop me.

It may seem foolish not to have assumed that a young woman, twenty-seven years of age, was quite capable of looking after herself in these days of feminine independence. Even presuming that she had gone to Clifford's Inn, what harm could possibly come to her there? Alone with Gollancz in the seclusion of those rooms of his, I knew I had no reason to fear any dastardly action on his part. Against my own inclinations I was convinced that, so far as his relations with women were concerned, his behaviour could not be questioned.

Was it Juniper herself I doubted? In the desperate state of her mind was there anything, under an influence of this nature, she might not do? All that indifference, all that cynicism and insolence, I knew, was only a mask, a kind of armour to protect the susceptibility of the emotions it concealed. Yet with my own feelings, how dared I doubt her?

This was not what it was that composed my fear. What I was afraid of—I may as well admit it—was the power of Gollancz over things which, in the ordinary habit of my mind, I should have scoffed at. The elder Crawshay-Martin had met his end in some relation to those ceremonies that took place in Clifford's Inn. My friend had taken his own life in circumstances that inevitably in my mind pointed to the indefinable influence of Gollancz. There were Juniper's and Claude Weaver's dreams. There was what I had seen myself in that room at Clifford's Inn. With every instinct of sanity I was still unable to rid myself of my apprehensions. At half-past ten I could abide them no longer. I could not sit there in idleness. If Gollancz followed these occult practices, then, notwithstanding how much I told myself he must be a charlatan, I was still afraid. Ringing up her club once more and hearing she had not returned, I left the Devonshire and went down to Fleet Street.

In some sort of concession to my consciousness that I was a man of science, practising medicine in the twentieth century, I would not take a taxi as though it were a matter of life and death. Could anything, in the heart of London, be more ridiculous? I walked. Should I have understood more of what I found if I had not wasted that half-hour? I shall never know that. Juniper will not be able to tell me. And it is no good concerning oneself with such speculations now. I did walk.

It was some time soon after eleven when I passed under the archway of the porter's lodge. Away from the noise of the buses taking the East Enders back to their homes from the West End theatres, the Inn was as quiet as that night before when I had come down there like a spy investigating the privacy of Gollancz's life. The same effect of remoteness fell upon me directly I found myself in those cobbled courtyards. Even with the actual experience I had had of the congregated charwomen, the typewriters clicking in the architect's office, of people coming and going in the light of day, the sensation of a deserted place, removed from all association with the world outside, was insistent. The echo of my own feet between the wings of those buildings was like thunder in the stillness.

The first thing I did was to go round to the courtyard from which I could see his windows. The curtains were drawn, but if there were any parting between them—which it was difficult to see in that darkness—then there was no light coming through. His candles were not burning unless, on this occasion, the curtains were so closely drawn that they shut out every wink of light.

For a few moments I stood there, staring up. But gazing at those blind windows was telling me nothing. The Inn was quieter that night even than before. No lights were burning anywhere. Every inhabitant of the place was asleep. Or, like the God of the Israelites, they were out upon some nocturnal journey. There was no one to ask anything. And even if anybody had come by, what could I have said?

At last I turned back to the other wing of the building and passed through under the wooden porch at the entrance to Number Eight. The old street lamp was burning on the staircase above the architect's floor. It was about the only light in the place.

I did not creep up the wooden stairs this time. Perhaps to infuse a sense of justification into myself, I trod the steps with firm determination. Any moment on my way up I expected a door to open. The lady's of the visiting card. I imagined an inquisitive head being thrust out to inquire what I wanted. But there was not a sound other than the hollow noise of my own footsteps.

Gollancz's door on the top landing was closed. I could not have expected anything else. But the thing that brought a sickness into my throat was the penetrating smell of incense. Lighter than air I suppose, it had all collected and hung there in the atmosphere under that sloping roof. I stood for a moment breathing it in, wondering what I should do next. There was only one thing to do. I knocked. There was no answer. No sound of a movement inside. I knocked again. Louder than before. No one was there. And yet, for some unaccountable reason in my mind, I was not satisfied. I suppose I ought to have felt a sense of relief that Gollancz was not in his rooms. If he was not there, then Juniper wasn't. And that was the most likely place in London, if they were together, where she would be.

Obviously it was no good going on knocking. I tried the door. It was locked. My next thought was to telephone again to her club. I went back into Fleet Street. Running almost, I went up to the Waldorf Hotel and telephoned from there. It was ridiculous in the highly-lighted civilization of that place to realize what was in my thoughts, the fears and suspicions they contained.

I received the answer I was dreading. She had not returned. I even requested that they should go and look in her room. But she was not there.

I admit then I was beginning to feel desperate. In that condition one thinks hopefully and inevitably of the police. From the commissionaire at the Waldorf, I ascertained the situation of the nearest police station, and went there. I actually ran there. By the time I was standing in the superintendent's office, I was out of breath. It may have lent some urgency to my request. I asked for someone to come up to Clifford's Inn with me. I had reason to suppose, I said, that a lady was there, and I was afraid something might have happened to her. I was a doctor. She was a patient of mine, I said. I gave them my card. I suggested she might be ill. Anything I could think of I told them that would not be likely to involve Juniper in any trouble. I didn't want them to suppose there was anything shady about it. But they could see from what I told them that it was necessary to do something, make some investigation, and they sent a sergeant along with me.

On our way back to the Inn, I tried to explain to him, as well as I could, the nature of Gollancz's occupation of those rooms. Remembering the type of intelligence I had met with in the sergeant in charge at Shipleigh, I made no endeavour to convince him of the occult nature of Gollancz's beliefs. He held religious services, I said, in his room. Burnt incense, and all that sort of thing.

"Like what they do in Rome," said the sergeant. But whether he meant actually the city of Rome or the more comprehensive Holy Church, I could not discover.

"And does this lady go and attend these services?" he asked.

"I've reason to believe so," I told him.

I was determined he should not think that Juniper was there for some improper purpose. But that undoubtedly was what he did think. A young woman in a man's rooms at that hour of the night had only one meaning to him. That was his experience of life, and it was not conceivable to him to depart from his rigid estimate of human nature. Murder, theft or immorality. These, to him, were the three main functions of human beings. He nodded his head. He emitted inarticulate grunts to all I told him. But that, I knew, was what he was thinking.

Possibly the smell of the incense on that landing unsettled the preconceived ideas in his mind a bit.

"Smells a bit holy—don't it?" he said, when he, too, had knocked on the door and we were standing there waiting for some answering response within.

After a second knocking, he examined the lock. It was an ordinary lock, capable of being opened from within, but effectually barred to the outsider. I looked on with interest as he took out a bunch of keys and, finding one to fit the lock, I could not help thinking what little security there is in all our patented precautions to preserve the common safety of our existence. Because the door opened as he turned the key, as easily as if he had been entering his own private house, and there we were in that dirty little threshold kitchen, with its rusty gas-stove, its sink, and the skylight, through the smutty glass of which I could see a misty twinkle of the stars outside.

The door into the other room was closed, but even there in the cramped space of that kitchen, the faint blue mist of the incense smoke was still hanging.

"Pouf!" exclaimed the sergeant, blowing it out of his lungs. And then he added: "I suppose I ought to knock on the door. We're only looking for someone—aren't we?"

He knocked, and there was no answer. He knocked again, and glanced at me.

"Nobody there," said he; "but we'd better just have a look inside."

He opened the door. If the smoke had not had the penetrating smell of incense, one would almost have thought the room was on fire. The windows were closed and the heavy curtains I had seen from outside were drawn fast across them. These had obscured the light, because there were candles burning. The seven-branch candlestick I had seen in that cupboard was standing on the deal table which, draped with a fine piece of material, had been made to look like an altar. All the candles in it were burning, low in their sockets, but through that blue mist of the atmosphere—like the accumulated smoke in a bar parlour on a Saturday night—their illumination was faint and uncertain. The dark blue ceiling, too, lent no reflection. The scarlet rose in the centre looked no more vivid in that haze than a dark smear of blood. Just around the seven flames of those candles there was a certain aura of light that did not reach the corners of the room. It was only after a moment, standing there at the door, that we could see it was empty.

If Gollancz had been celebrating his Mass, then the communicants were gone.

"Well, your lady must have said her prayers and hopped it," said the sergeant. There was no surprise in his voice. It might have been his habit to look in at the private sanctum of a Rosicrucian every day of his life. But I was not to be satisfied with that one cursory glance. The curtains were drawn across that L-shaped portion of the room, and, taking the seven-branch candlestick in my hand, I pulled them apart.

How had I known she was there? I can only say I had. Suppressing the exclamatory impulse in my voice, I said quietly:

"No—she hasn't gone. She's here."

She was lying on that bare bed, couch, whatever he called it. Over the clothes she had worn when she came up to town, there was a dark blue robe, such as I had seen hanging in the cupboard. It never occurred to me that she was dead. I had no fear like that. By the light of the candles I could see the pale colour of her cheeks.

"She's just asleep or fainted," I said as the sergeant joined me and, handing him the candlestick, I went across and leant over her, feeling her pulse.

It was beating more or less normally. Her breathing was deep. I had said it was sleep or a faint to satisfy the sergeant's mind. But it was no ordinary unconsciousness.

"The heat and the smell of this incense," I explained. "Just pull those curtains and open the windows," I told him. "Then we'll get her across there so that she can breathe a little cool air."

He did what I told him, but I was none too certain, even as I said it, that any ordinary means of resuscitation would revive her. If this were a trance under the hypnotic influence of Gollancz, how could I hope to get her back?

But after a few moments, when we had carried her to the open window, I could see her breathing was becoming less deep. Once or twice her eyelids twitched. Her lips gradually parted, and then at last her eyes opened. It was obvious she did not know where she was. This return to consciousness was only partial. She recognized me, it is true, but she did not know why I was there. As for the sergeant, she didn't appear even to see him.

"Go down into Fleet Street," I said authoritatively, "and get a taxi. In a minute or two she may be able to walk down. If not, we'll have to carry her."

He went at once, and I was left alone with Juniper in Gollancz's room.

CHAPTER XIV

He must have been gone about ten minutes. There is no need to describe my sensations, holding her there for that time in my arms. I knew then that, wise or unwise, I should delay no longer in telling her what was in my mind as soon as she was physically able to hear me. Already I felt a fool in not speaking before. Perhaps this might never have happened. Whether or not, it would at least have established an intimacy between us. I knew she did not resent my interest in her. She might probably have consulted me before she had come here to this room in Clifford's Inn. She would have let me know she was coming up to town.

Discretion is all very well. One can be too discreet. One can know too much of the psychology of women to know how to deal with them. That was the disadvantage of being forty-five. A younger man would not have waited. A younger man could never have walked all the way down into Fleet Street. He would have taken a taxi, even if he had not got the money to pay for it. And even that half-hour might have made a difference.

Only once during those ten minutes of the sergeant's absence did she say anything. In a distant voice, that gave me the impression not of the difficulty of speech but as of hearing someone talking in another room, the voice of a person removed some distance away, she asked where she was.

"You're all right," I said. "I'm Dr. Hawke."

She nodded her head.

"I'm looking after you," I added. "There's nothing to worry about."

"I'm not worrying," she said. And she closed her eyes as though, unwillingly, she were returning from some place she was loath to leave.

And then the sergeant came in with the information that he had a taxi waiting in Fleet Street by the Clifford's Inn passage.

Holding on to my arm, she was able to walk there. Not by any means the active movement of a body in the full possession of its vitality. She went down those stairs hesitatingly, like a sleepwalker having just got up out of her bed. I was not sorry when I saw her finally in the taxi.

"Tell him to go to Arlington Street," said I—and I gave the sergeant the number. "Perhaps you'd better come with us," I added, seeing a look in his face. "I'm going to take her back to my house. She may want attention during the night."

Evidently he was not quite satisfied. I don't blame him. He

came with us to Arlington Street. As we parted at the door, he said:

"I've got to make inquiries into this matter, you know, sir. 'Course it may be all right. Don't say it isn't. But a young woman in a strange place—that condition—you follow me what I mean?"

I quite followed him.

"You'll find," said I, "that it's what I said. A religious ceremony was being held there. She was evidently overcome by the heat of the room, and fainted. That's all. Whoever was there may possibly have gone out for a doctor. Lucky I came. Still, you must do what you have to do."

For one instant I had a thought of tipping him a ten-shilling note. A young man might have obeyed that impulse. But in a moment I saw the possibility of its rousing his suspicions. There are advantages and disadvantages.

"Very well, sir," he said respectfully. "You'll probably see one of us come along to-morrow morning."

"I'll be here," I said, and I closed the door.

It was after twelve o'clock. I roused the maid. She got a room ready. For the little while that that was being done, Juniper lay on a settee in the room that used to be our drawing-room. For the last ten years or so, I had made it into a kind of study. During that quarter of an hour her eyes were mostly closed. Not in an unconsciousness. I sat and watched her. It was more a kind of fatigue, as though now the normal demands of her nature had asserted themselves and she wanted to go to sleep.

Once she opened her eyes, looked at me for almost a minute, and then said:

"How did you know I was there?"

I told her that Mrs. Aubrey Weaver had rung up.

"She was worried about you," I said. "She asked me to inquire at your club."

"But how did you know I was there?" she repeated.

"You'd told me that was where Gollancz lived," I replied. "When I found you weren't at your club, I had to look somewhere. Don't worry yourself about it now. Your room'll be ready in a minute. You want some sleep."

She closed her eyes again for a little while, then, opening them once more, she asked why I had not taken her back to Dover Street.

"I thought you wanted looking after," said I.

A smile of cynical amusement, more like herself, flickered about her lips.

"I suppose you thought," she said, "that a woman arriving at her club after midnight in a semi-conscious condition might be reproved by the committee. I haven't read the regulations. You're probably quite right. Nice to have a man to think of these things for you."

Just for that moment, it was the Juniper I knew. But having said that, the distant look returned to her face, as though she had forgotten and had heard a voice calling her back. Her eyes closed again and she said nothing else. When the maid came down to say the room was ready, I told her to help Juniper to get to bed. She followed the girl upstairs without a word. Without even saying good night. She had forgotten my existence. I sat in the study, trying to think out what had happened and all it meant. It was three o'clock in the morning before I went to bed myself. Did I sleep? I don't remember it.

First thing when I got up, I rang up Stoke Charity to let Mrs. Weaver know that Juniper was all right. I gave the message to a maid, as casually as I could, just to say that she was probably returning that day. Then I ate some kind of a breakfast. I had not finished when they told me Juniper had asked if I could come upstairs and see her.

It seemed strange knowing there was a woman in the house. Impossible to describe my feelings as I went up to her bedroom.

She was sitting up in bed, dressed in what women call a camisole, I suppose. I hadn't thought what kind of garment she was going to sleep in when I brought her back to Arlington Street. In any case, it would have seemed peculiar to send to the club for her luggage.

Her arms were bare. It was not the kind of apparel a woman expects to be seen in. But she was quite indifferent to fussy ideas of modesty. Nevertheless, I may have imagined it, but I thought she, too, was conscious of the strangeness of the situation.

Alone there in the house with me at that hour of the morning. If, indeed, she did know what was in my mind about her, she must have been. But she was not bothered about her bare arms or the inadequate substance of that garment about her shoulders.

Every woman who possesses it must know something about her own beauty. Juniper was beautiful then in that queer, personal way of hers. A beauty that essentially belonged to her. And a false modesty, when a woman realizes that, I suppose is an entirely insincere sentiment. It may have been the means by which our Victorian mothers attracted our Victorian fathers. But it has no place in the modern young woman's concept of honesty.

It seems ridiculous, with my experience as a doctor, but I think she was easily the more self-possessed of the two of us when I came into the room. It was probably nothing less than a feeling of awkwardness that made me go straight across to the window and draw the curtains a little to let in more light. When I came and leant on the railing at the foot of the bed, having by that time assumed what I knew well enough to be my bedside manner, she asked me why I had done it.

"Are you one of those who dislike the glare of light first thing?" I replied.

She said she didn't mind. She only wanted to know why I was behaving like a waiter in a foreign hotel.

That opened the way to a moment of laughter, but I could see at once it was not her mood. Obviously she could still be the Juniper that fascinated me, but there was another woman there as well now. It cannot be possible for the whole nature of anyone to change in a night. The cynicism, the humour, the attractive insolence of her was still there. But whatever had happened at Clifford's Inn, I could see she had discovered something that was new and strange to her whole conception of herself. The one side of her nature was struggling with this other. It was like a wrestling in the wilderness. She could not herself have told which was getting the upper hand.

"Did you mind me sending for you?" she asked, as I stood leaning on the bed-rail.

"No," said I. "Not a bit. Why should I?"

"I didn't want to get up," she went on. "I just wanted to lie here and think. Then I found I couldn't think. All my thoughts got in a heap. I wanted you to come and help me pick 'em out."

It was the first actual sign of friendliness and confidence she had shown me. I moved away and came round to sit on the edge of the bed. She shifted her feet to make room for me. Women are queer creatures. Much more readily than men can they fit themselves into a situation. She was more at her ease than I was.

"Let's have 'em, then," I said. I did succeed in accompanying that with a smile. "Spread 'em out and we'll pick 'em over."

Then she was silent for a bit, with her knees cocked up in bed and her hands clasped round them. Up to a certain age, women can look like children in bed. She looked like a child, thinking out its first problems of the universe.

"It's so difficult," she said at last. "I don't know where to begin. I suppose nobody's just one person. Not unless you're terribly ordinary and commonplace. All the time life, nature, is trying to make you one common creature, bearing children and housekeeping if you're a woman, begetting children and working if you're a man. The old curse of Adam and Eve, I suppose. Nature shutting you out from God."

These were surprising thoughts for a young woman of her age to be thinking. But what astonished me most of all, with her kind of agnosticism, was that introduction of God. It was the first time I had heard her use the name, other than as she had said it in the garden at Stoke Charity. A kind of cliché, as she had called it. Her Gentleman of the Old Testament.

"And have you discovered," I asked, "that you're two different people?"

"Yes, two absolutely different people. There's somewhere else," she said mystically, "than what we suppose to be the world. There's something else than what we just suppose to be living, eating and drinking, and people making what they call love."

"Did you discover this wisdom at Clifford's Inn?" I inquired satirically.

"Yes." My sarcasm had not reached her. "He showed me. Gollancz. What is he? No good just saying he's a Rosicrucian. Rosicrucian's only a word. Words are only things we kid ourselves with. We call ourselves Christians, but we aren't Christians, any more than we're Jews. Lord! How Christ must laugh at us! Or be sick of us! Or whatever sort of thing He feels!"

I had never seen her in this mood. I should never even have conceived it possible to be a mood of hers. The cynicism of it was all that was like her. But, beneath that, there was an underlying sense of the mystery of her own being which was the last thing I should have imagined would have touched her mind or given her a moment's thought.

"Wouldn't you like to tell me what happened last night?" I asked. Until I knew that, I felt it impossible to understand anything.

At first I thought she was going to tell me nothing. An expression of reserve, almost of secrecy, settled down upon her face, shutting me out of all sight of her mind.

"Don't, if you don't want to," I added quickly. I could even hear myself the jealous sound of my voice. Possibly she heard it too. Perhaps a woman is roused to some kind of sympathy for a man when she knows he's in love with her. Whatever it was, something dispelled that look of secrecy from her eyes. She had withdrawn her body against the pillows. Now she leant forward with her head resting on her knees, her eyes staring, regarding me abstractedly as though my face were a written book and she were searching for some definition in it that would enforce her understanding.

"I don't mind telling you," she said. "Why should I mind? I'd met Mr. Gollancz a few days before. I'd dreamt I should meet him. I went to meet him."

She didn't say where. Evidently she thought I didn't know.

"He told me to come to Clifford's Inn. He told me to come there last night at nine o'clock."

It was no good interrupting her with comments upon the folly of doing a thing like that. I may have felt like a schoolmaster, concerned with her behaviour. I wasn't so much of a fool as to show it. I said nothing, and let her go on.

"I went there. He was alone. He opened the door. I went into that room. You saw it?" I nodded my head. "The blue ceiling. That scarlet rose. He was in a long white robe. Sandals on his feet. He was like a monk."

There was no need to tell her I knew. It was only necessary to signify with my eyes that I understood. She was not waiting for any word from me, anyhow.

"There was just a table in the room. There were no chairs. He gave me a blue sort of robe to put on. I put it on. I suppose I felt the clothes I was wearing were ridiculous, there. Then he told me to sit down on a rug on the floor. I did everything he told me. It didn't seem possible that one could refuse. It would have seemed silly to refuse. I did sit down. He lit some more candles. Then he sat down himself. Not near me. The candles were between us. I could only see his face through a haze of light. It sort of all shimmered with the flames of the candles. As I looked through them, even his eyes seemed like two flames. I'm not talking nonsense. I'm telling you what happened."

I was afraid she was going to stop. It was evidently an experience she could hardly believe herself. As she put it into words, it sounded incredible to her. For a moment I knew she was thinking it was better to leave it there in her mind, without words. Just as it was.

"I know it's not nonsense," I reassured her. "You needn't be afraid I shan't understand. Everything that happened to you last night has a rational explanation."

I said that to give her confidence. But did I believe it? How could I, rationally, have explained many of the things I felt had happened concerning Gollancz? I wanted her to go on. If I failed to give her rational explanations afterwards, that couldn't be helped. But already her mood had changed. I had not been able to prevent that. She suddenly went off into vague questionings.

"Do you believe," she asked me, "that the only morality in this world is in the will and the mind of each of us? Do you believe there's no such thing as vice or virtue as one understands them? That we pass through phases and planes of our existence, by our will to do what we desire to do, and that when we deny and suppress our real desires we are denying our absolute selves, the experience of life that is the very substance of their meaning?"

"A very comfortable morality," I replied. "To do just what you want to do."

"Oh, yes—but you have to be sure that you want it. Not just

the mere pleasure from what you do. Not something that's going to make you a slave to your wants—like Claude and his drug—but something, when you've done it, that's going to make you freer than you were before. Do you believe that?"

"Is that what Gollancz told you?" I asked.

"He told me thousands of things," she said. "I don't know how long it was he sat there with the flames of those candles between us. It might only have been a few minutes. I lost all count of the sense of time. And it was all true. He knew my mind as if it were inside his own and he was speaking to me with it. Sometimes I could almost have believed it was me, talking to myself. Daring to tell myself the absolute truth. He knew all about Claude. He knew everything."

"Did he know about me?" I asked.

"What about you?"

"About me and about you?"

She stared at me.

"What?" she repeated.

"That I love you," I said.

I said it without emotion. I said it as though it were as plain a fact as my sitting there at her bedside.

"Didn't he tell you," I went on, "that it was the desire of my life and every thought I have, to give you such happiness as I could and to protect you from everything that threatened you? Didn't he tell you that?"

She was still staring at me. She didn't speak. She only shook her head.

"So there is something he doesn't know," said I, with a note of triumph. Which was ridiculous. Because it was not what I felt. I was sure he must know. It was not difficult to credit him with that. But why hadn't he spoken of it to her? Was it because it was something he had not the power to oppose? The only thing in which the will of my desire, as he might have said, was equal to his own?

"Go on telling me," I urged her. "I haven't said that to stop you. I expect you knew it. I've only put it into words. It isn't any more real than it was that first evening you dined with me, or than it was the other day when we sat in the garden at Stoke Charity.

Anyhow, I'll never let it worry you. I promise you that. I'll never speak of it again if you don't want me to. I'm a friend—that's all—if that's what you want me to be. Go on. Tell me. What happened then?"

But whether she was glad or sorry to hear what I had said, it had effectually broken the clear thread of her story. She tried to go on, certainly, telling me how Gollancz had offered to show her the life beyond what she called living, the world beyond what she knew to be her world.

Whether she had wished for this experience or not, she didn't say. She gave me to understand that there seemed to be no question of refusing it. He had lit the incense in the brazier. Sitting there with the blue smoke of it illuminated by the candle light between them, he had spoken things that had sounded with understanding in her ears at the time. But, as words remembered from a dream, they had no sense to her then.

The state of hypnosis is induced by confusing, bewildering the sight, concentrating the eyes upon a certain object until the sight becomes obsessed by it. There seemed no doubt to me, from what she said, that he had confused and bewildered the sense of her hearing with his words. The smoke, too, as she watched his face through it, became a blue globe, filled with the beams of candle light. She told me that.

"Like a bubble," she said. "All moving."

I could feel what she meant. The lights and colours in a soap-bubble pass through it in moving prismatic currents—never still. I suppose if one could keep a soap-bubble long enough intact, one could hypnotize with it as easily as with a ball of crystal. And the pale blue smoke and the candle light had become like that—like a bubble to her. With the face of Gollancz gazing at her out of the centre of it. The odour of that incense in her nostrils. The sound of his arresting voice reiterating itself upon her ears.

There was the rational explanation I had to offer her. She had been hypnotized. All those sensations she had had of passing up a stairway of light, of the opening of a dark gate and an emergence into some dazzlingly lighted space, was pure suggestion to the mind in a state of hypnosis.

"The last thing I remember him saying," she told me, "was

that the knowledge of the alchemists was only symbolized by their transmutations of the common metals into gold. 'The fire of the alchemists,' he said, 'dissolves our weariness into ecstasy, it burns the sweet madness of our dreams into the living truth. The soul it transmutes from the earthly body of death, and out of the deepest darkness it creates the dazzling light of God.'"

So far as that she had gone in her description of what had happened the night before. I had the feeling there was a great deal more she had not told me. It may have been then that she passed into that state of unconsciousness in which I found her. She did not say. Suddenly, as though a nerve storm had broken down her control, she turned away. She buried her head in the pillows and her bare shoulders were shaking with sobs. I could just hear her voice, stifled by the pillows.

"It's no good your telling me," she was crying. "I can't help it! I must! I must!"

I didn't waste any time then asking her what she meant. If it was what I had said she was talking about, it was not the moment for me to discuss it then. What it was she couldn't help, I didn't ask her. What she must do, I couldn't guess. She was in a nervous condition of exhaustion. I went downstairs and got her a dose of bromide. When she had taken that, I pulled the curtains across the window and told her to get some more sleep if she could.

"At any rate lie quite still and try and get a bit of rest," I said, and I left her.

Leaving instructions with the maid, I went off to the hospital. There was nothing really to worry about. Indeed, I felt the more I kept out of her way the better.

For the rest of the morning, I went the round of my patients. I had not finished until after one o'clock. As I opened the door of the house in Arlington Street, the maid came out of the waiting-room at once to meet me.

"What's the matter?" I asked.

"Mrs. Weaver has gone," she said. "She got up about an hour after you went. She left this note, and told me to give it to you when you came in."

I took the letter into my consulting-room. I felt no inclination to open it there in front of the maid.

This was the second time I had seen her handwriting. A peculiar, individual scrawl. Not the gigantic, egotistical caligraphy of those women who are obsessed with the importance of their personality. Indeed, it was small, inclined to be scratchy, and somehow or other as I looked at it, very like her—cynical, rather amusing, and yet conveying a force of emotion in the speed with which the letters had evidently been made.

There was no formal beginning. It just said:

Thank you. I know how good you've been and meant to be. Don't worry about me any more. I've gone home. I know you mean it for what the Sunday school teachers call—the best, but don't go there again. Bless you. Juniper.

That beatitude and the signature of her Christian name gave me a hope which all the rest of the letter, as I proceeded to think over it, dashed to the ground. She told me not to go there again. Of course, to Clifford's Inn. Which only meant that she intended to go there again herself. She had not finished with Gollancz, then? He had got a hold of her. Would he let her go? I stood there by the side of the desk in my consulting-room and I have never felt so powerless, so at my wits' end before in my life.

CHAPTER XV

I had rung up later that day to hear if Juniper had returned safely. The maid at Stoke Charity said she was there. Did I want to speak to her?

"No," said I, and on second thoughts I said "No," again, and hung up the receiver.

What would there have been to say if she had come to the phone? For all the mechanical wonders of electric wave lengths and living wires, there is no contact of minds in conversations like that. I knew the only power I had in conflict with Gollancz was the power of my will. A function of which the psychologists know nothing. The power of his will over her was hypnotic. Whatever that may be. No one really knows. The power of mine was emotional. And when you come to think of it, are we not really as ignorant of that?

Whatever his power might be, I was still convinced it was the book and not Juniper herself he wanted. But so long as that manuscript was in the possession of Claude Weaver—and I knew of nothing in the limitations of the law that could take it from him—what could I do? Buy it from him and give it to Gollancz? But what sum of money would he want? Even two thousand pounds would have strained my financial resources to their limit. But he had refused two thousand. Besides, wouldn't the thought of giving in like that have been repugnant to anyone! It was not likely I should win Juniper from him that way. The power of money was not the kind of power that would have any effect upon her. It was only by convincing her that all I felt was less centred upon those desires he talked about; that it was her happiness I cared for as much as my own: that I could hope to succeed against the force of his will.

One friend only I had to help me in this. It sounds preposterous. The mother of the man whose wife I was in love with. As bizarre and improbable as that, the situation was. And yet there were things Mrs. Aubrey Weaver had said to me, which made it not seem as improbable as it sounds. Her affection for Juniper, which she had shown me so plainly, was one that had nothing to do with relationship. It was deeper than that. She cared for that young woman, not because she was her daughter-in-law, but simply because she was a young woman. Because, as she had seen the lives of women, they were tragic. Because she knew that in Juniper's marriage, even to her own son, her life was tragically being wasted.

As for Claude Weaver himself, even though he was flesh of her own flesh, she knew there was no curing him of his drug mania. She had said herself that sometimes she wished it was all over. As also, doubtless, she sometimes wished she had never been a wife. As I can even conceive her wishing she had never been a mother.

But believing in her sympathy to that extent was a very different matter from asking for a practical expression of it in this affair. I did not see how I could do anything in that quarter, and for days I waited on in London, hoping to hear either from Mrs.

Aubrey Weaver or from Juniper herself. But I heard nothing. The police had not called on me the next morning after we had found Juniper in Clifford's Inn. In a distracted moment, I almost wished they had. That they had found cause to suspect Gollancz of something that came within the province of the law, and that the whole affair would come out in the light of day instead of being shrouded as it was in the dim glimmer of his candle-light.

That, I knew, was only a counsel of desperation. For her sake it was the last thing I could have wanted to happen. As the next two or three days went by and no one appeared from the police station, I was really relieved.

But what had become of Gollancz that night, and why had he left her alone in his rooms? Of that I knew nothing. She, at least, had been unable to tell me. That the condition in which I had found her had been hypnotic I was quite certain. But whether it had been of his imposition or she had merely passed into the trance, listening to his voice and watching, what she described as that globe of the curling smoke of incense, it was impossible to say.

Yet what a situation for a woman to be in, in the hands of an unscrupulous man! I felt sick as I thought of it. Nevertheless, the one thing of which I was certain was that Gollancz had no designs upon Juniper herself. It was her will I had to free from his. He held it and he did not wish to hold anything else. But, my God, that was bad enough! Indeed, wasn't it the worst thing that could happen to her? For what was my knowledge in the labyrinths of psychology compared with his? With all the scientific training I had had, I felt almost like a child in his hands. Calling it chicanery, persuading myself he was a charlatan, didn't help. He had the will of the woman I loved in his control, and nothing, it seemed, that I could do could wrest it from him.

A week had gone by and I had heard nothing, except that she was back safely again at Stoke Charity. It was something at least to know that she was out of London. Yet what obstacle did any distance present to him? He was with her in her dreams. In her dreams he had called her to meet him in Whitchurch. How could I think of her as safe, wherever she was?

It is not difficult, then, to suppose my state of mind when, at the end of that week, I saw Gollancz himself one day in London.

I had been down to a firm of medical instrument makers in the Strand. My chauffeur was driving. I was looking at the crowds of people on the pavement as one does, listlessly, seeing none as individuals. Just realizing the mass of humanity passing up and down the street. Much as you look at ants swarming on an antheap. I saw no more than the jumble of hats and faces and legs moving, and then, suddenly, in the midst of that crowd, my eye picked out a black sombrero hat. How instant must have been the working of that function which communicated the arresting intelligence to my brain.

"Pull up by the side of this kerb!" I almost shouted to the chauffeur. "Then take the car up behind the Lyceum Theatre and wait for me there. Don't know how long I shall be. Wait for me."

It was scarcely a moment before I was out on the pavement, but when I looked in the direction of the Law Courts, which was the way he had been going, the sombrero hat was nowhere to be seen. I crossed the street under the mudguards of hooting motor-cars. There was only one turning he could have taken. I pushed my way through the clusters of people waiting for buses at the corner and looked down the street leading to Waterloo Bridge. And there in the distance, over the heads of the hundreds of people coming and going, I could see it. Just as that morning in the Haymarket Crawshay-Martin and I had watched it floating away over the waves of heads until, in Piccadilly Circus, it was lost in the trough of that sea of humanity.

How long a pursuit it was going to be or how it would end, I never paused a moment to consider. The thought of that man was so predominant in my mind, and had been all those days, that the mere sight of him was quite sufficient to draw me like a magnet. Dodging in and out between the pedestrians, I succeeded in lessening the distance between us. It was not my intention to get too close, but close enough to be able to see if he turned off anywhere or disappeared into any of those shops on the other side of the bridge.

But he kept straight on, never looking behind him, or to right or to left. His eyes, as I could imagine them, completely oblivious of all the men and women about him. His mind lost to all the distractions of human interest. I was near enough to see people turn round and look after him when he had gone by. But there was nothing surprising in that. In all the crowds of faces one sees in London streets, there occasionally is one that draws the wearied eye and forces one to look back. His certainly would have done that. No one with the faintest impulse of observation could have passed him by with indifference.

My only fear that he might look round and discover me following him was evidently quite superfluous. I suppose I had some idea that he could sense an antagonism as near to him as that. If I had thought it out at all, I might have realized how unreasonable that was. In the physical consciousness it was only possible he could be aware of what any of his five senses could register upon his mind. And with the habit of his concentration in what he was doing, it was most unlikely he would be looking about him. People stared at him as he went by, but he was aware of none of them. Straight on he walked through the stream of those moving bodies as though nothing could turn him from the object of his destination.

It was not long before I learnt what that was. He turned sharp to the right down the street to Waterloo Station. I was just in time to see him pass through the gates into the station itself. Then I quickened my pace to get nearer to him. In the booking-hall I concealed myself behind a pile of luggage while I watched him go to the ticket office. The transaction of buying his ticket only took a moment. He went away from there into the main body of the station.

I was quite aware how ridiculous it would have appeared if anyone I knew had seen me, a doctor with a practice in the West End, hiding, like any little private inquiry agent, behind a pile of luggage. But if all the actions of the most sedate of us could be observed in our everyday life, I fancy that even kings and prime ministers might find it difficult at times to account for the reasonableness of what they did.

So much had the obsession of that man been centred in my mind for the last few weeks that what I did that morning was reasonable enough to me. I could not have done anything else. Directly he had left the ticket office, I went to the same counter before the memory of the clerk inside could be confused with the demands of other travellers.

"You saw a gentleman just now with a black hat—wide brim."

"Yes, I saw him," said he.

"Did he get two tickets?" I asked.

"No—he only got one."

"Oh!" said I. "He said he was going to get mine. I want another, then—same place. Did he take a third class?"

"Yes—third. Third return."

"Third return then for me," I said. "How much?"

He named the sum, and punching the date on the ticket he slipped it across the counter to me. I saw the destination as it lay there. It was Whitchurch. Whitchurch, just a few miles from Stoke Charity.

So far as having obtained the information I desired, I might easily have left the ticket there in my haste to get away. There was no sense in travelling in the same train with him. The last thing I wanted was that either he or Juniper should know I was concerning myself in this matter. The ticket had completed its service so far as I was concerned, but I did have my wits sufficiently about me to pick it up off the counter, thrust it in my pocket, and depart.

There was no necessity to follow Gollancz any longer. Whether he sat in a smoking compartment or not was of no interest to me. I knew where he was going. Nothing I could do would stop him. I found myself striding out of the station almost breaking into a run. I could not waste the time to walk back over Waterloo Bridge. I jumped on to a bus and jumped off again as it was held up in a jam of the traffic coming into the Strand.

Behind the Lyceum Theatre my chauffeur was still waiting. I got into the car and told him to drive home. In ten minutes I was back in Arlington Street. In half an hour I had made all arrangements for my absence from town for the next two days if necessary. Within an hour I was driving by myself on the Portsmouth Road, making for Whitchurch. By four o'clock that afternoon I had engaged a room at the principal hotel there. But what was my object? What was I going to do? All the way down in the car I had tried to think out some plan of action, but how was it possible to plan anything until I knew something more of what Gollancz himself intended to do?

My first instinct had been to get within touch of Juniper. I had done that. Stoke Charity was only seven miles away. But after that letter of hers, I believed it to be unwise at that juncture to let her know where I was.

There was only one person with whom I could communicate. Juniper's mother-in-law. There was only one means of communication by which, if I was careful, I could conceal the fact of my being so close. I went to the public telephone in the post office, asked for the number of the Court House, and shut myself in the sound-proof telephone-box.

When the mind is vital and alert with more than ordinary activity, all sorts of ideas and memories come without bidding to its assistance. I had remembered the name of the woman whom Mrs. Aubrey Weaver had told me did her sewing for her. The woman who lived in Alton and had seen Juniper that day with Gollancz in the street. When the maid at Stoke Charity answered the phone, I told her that Mrs. Collins, from Alton, wanted to speak to Mrs. Aubrey Weaver.

In half a dozen different ways that ruse might have gone all wrong. Mrs. Collins might at that moment have been at the Court House. Mrs. Weaver might have been unable to come to the phone and Juniper have taken her place. I had to take my chance of these contingencies, and luck was in my way. With a considerable sense of relief I thought I heard Mrs. Aubrey's voice. But I confirmed it first before I gave myself away.

"Is that Mrs. Aubrey Weaver speaking?"

She said it was.

I told her then it was Dr. Hawke, and it may have been my imagination, but I thought I heard her mutter, "Thank God!" as she stood in front of the instrument. It was not loud enough to take any notice of. I went on quickly to inform her I was in Whitchurch. That I knew Gollancz had gone down that morning, and assumed he must have been going to meet Juniper.

"You told me to take care of her," said I, I suppose because, to the mother of Claude Weaver, I felt my action needed some kind of justification. "So I came down here at once in my car, to be near if I were wanted. I rang you up directly I got here to warn you. If Juniper goes out of the house on any pretext whatever, believe me it will be to meet him."

"There's no need for her to go out of the house," she replied.

"How do you mean?"

"Mr. Gollancz is here."

I don't know that I was so much surprised at that as aware of the conviction that he must have something very definite to do if he felt his actual presence was necessary, there in that house.

She went on to tell me that it was Claude and not Juniper who had informed her that Gollancz was coming. About the book, he had said, but had been very indefinite in his information. I gathered that during the last week in which I had heard nothing, his mania for his drug had been very acute. Twice in the middle of the night she had heard him screaming for Juniper.

What those women must have suffered in the house with a man like that!

"How long is he going to stay?" I asked.

She did not know. A bedroom had been prepared, but he had brought no luggage with him. At the moment that she was telephoning to me, Gollancz and Juniper were sitting in the garden.

"I can't see, I can't see," she muttered pathetically over the telephone. "I can't tell you what they are doing. I can only hear Juniper's voice when she speaks to him."

"What about her voice?"

"It's so unlike her. You know how clear her will is with everyone. You can feel it as she speaks. It's all gone with him. She talks as she would talk in her sleep. I know so well what she's feeling. When I hear him speak, it takes me right back to those days in the library at Malquoits. My voice, I know, has become the voice of an old woman. I can hear it myself as I speak. But he hasn't changed at all. It might have been yesterday he was talking to me there. It's like a memory made alive. I assure you, Dr. Hawke, it frightens me to hear him. There's something about it all we don't understand."

I knew that well enough. But I wasn't going to distress her still further by telling her how much there was.

"Has he recognized you?" I asked.

"Oh, yes. At once. He made no concealment of it. I don't know why I should suppose he would. Not concealment, anyhow. Much more likely he would have completely forgotten about me. He never took any notice of women. But he hadn't forgotten. 'Miss Crawshay-Martin,' he said as he held my hand. I can't describe to you how much more he seemed to say without any words, when he just said that."

For a moment I did not interrupt her silence. Even over those wires, I felt it to be something it was better for me not to disturb. When she spoke again, a moment later, it was in a more controlled tone of voice.

"He has been upstairs to see Claude," she informed me. "He only came down about a quarter of an hour ago. Then he went out into the garden with Juniper. I don't know what he and Claude talked about. Though I believe it was that book. Claude has been at work again translating it. He reads me some of the parts in English that he's done. It's very like those things my father used to talk about. The influence of the stars. The star of Solomon. The sacred Pentagram. All things that mean nothing to me, or to Claude for that matter, but which, in the book, seem to have extraordinary significance."

It was strange how much I found myself relying on my instincts in all that concerned Gollancz and his movements. Facts counted for nothing. It was what I felt I knew that I acted upon. And here, as she told me this, I had the certain conviction that it was because of this ambition of Claude Weaver's to translate the book that Gollancz had come down himself to Stoke Charity.

Already, with the power of his will, he had endeavoured to interrupt that operation. In his sleep, Weaver had been led to the place where his drug was concealed and had nearly ended his life then. But the chances of circumstance had been against Gollancz. With all his will he could not oppose chance. Weaver had recovered. He was continuing with that self-imposed job of translation, little realizing that by doing so he was violating the secrets of the Brotherhood of the Rosy Cross. To Gollancz, a sin against the Holy Ghost if ever there was one. But could he suppose the risks he was taking? I little imagined that he did. Gollancz had come down there to put a stop to it. However, in this he was dealing with a man who, in the diseased condition of his mind, was incapable of all reasoning. Then what would Gollancz do? How would he achieve his object? I could not conceive of him leaving that house until it was accomplished.

"What makes you say you think it was the book?" I asked, when these thoughts had passed through my mind.

"I don't just think, I know it was the book," she said. "I went up to Claude's room soon after. He was talking about it. Excitedly. He kept on repeating how he had had that offer of two thousand pounds and saying he wasn't going to part with it for less than five. Not to anyone. He kept on saying that. 'Not to anyone!'"

"As though Gollancz had asked for it?"

"Yes—it sounded like that, though he didn't say so."

"And where is the book now?"

"He has it locked up in a safe," she told me, "and he's got the key. He won't tell any of us where it is."

I was not in a mood to realize the interest of all this. The occult power that Gollancz had over the unseen, the immaterial, while in the face of anything as material as that safe he could do nothing. The modern man of science with a charge of gelignite would have blown the safe open and taken the book. But these were not the methods of Gollancz, even if he had known how to use them. Still, I confess, I would sooner have had to meet the housebreaker, with his oxyhydrogen drill, his jemmy and his life-preserver, than this man who could break his way into the hidden and unknown places of the human mind.

"Well, I don't see that you can do anything just now," said I. "It's no good my coming over to Stoke Charity. It would only aggravate Juniper."

I told her then of Juniper's letter to me. I did not describe the condition in which I had found her in Gollancz's rooms. That seemed unnecessary. There was no need to increase the apprehensions she already had. But I assured her that for the moment I thought it unwise for me to come over to the Court House.

"I'm near at hand," I told her. "You needn't worry. The telephone number of my hotel here is 843. You can call me up at any moment and tell me what's happening. If you really think it necessary, I'll come. But, believe me, there's one way you can get rid of that man at once."

"How's that?" she asked.

"Get that book for him," said I. "Get it anyhow. Steal it from your son if it's necessary. He's tampering with things he doesn't understand. That none of us understand if it comes to that. After all, what's two thousand pounds compared with his life or Juniper's safety? Get that book. That's what I'm telling you. And remember—if you want me—I'm here."

She promised she would do what she could and said good-bye then, reluctantly, as though, even over that distance and with the mechanical contact of the telephone, I were the only person she could rely upon. Her voice seemed to fall away rather than to stop.

I could see her in my mind, with her blind eyes, feeling her way through the passages of that house, all senses but sight quivering to know what was going to happen next.

CHAPTER XVI

The number of things to do in a country hotel when one cannot leave the house are extremely limited, and none of them of an absorbing nature. Such literature as is to be found lying about on the tables in the lounge is offensive with its shameless purpose of advertisement. Sometimes there is a billiard-room, and then it is possible to pass away an hour or two with bonzaline balls and cues without tips. But there was no billiard-room in the hotel at Whitchurch and, so far as I was concerned, it was not merely a question of an hour. I had to wait there until Mrs. Aubrey Weaver called me up on the telephone. She might not call at all.

By the end of my solitary dinner, I could have repeated the whole of the attenuated issue of a London evening paper off by heart. And yet all the time it was impossible to concentrate my attention on anything. In all my thoughts I was out there at Stoke Charity, wondering what they were doing at the Court House. Starting at every sound of a bell, as when a bicycle passed in the street outside. Wondering again and again whether it would be wise to ring Mrs. Aubrey up a second time, and knowing well enough the subterfuge of Mrs. Collins, once used, was exhausted. It would no longer be convincing at that hour of the evening.

Rejecting the cup of coffee they brought out to me in the lounge—on its own grounds, as one might say, which made it like mud in the cup—I sought out the landlord and dragged him by means of a proffered drink into conversation with me. He was quite ready to talk to a stranger about anything and anybody in the neighbourhood. From the advantage of his position as hotel keeper, he would have had me to suppose that he could see most of what was going on. It was not difficult to lead him round by places of local interest to the Court House in Stoke Charity.

His ideas of Judge Jeffreys and the Bloody Assize were not what one would call authentic history. Even his conceptions of abstract justice in his own times were strangely biased by opinions on the licensing laws and the drink regulations. His whole view of government, in fact, was of a system of rights and injustices that personally affected him as the proprietor of an hotel. It might have been a world of hotel proprietors. When in the course of our conversation I informed him I was a doctor, he accepted that, but seemed to infer that legislation was not intended or designed for the likes of me.

The one other class in life of whose existence he seemed dimly conscious was the country gentry, and this led him quite naturally from Judge Jeffreys, who had presided at the Court House, to Claude Weaver, who owned it.

"Gentlemen, of course, have their own ways," said he, "but I must say he's a good customer whenever he comes in here. He gets a bit on, you know, at times, but he's genial. I will say that for him. He's genial."

As a testimonial of character from an hotel proprietor, I was made to feel that geniality in a gentleman was one of the highest credentials. All the same, I was curious to know what lay behind that qualification of Claude Weaver—having his own ways. What ways?

"Do you mean his behaviour's a bit peculiar at times?" I asked.

He looked at me with a slant of his eyes as though to determine whether my curiosity was entirely justified by the fact that

I was having an idle drink. Taking the chance that it was, rather than lose it, he said:

"Did you never hear of that case of a nigger bein' had up for sellin' drugs in London?"

I shook my head. I was prepared not to know anything.

"Well, p'r'aps not. They tell me it was kept out of the papers as much as possible. But Mr. Weaver was the gentleman the drugs was sold to."

Knowing me then to be a doctor, he looked at me as though, out of the pure generosity of his confidence, he had presented me with a case which would materially add to my medical experience.

"Seeing him casually, you know," he continued, "you'd never think he went in for things like that. Pleasant spoken, he is. Well—what I said. Genial. But they tell me he's fair awful at times when the habit's on him. Beats his wife, they say. Nice young woman, too. Smart. You know what I mean."

So it was common property as far as Whitchurch. To the knowledge of an hotel proprietor, Juniper was a beaten wife. A woman degraded by her husband, to be pitied in the proprietor's estimation as he would have pitied a drunken tinker's wife. I felt my blood boil.

"And you'd never think it," continued my companion. "Well, not if you knew the gentleman as well as I do."

He inferred an intimate acquaintance, but one which by the sacred laws of friendship he was not at liberty to talk about. Not, anyhow, on an empty glass, which has a terminating effect upon the confiding conversation of this class of gentleman. But that was a matter that was quite capable of readjustment. I had only to say, "Another sherry?" and with a degree of diffidence mingled with surprise that did him justice, he said:

"Well—I don't mind if I do."

With this generosity on my part, I felt I was fast approaching that qualification of gentility which would entitle me, together with innkeepers, to a more lenient legislation of government. But, in my own estimation, I could see myself as little better than a private inquiry agent. One of the most despicable occupations it is possible to conceive. The only exoneration I felt I deserved was that at least I was doing my own dirty work myself. Moreover, I defy anyone not to have done the same in my place.

Here was a garrulous hotel proprietor who evidently knew something of the private life of the man who was wrecking the happiness of the woman I loved. Well, the man who would not have encouraged him to talk would either have been less or more than human. I admit that was not the only other glass of sherry I treated him to. But I do not suggest for a moment that what he told me was under the alcoholic influence of his wine. He drank slowly and sparingly, as a man must if he has to live in the close vicinity of a bar parlour. It was only that when his conversation flagged—ran out, as it were, with the wine in his glass—I made a point of having it replenished.

"You'd never think what?" I had said, as we held up our second glasses in the air to each other, for he was punctilious over the formalities. "Do you mean you'd never think he was a man who beat his wife?"

"Yes, that's what I did mean—judging by—judging by things I saw, you know."

"What things?"

He was inclined to be mysterious here. He looked at me and then looked away. Gazing into a distance of his memory, he pursed up his lips dubiously as though he were wrestling with his conscience and were not quite certain how strong an opponent to his desires it was. It was evidently something he thought better not to talk about but found very entertaining to say. As a wrestling match, it proved to be a one-sided affair. His conscience never really stood a chance. Clearing his throat after the still, small voice in him was silenced, he said:

"We had an extraordinarily pretty girl here in the bar. Real flier, she was. You know. Expensive silk stockings and a nice pair of legs."

I could quite understand that that was what my companion would have called a pretty girl. It was only necessary for me to nod my head.

"Well, he got very pally with her. The way a gentleman might, you know, coming in for a drink, just like you or me 'ud be sitting here. And I must say his manners to her, all I ever saw of 'em together, were—well, you might say he treated her like a lady. Well—I happen to know he did. Never think he was the sort of man to lay his hands on a woman. I know that. She told me herself. Before she left to get married."

He paused a moment on the verge of another confidence. Possibly the still, small voice in him was not quite silenced, after all. It raised itself, as you might say, on its elbow. He had only inferred things in what he had said. Before the confiding of an actual fact, his conscience for the last time had lifted its head and looked at him. But it was getting on for ten o'clock. I was the only visitor in the hotel. The sherry was not a bad wine. I had told him to get his best. It was a moment when the infidelities of married gentlemen of the county were an absorbing topic of conversation to him. His pause was of the shortest duration. With a glance about him, he leaned a little nearer to me:

"As a matter of fact," said he, "he stayed the night here once or twice when his wife was up in town. And the girl, of course, lived in the house too. Well"—he winked at me—"I knew," he said. And with that, I suddenly felt sick of it all. Sick of hearing these confidences. Sick of his insinuating voice. Sick of the sensation that indirectly he was talking about Juniper, associating her with a barmaid of loose morals and silk-stockinged legs. Sick, most of all, of the thought that in all probability she must suspect these infidelities, or must at least know that with his visits into Whitchurch there was scarce a soul in the neighbourhood who did not know of the beastliness of her life.

"Well—that's a matter between the barmaid and him, isn't it?" said I. "One can imagine all sorts of things, and still be wrong."

"But why did he stop at the hotel here," he asked knowingly, "with his own house not more than seven miles away?"

"People who are addicted to the habit of drugs," said I with a weight of authority in my voice, "are liable to do the most unaccountable things. I wouldn't go round saying that about this Mr. Weaver, if I were you, it might get you into trouble."

Probably he felt the wisdom of my advice, because he thought he heard his wife calling him. Excusing himself, he hurried out of the lounge, and when he came back to his half-finished glass of sherry, the name of Claude Weaver did not pass his lips again. He went on to other matters, in which he revealed just as unlikeable a personality, but kept himself to safe ground. It was nearly eleven o'clock. The bar was closed. His wife had gone to bed. We were the only two still up in the establishment when the telephone bell rang in the silence of the house like a fire alarm.

I jumped at once to my feet.

"That's for me," I said emphatically. "I've been waiting for a call. Don't you bother to stay up. I may be some time. I know my room. I might even have to go out to see a patient. But I can easily get my car out of the garage."

The telephone was in a cupboard at the end of a passage. It was lit with electric light, but even with the door closed I could not suppose it was absolutely sound-proof. I left him there, finishing his third glass of sherry, and, leaving the door of the cupboard slightly open so that I could hear when he went up to bed, I took off the receiver.

"Yes," I said. "Hallo!"

It was Mrs. Aubrey Weaver's voice. Pathetic, it sounded to me, in its distress.

"I want to speak to Dr. Hawke," she said.

"It's Dr. Hawke speaking," said I. "Try and not ask me any questions. It'll be difficult to answer. Just say what you've got to tell me, and don't mind if my answers sound a little abrupt."

From where I was I could hear Mr. Willett, the proprietor, moving about from one room to another. Ostensibly locking up. But I had a definite feeling that his interest in the landed gentry was extending to me. A London doctor in a country town, called up on the telephone by a patient at eleven o'clock at night. To a man of his inquiring nature, that was a circumstance not to be ignored. It was my impression he would find a few odd things to do before he went to bed.

"I don't really know how to begin," she said distractedly. "I ought to tell you everything that's happened because you might think I was fussing myself about nothing."

"Look here," I replied, "tell me candidly, would you like me to come out there? I will if you think there's anything I can do."

Her answer to that was immediate and unequivocal.

"No—no. I don't think you'd better do that," she said. "At least not now. Not yet. I may be worrying myself quite unnecessarily. It's not being able to see. I feel so helpless. I thought I'd grown accustomed to my blindness. I've even thought sometimes that it gave me an additional sense that other people lacked. It doesn't here. I don't understand. It's—it's more than I can understand."

"Well, go on," I encouraged her. "Try and tell me what you can."

I said no more than that. Mr. Willett's footsteps in the passage outside the cupboard door were a sufficient deterrent to any loquaciousness on my part. After hearing me say a few things like that, he might probably feel he was wasting his time, and go to bed. I was determined to give his curiosity no satisfaction. With that vague encouragement, she continued:

"We all had dinner together. Claude is up again. But after that last bout, I have felt in his voice lately an irritability, easy with my blindness to detect, quicker even than Juniper, that the hunger was coming back to him again. That has been his peculiarity. I know usually in these cases the habit is a continual one. But, like his father, he must be of a very strong constitution. It comes in bouts with him as it did with Aubrey. For a time he can give it up altogether. That's not usual, is it? But lately those intervals have been getting shorter and shorter. It's not more than ten days now since the last, and this evening at dinner I could feel the storm on the point of breaking. Oh, you don't know what it's like, Dr. Hawke. You don't know what it's like. One's own son. It's terrible."

"Try and forget that," said I, encouragingly; "just go on and tell me what's happened."

Mr. Willett passed back again down the passage. I may have imagined his footsteps to slacken as they reached the cupboard door. But he could only have realized from what I said that he was going to hear nothing to satisfy his curiosity at this end, and at last I heard him mounting the stairs on his way to bed.

"Well, soon after dinner," she continued, "Claude went to bed. That was a sign. Juniper and I knew quite well what it meant. Whenever he's like this he wants to get away alone by himself. God knows what he does. Whether he tries to fight it down or not, I don't know. He never succeeds. But that is always a sign when it's getting the mastery over him. I could hear the fear in Juniper's voice when she offered to go up with him. He almost shouted at her when he said he didn't want any interference from her. Interference! When the poor child was only trying to do her best."

"And what," I asked, "was the other one doing while this was going on?"

"Nothing. Nothing, of course, that I could see. And nothing that I could hear. But I assure you I wish he had. Said something—even done something that I could hear and understand. From him there was absolute silence, and yet never for an instant could I forget he was there. I just felt him watching, waiting, as though he knew all that could happen, all that was going to happen, and had only to bide his time."

"For what?" I questioned her.

"I don't know. I don't know!" she repeated.

But I felt I knew. Once before I had said it to Juniper. Over and over again my mind was saying it to me then. He was waiting for Claude Weaver's death.

"Don't you think I'd better come out there at once?" I said sharply.

"No—really, no! This may be all my imagination. After what you told me about that letter of Juniper's, I think it might only aggravate everything and everybody. At any rate, I'll tell you what's happened, and then you can judge for yourself. Juniper and I and Mr. Gollancz sat down there in the hall. He talked about strange things. Things something like he used to talk to me about in the library at Malquoits. Oh, it was exactly like being there again when I was a young girl. Only now he was saying them to someone else. Someone of the next generation. And as though I were not there. As though I never existed. And to Juniper as if, as a woman, she didn't exist either. But from the sound of her voice whenever she answered or asked a question, I could hear that she felt, just what I felt myself those forty-odd years ago. She's fascinated by him, Dr. Hawke. Her will is not her own. I know. Because that was what I felt. What I said I would tell you one of these days. I tell it you now. If the conventions for young women had not been what they were then, I don't know what I should have done. And that was what I could feel with her. I—I couldn't bear it. It—it—oh, it sounds terrible to say it, but it's the only way I can explain. It was as though she were standing there, stripping herself for him and—and he wasn't looking at her. I suppose I oughtn't to have done it, but at last I got up and went to bed. I said good night to them, but they didn't answer. I was actually crying, whimpering like a child as I went up the stairs. And I can believe they neither of them knew I had gone."

It was more than I could bear to hear her stop. I felt I couldn't hear any more, and yet I must know.

"You left them there alone!" I exclaimed.

"Yes. But not for very long. I promise you it was not for very long. I had not been in my room for more than five minutes before I felt convinced it was my duty to her to stay there by her. Blind as I was, I believed that my presence between them could save her from herself if not from him. I had not begun to undress. I had been standing in the middle of the room, doing nothing, just clasping and unclasping my hands. At last I went back. The passages in the house are very heavily carpeted, and I don't suppose they heard me coming. As I came out on to the landing above the hall, I heard her say something. Oh, I can't tell you what she said!"

"You must tell me!" I insisted. "I must know!" And in the stress of my emotion, I added: "Juniper means more to me than any woman in the world. I'd give my life for her. I must know!"

Did that surprise her, shock her? It would be impossible to say. Perhaps, as I had thought before, she knew it already. Whether that was so or not, she made no comment on what I had told her. She just repeated what Juniper had said. The tone of command in my voice, the importunate sound of my will, must have been greater in that moment than any conception she had of conventionality. She gave me Juniper's words as exactly as she could remember them.

" 'It's all very well telling me we belong to ourselves'—this is what she was saying—'once, perhaps, I had a sort of idea that I did. I haven't had it any more since those dreams.' What dreams she meant, I don't know. I'm just telling you what she said. But plainly I heard her say that. 'I haven't had it any more since those dreams. Since then the whole of my will belongs to you. My body, my soul, all of me does. You can do what you like with me. I don't care. Take me now if you want to.'"

Each thing as she repeated it was like a blow in my face. She might have had some heavy implement in her hand, was striking me with it, and I was powerless to prevent her. I couldn't tell her to stop. I had to let her go on. Even then, when she paused and I felt there was still more to come, I hadn't the will to say: "That's enough." All the hopes I'd ever entertained of my chance with Juniper were being crushed out of existence. I could only stand by and see them being annihilated.

"That was what she was saying, Dr. Hawke," Mrs. Aubrey continued after that pause. "You may think it utterly wrong of me to have stood there and listened. I couldn't help it. If I could have moved, I would have done. But don't you see it was my own life being lived again in another generation. In those days when I was a girl, the words that Juniper was saying couldn't have got away from my tongue. I couldn't have spoken them. But they were all that I'd thought. Everything I'd felt when he used to talk to me in the library at Malquoits. Only then he'd never let me get so near to him as she was. Near enough to say things like that. Perhaps if he had, I should have said them, too. There's not so much difference in generations as all that. Women have always been much the same when it came to their passions. But, somehow, I feel he wants more of Juniper than he wanted of me."

"Why?" I exclaimed at that. "What does he want of her? What did he say?"

"For what seemed quite a long time as I stood up there on the landing, he said nothing. But the silence wasn't empty. You mustn't suppose that. I don't know what happened. I don't think either of them moved. Of course, I couldn't see, but I should have heard them if they had. I promise you if I thought anything had been happening, I should have forced myself to go downstairs. There was an absolute silence after Juniper had spoken, and then at last he said: 'We do not yield ourselves to the angels, or even to death utterly'—I'm telling you his exact words—'except through the weakness of our will. Your will is not weak,' he went on. 'You will do what you desire to do.' I heard her asking him what that was, and he said: 'You will take your freedom. Death will not stand in your way when it comes to the moment for you to choose.' And then, as though she knew what he meant, though I didn't, she said: 'When will it come?' And he said: 'Very soon.' Perhaps it was because I didn't understand what they were saying then, that my mind began to assert itself over my body. I felt I could move again, and making some noise to warn them—I think I coughed—I walked across the landing and came downstairs again. 'I thought you'd gone to bed,' Juniper said. Her voice was cross. Quite unlike her. I know she didn't realize she was speaking to me like that. I told her that when I got to my room I felt worried about Claude, and knew it was not a bit of good going to bed. 'You ought to go to bed,' she said, but in answer to that I just found the chair I usually occupy in the hall, and I sat down."

"What did they do then?" I asked sharply. Perhaps there was in my voice the same note of impatience as in Juniper's. I couldn't help it. Anyhow (indeed, a blind angel) she took no offence.

"He did nothing. But Juniper asked him if he would come out into the garden with her. I was just going to implore them not to leave me. To pretend that, in that state of nerves, I could not bear to be left alone. Because, if Juniper had gone away with him then, God knows what would have happened to her in that mood and state of her mind. But, thank heaven, at least he saved me from that. 'We'll stay here,' he said. 'Perhaps you may be wanted. You don't know.' How could he possibly have known what was going to happen in the next few minutes. Because it was true enough what he said. We all sat there in silence for a few moments, and then there was the noise of a door being flung open and the sound of feet running along one of the corridors upstairs. I knew at once it was Claude. I could hear the sound of his desperate breathing as he came. He rushed out on to the landing above us. His voice was like the voice of a man gone mad. Oh, I've heard it like that before, Dr. Hawke. He screams when he wants his drug. He calls Juniper by the foulest of names. He shouted at her then down into the hall and told her if she did not get it for him then he would—— Oh! I can't say what he said. For a few moments she did not move. Usually she tries by what she says to calm him down. She promises to get it for him if he will go back to bed again. To-night she didn't speak. She let him rave on up there. I couldn't bear the sound of his voice any longer. I had to come and telephone to you. What do you think I ought to do? Ought I to persuade her to give it to him? He may go on like this all night if she doesn't?"

"Can you hear him from where you're telephoning?" I asked.

"Oh, yes. You can hear him all over the house."

It might have been the wires, but I imagined I could myself. The high scream of a man who has lost human control. In that silence of the hotel, with everyone in bed, not an easy sound to listen to.

"I think you'd better let me come out," I said.

"But what could you do?"

"I could give him a dose that'll keep him quiet. Shall I come?"

I waited for her answer. She did not reply.

"Shall I come?" I repeated.

Still she did not say. With the momentary cessation of her voice I was sure then I could plainly hear the screams of Claude Weaver. A hollow sound through that telephone.

"Shall I come?" I called out for the third time. And still there was no reply. The screams continued a moment longer, and then they stopped. It was all silent. Just the faint buzzing of the wires.

CHAPTER XVII

I could stand the suspense of this no longer. Even with the voice of Mrs. Aubrey Weaver informing me what was going on in that house, it was difficult enough to stay there, listening and doing nothing. When, without hanging up the receiver at the other end, for I was sure it was Weaver's voice I had heard, she had left the telephone as though for some desperate necessity, I severed the connection at my end and came out of the cupboard. Wanted or not wanted, I was going out there and, seizing my hat, I went out to the garage for the car. It was locked. That fool of a Willett might have told me so. I had to come back into the hotel and ring a bell to rouse him.

It was not much rousing that he required. It was a mere exercise of optimism on my part when I thought he had gone to bed. Attired in a Jaeger dressing-gown, with his hair on end, even his eyebrows bristling, he appeared at once in answer to my summons, looking the picture of inquiry. When he heard it was the key of the garage I wanted, he insisted on accompanying me out into the yard. It was impossible to shake him off. Shooting oblique questions at me, he did his best to find out who it was in the neighbourhood of Whitchurch who was in such desperate need of a doctor at that hour of night.

In his association with the landed gentry, he felt he ought to know. There might, he said, be some little thing one way or another that he could do. One never knew.

"One never will know," said I.

A remark like that had no effect on him. He stood by, still persisting in his questions while I got the engine started. How far was I going?

"A few miles," I replied.

"Do you know the road all right?"

"Quite all right, thank you."

"It isn't in the direction of Stoke Charity by any chance, is it?" he asked sharply.

The idea had suddenly jumped in his brain. Our conversation that evening. The advice I had given him. He was a little nervous, but fully alive to the possibility of anything that might be happening at the Court House.

"A man of more sensitive perception than yourself," said I, exasperated by this time, "would have realized long ago that I had no intention of admitting him into my confidence." And I raced the engine to get it warm, so that any further conversation was impossible.

He stood there in the yard of the garage in his Jaeger dressing-gown, watching me drive out into the High Street. I've no doubt, from the expression of his face, his sleep was not going to be any too comfortable that night. A man's memory trying to recall the unwise things he has said, is not an easy bedfellow.

Half-way out of the town, my engine refused to pull. Mr. Willett was bad enough. This was worse. I have driven a car for nearly twenty years, but am no mechanic. It was either carburettor or ignition. But between those two possibilities, mysterious worlds existed in the bowels of the engine for me. I got out and looked at the plugs. Testing them with a screwdriver, I found they were all sparking. It might be the distributor. But the distributor, as far as I was concerned, was like a conjurer's box of tricks. I was just going to get in and try her again, desperately, as ignorance inclines one to, hoping that, perhaps, it was pure contrariness on the part of the machine, that whatever had been wrong had by some miraculous happening suddenly come right. And then I remembered I had closed the choke to race her up when Mr. Willett was talking to me. I had been trying to run her on undiluted petrol vapour. These things happen to anyone. But I had lost ten minutes. A quarter of an hour later I was tearing into the drive of the Court House.

The lights were burning in the hall. One of the windows as well on the west side of the house was lit. It was not more than half an hour since I had heard Mrs. Weaver's voice break off into silence on the telephone. Little more than thirty minutes, yet it seemed as though I had lived through the best part of a lifetime. My mind was not in any state to think of ceremony. I went straight to the hall door to open it. It was locked. Ringing the bell would have been no good. I knew the servants were in bed. I thumped on it with my fist.

For those few moments while I waited there in the darkness, my imagination seemed capable of conceiving anything. I cannot recollect a worse minute in my life than that. Was it a minute? A few seconds, with the kind of apprehensions I had were sufficient to have the full weight of time. I was just about to hammer with my fist again, when I heard the bolts being drawn back, and the door was opened. The warmth and light from the hall streamed over me and against it, in a black opaque mass, stood the figure of Gollancz.

Looking back on that moment, I wonder sometimes how long we did actually remain there without a word passing between us. I, standing on the doorstep with the flood of the light on my face for him to see every expression that passed across it. He, inscrutable, as you can well suppose, in the density of that silhouette he made against the light beyond. Certainly he was the last person I expected to admit me. I had scarcely recovered from my astonishment when, with what I can only describe as a smile in his voice, he said:

"The doctor. Opportunely. I think, doctor, you had better go straight upstairs to Mr. Weaver's room. Do you know the way? Or can I show you?"

Knowing what is known, what I have already recounted from my conversation with Mrs. Aubrey Weaver, it may seem as though all this was said with the most refined of irony. But it was not. Irony was not a weapon of his equipment. Always he gave one the impression it was his use of the absolute truth that made the disconcerting quality of his remarks. He would not have stooped to the common employment of satire. His mind was beyond that. On the two occasions when he had spoken directly to me, in the passage at the "Scarlett Arms" and in his rooms at Clifford's Inn, the apparent sarcasm of what he had said, lay in the scrupulous exactitude of his statements.

I have said there was a smile in his voice. But it was the smile, not of a man who is amused at the discomfiture of another. Rather, it was the smile of one who is watching the events he has foreseen, verified by circumstance. He had expected me. At that hour of night. And there I was. He made way for me to pass into the hall.

I took off my hat and turned—perhaps in astonishment—to look at him as he closed the door.

"How do you know I've come to see Mr. Weaver?" I asked.

"But you've heard," said he, "what happened on the landing up there? About an hour ago. He was demanding his drug. His wife has given it to him. Don't you know the condition he is in?"

"No," said I abruptly. "And how do you?"

"One uses one's intelligence," he said quietly. "As you do, within your limitations, when you diagnose a case. Or do you refuse to admit the quality of instinct in your profession? Possibly you do. Most doctors refuse it. They hold to the principles of science. But my impression of you is that at least you are honest. I have told you that before. I was here when Mr. Weaver came from his room on to the landing. A man in that condition is not far from his end. But you heard all this."

"How do you know I heard?" I exclaimed.

"Didn't his mother telephone to you? But aren't you wasting time with these questions, Dr. Hawke? You must be quick. They are both up there. They're waiting for you."

What more could I say? It was quite true I was wasting time. I turned away from him in exasperation and went upstairs. In the hall below, he stood watching me. I could feel that, but did not look at him again.

The door of Claude Weaver's room was ajar. I knocked and, without waiting for admission, went in.

Naturally, I have been present at many death-bed scenes. None, I think, quite as strange as that. The first impulse of one's eyes, of course, is to the patient. In the nature of one's occupation, one can be conscious of little else. A glance is often enough. There is little doubt about the approach of death. It is easily recognizable.

Here I knew in an instant. The moment I had seen his face, heard the note of his breathing. But it was not at him alone that I looked. There was his mother kneeling by the side of the bed. Her hands were holding one of his. She was not crying. There was no distress in her attitude. It was just as though, in that condition, he had become to her like a child again; and patiently, forgivingly, affectionately, she were leading him by the hand into a dark place where he was not certain of the way.

But it was Juniper herself in that picture who, apart from all the impulse of my emotion, arrested the attention of my glance. She was standing at the end of the bed, looking down at him. The man who had made such wretched havoc of her life. The man for whom her hatred could only have been intensified because she had had to live with it, locked up inside herself for all the years they had been married. She was watching him, passing out, making way for her freedom, but there was no pity in her face. Not a trace of it. Any tenderness, any charity consistent with her nature was gone. Remembering the words I had been told she had said to Gollancz, I could see she was still the same woman who had spoken those. For a moment I stopped and took her arm. She did not even turn to look at me. Then I went over to him, lying on the bed.

There was no question about it. It was too late. I did what I could, but there were no signs of recuperation from the state of coma into which he had passed. He responded to nothing.

"What dose did he take?" I asked.

In a voice strangely unlike her own, Juniper directed my attention to a little bottle that was on the bedside table. I picked it up. There were a few tabloids in the bottom. I looked at the label. They were eighths of a grain.

"Do you know how many there were?"

"Fourteen," she said without hesitation.

"There are only three there now," said I.

"Yes."

"Do you mean to say he took eleven? More than a whole grain?"

"Yes."

I stood up.

"I can't do anything," I said frankly. "He's beyond the reach of any antidote. He may last a few hours. He may go any minute."

Mrs. Aubrey Weaver made no sign of distress at that. Her hands left his and I saw them feeling for his face. She raised herself to lean over him and kissed his forehead. It was a child she had kissed. Not that man. Then she stood up from the bed. Finding her way down to the foot of it, she reached out to touch Juniper. I saw their hands meet. I imagined a pressure as they held a moment. But not from any sign in Juniper's face. Then Mrs. Aubrey began to feel her way to the door, touching pieces of furniture that she knew.

I hurried forward to help her.

"Thank you," she said. "Don't bother. I know my way. There's something I want to do. I want to do it now. You stay here with Juniper."

She went out, moving slowly through her perpetual darkness, and closed the door behind her.

Nothing happens, in the accumulation of circumstances, that has not happened frequently before. I am quite prepared to admit that. It is only one's personal view of their significance that alters them. I have known of a man and woman standing at the deathbed of the woman's husband and, at the moment of his passing out, becoming aware of a love for each other which, in the husband's lifetime, they had not dared to recognize. Of course, there have been situations such as Juniper and I found ourselves in then. But hardly one that resolved itself as this did.

It was a long while after the door had closed before either of us spoke. Honestly, myself, I was at a loss for anything to say. It was she who spoke first.

"Are you sure of what you said just now?" she asked.

"Which thing I said?"

"That he can't live?"

"Quite certain," I replied calmly. "The depression of the heart's action with a dose like that is impossible to recover from. If you listen to his breathing now, it's fainter than it was a few moments ago."

We listened for a moment or two. The sound of it was so faint that it might have been no more than the breathing of a very young child asleep. She had been watching his face. Then, without any emotion, she looked at me.

"I killed him," she said.

There was no change in her tone of voice. It had that same unapproachable distance about it. It was imperturbable, emotionless, and cold.

"For God's sake, don't say a thing like that!" I exclaimed.

"It's true," she replied.

"Even if it were true," said I. "But I don't believe it! Not for a moment! You haven't said that to your mother-in-law, have you?"

"No. I don't suppose there's any need. She probably knows."

"I'm perfectly certain," said I, "that such a thought has never entered her head. She's been telling me on the telephone what's happened. That's why I'm here. For God's sake, don't say that again!" I implored her. "You don't realize the consequences if anyone heard you. Of course, you didn't kill him. He's taken an overdose. As he did before when you went up to London. Only, this time he's finished himself."

She stood there, still in the same position, looking at me and shaking her head.

"He snatched the bottle out of my hand," she went on calmly, as though she had never heard my advice, "and I let him take it. I could have stopped him. But I didn't want to. He told me I didn't want to. And he was quite right. I wanted my freedom. He said so to me. I was just going to take the bottle away from Claude, when he laid his hand on my arm. He knew my mind better than I really knew it myself. We don't really know ourselves. We're afraid of what we really are. I've wanted Claude to die. For a long time I've wanted it and never knew. He showed me my own mind. He knows I killed Claude."

She was talking in the same kind of voice as that night in Arlington Street when I had brought her back in the taxi from Clifford's Inn. But who was she talking about? He had told her? He had laid his hand on her arm? Who did she mean? I asked her if she knew what she was saying.

"Oh, yes," she replied. "I know quite well what I'm saying."

"Who do you mean, then? Who laid his hand on your arm?"

"Gollancz."

"Where?"

"Here."

"In this room, do you mean?"

"Yes. Where else?"

"But he was downstairs."

"Oh, no." She smiled. "Here. I saw him."

"But ask your mother-in-law. He was in the hall. She was with him."

For the first time that night she looked at me with the consciousness of the Juniper I had known. The Juniper my heart had gone to.

"How do you know?" she asked.

"Because Mrs. Aubrey was telephoning to me, only three-quarters of an hour ago. I've been at Whitchurch. I knew Gollancz was coming down here. I came down to Whitchurch to be near you in case—anything happened. She telephoned and told me how he had become mad for his drug."

"Well? And then? And then?"

"Gollancz was in the hall. She told me so. She telephoned to me twice this evening. Once, before your husband came out on to the landing and the second time just after."

"Yes, well, then? While she was telephoning the second time?"

"But it was only a few moments and Gollancz was there in the hall. She told me so. With her."

"But I saw him!" she repeated.

"Did you see him come into this room?"

"No. I suddenly found him here."

"Was the door open?"

"No. Closed."

"Wouldn't you have heard it open?"

"I suppose I should."

"And you didn't?"

"No."

I took her arm and held it tightly in my hand, forcing her to look at me.

"Are you absolutely sure it was Gollancz?" I insisted.

"Perhaps more certain than I am that you're here. Now, in this room. When I believed you were in London."

"And he persuaded you not to interfere when your husband snatched the bottle out of your hand?"

"It was not a question of persuasion," she persisted, quite calmly, as though she never realized the significance of the charge she was making against herself. "I tell you, he didn't do anything. He just showed me my mind. As you show a person a picture. I wanted Claude to die. I wanted him out of my life. I hadn't really known it till that moment. Then, when I did know, I killed him."

"For God's sake, don't go on saying that!" I begged her. "If anyone killed him——"

I stopped. In the same moment, as it might have been, she had stopped listening to what I was saying. We had both turned and looked at the bed. The faint breathing had ceased. The body of Claude Weaver, there in the room with us, had suddenly assumed the look death brings with it. The appearance, even in a crowd, of being alone. He had passed out.

CHAPTER XVIII

How long it was she stood there looking at him, I could not measure in my memory. What her thoughts were, I don't pretend to know. At last she turned her eyes with a question at me, and I suppose a movement of my head signified to her that he was gone.

At first she seemed hardly to realize the actual fact of death. Indeed, as she told me afterwards, she had never seen anyone die before. Then, suddenly, for a moment, she was shaken with trembling as though a material consciousness had at last asserted itself. With an effort of will, she regained control of herself. Her voice became quite self-possessed. The old note of insolence was recognizable in it again as she said:

"Well, what does one do now? Tell the police? Give oneself up? May as well do the thing properly as it's usually done. A pity not to be conventional."

I took both her arms in my hands and forced her to look at me.

"This isn't the sort of moment to remind you," I said, "of what I told you when you were at Arlington Street. But don't forget it. It means more even now than it did then. Perhaps you realize by this that that man's influence over you isn't a normal one. If it did happen as you say, if it could have been prevented, if the bottle could have been taken out of his hand in time, the responsibility belongs to Gollancz that it wasn't. As I was going to say just now, if anyone killed your husband, it was he. But the facts are, your husband killed himself. However, if you're going to be so foolish as to persist in what you're saying, then come downstairs at once with me and face Gollancz with it. He must answer for what's happened, if anybody does. Not you."

Still holding her by the arm, I led her out of the room. She was peculiarly docile for her. Whatever was to be the outcome of it all, she had entirely resigned herself. I don't think she cared. In that moment of trembling she may probably have realized the possibility of capital punishment for the crime of which she was so carelessly and recklessly accusing herself. I only suppose that. In her mood now, she appeared indifferent to everything.

As we came out from the passage on to the landing, she released herself from the hold of my arm and looked down into the hall. Gollancz was standing there. Alone. Her gaze as she stared at him had the look of an animal's. Fascinated. I realized then, watching her, that in controlling her will he had isolated the lower side of her nature. She had no command of herself.

She was not Juniper, not the woman I loved. She was the mere animal being of herself without the spiritual essence that made her human. The creatures probably we all are without the higher exercise of our wills.

It was while I stood there, watching her, realizing this, that Mrs. Aubrey Weaver came into the hall below. She was carrying something in her hand. I knew what it was at once. The Book. It was the Studion manuscript. This was what she had wanted to do. She had found the keys of the safe. She knew, as I knew, as I had told her, there was only one thing that would rid that house of the influence of Gollancz. She had lost her son. To save Juniper, she had done what she was doing then. In silence we watched her put the book into Gollancz's outstretched hand.

"You've wanted this a long time," she said.

He smiled as he took it from her.

"You might have given it to me years ago," said he. "It would have saved a lot of trouble."

I glanced at Juniper's face, wondering what she was thinking of all this. And it was utterly changed. As though in that instant of Gollancz gaining at last the object of his desires, he had released her will and she was herself again. There was a horror in her eyes now. She was gazing down at him with an instinctive hatred, as she must often have looked at Claude Weaver when he was alive.

And the sight of that look had an instant's effect upon me. Gollancz had got what he wanted. His will had set hers free. But in the long conflict that had been carried on between us both, beginning that afternoon in the garden at Malquoits when I had urged Crawshay-Martin to bid at the auction against Mr. Bannerjee for the book, I was determined he should not get away with it as easily as this. Hurrying down the stairs into the hall, I said, as I reached the last step:

"I don't think this business is quite as simple as all this."

He turned with an imperturbable expression on his face.

"Nothing could be simpler, Dr. Hawke," he replied quietly. "Mrs. Weaver has given me this book of her own free will. There's no need for me to inflict my presence here any longer."

"But Mr. Weaver might have something to say to that," I rejoined.

"Probably. If he were alive."

"How do you know he's not alive?" I asked.

Juniper had followed me downstairs. She was standing beside me then.

"You have the science of your profession," he replied. "It's for you to tell us whether he is or not."

"Very well, Mr. Weaver is dead," I exclaimed. It was quite obvious he knew that as well as I did. "But there's a question that still remains as to how he did die. He took an overdose of heroin. He snatched the bottle out of his wife's hand. But you were up there in that room, and you exerted your will and influence to prevent her from taking it away from him. If there are any questions of Claude Weaver having come by his death in an unnatural way, it is you who will be required to answer them. You were there in the room when it happened. You persuaded Mrs. Weaver to do nothing."

He put the book inside his coat. A protective movement, as though I had threatened that. The only movement he made. His face betrayed no emotion. No resentment. Nothing at all.

"If there were any question of how Claude Weaver came by his death," he said, "I'm afraid you'd find it difficult to prove anything, Dr. Hawke. But there is no question. Claude Weaver killed himself. As his uncle did. Even if his wife likes to declare she did not prevent him, her statements would be regarded as those of an hysterical woman. In her absence he had nearly killed himself a short time ago. It was not likely he would escape a second time. But the point is you won't allow her to make any such statement. She will not want to make it herself. And what she may say about me is unimportant."

"Do you deny you were there!" cried Juniper. "There in the room! That you spoke to me! That you told me to do nothing!"

I looked at him to see what he would say to that. He made no answer. Instead, he turned to Mrs. Aubrey Weaver. The old lady seemed to respond to that glance, which she could not have seen. She felt her way across the hall to Juniper.

"He wasn't there," she said. "He wasn't in the room. He was down here in the hall."

"Not all the time!" Juniper declared.

"All the time," repeated Mrs. Aubrey. "I was here myself. When I came back from telephoning to Dr. Hawke, when I heard Claude calling out my name, you were here. You were just going upstairs. I never left the hall after that."

"But are you sure he was here?" I asked. "You couldn't see him. Were you speaking to him?"

"For a little while," she replied. "After Juniper had gone, I said something about Claude. He answered me. I went on speaking. I asked him if he thought there was any hope of Claude ever mastering himself of the passion for his drug. There was no answer. Three times I spoke to him and there was no reply."

"That was when it was, then," interposed Juniper. "You couldn't see him. He must have crept upstairs then. As quietly as he came into the room, because I never heard him."

"No, he was here in the hall," the old lady persisted. "I know."

"How do you know?" said I.

"When he didn't answer," she went on, "I was still sure he was here. I said his name two or three times, but I was still certain he was in the hall. Then I got up. I felt my way from chair to chair. And I did find him. He was here."

She stopped abruptly at that, and I looked at Gollancz. His eyes were directed at her. It was as though with his will he were commanding her to say no more. As her voice broke off, he turned to me.

"Can it advantage you, Dr. Hawke," he said, "to inquire any more? This lady says I was here in the hall with her. Do you think you can understand the observations and fancies of Mrs. Claude Weaver's mind? Why not leave those things alone of which you and the science in which you trust cannot hope to know anything?"

"I refuse to leave them alone!" I exclaimed. "Mrs. Weaver says you were down here in the hall. I have no reason to disbelieve her. But neither have I any reason to disbelieve Mrs. Claude. What was he doing?" I asked. "Why wouldn't he answer you?"

"He was asleep," she said.

"Asleep!"

"Yes."

"How do you know?"

"I shook his shoulder and he didn't move. He was lying on the divan there below the stairs."

"How was he lying?" I demanded sharply.

"He was lying stretched out, with his hands folded in some way underneath his back."

In the contest of my will with Gollancz, I had drawn that out of her. She told me afterwards she could feel the conflict of our wills, and that for that instant it was mine she had obeyed. But beyond that I could go no further. No further because, as he said, these were things that were outside the grasp of my intelligence. The moment she had described that attitude in which he was lying, I knew what I was up against. I could say nothing, because, frankly, I understood nothing. No more than that charwoman at Clifford's Inn who, when first she had found him like that, had rushed out in her ignorance for a doctor.

The law, like science, deals only with physical, with material, facts. If a crime, in the eyes of the law, had been committed in that house that night, the fact of Gollancz's body being there, where Mrs. Aubrey Weaver had proved it was, was sufficient to exonerate him. His influence upon Juniper could have nothing to do with the facts. His appearance to her in that room would only be regarded as an hallucination. Then, what were the facts as the law would understand them?

In a demented condition of mind, Claude Weaver had snatched the bottle of tabloids out of his wife's hand and poisoned himself with an overdose of heroin. There was nothing else for the law to judge of. The verdict, as it had been at the coroner's court at Shipleigh on the body of my friend, Crawshay-Martin, would be one of suicide. They would instance that case and an instability of mind would be said to be in the family.

I knew all this, as surely as I knew my own powerlessness to prove it otherwise. As surely as I had found it impossible to convince the sergeant of police at Shipleigh. "If you're going to talk about spiritual matters," he had said—or something like that, "the person you want to see is the Vicar over at the Vicarage." All he had required of me were the facts. But were the facts the truth? I knew they had no more to do with the truth then than they had now. And, turning to look at Gollancz from the confusion of these thoughts, it was quite plain to me he was certain of my impotence.

He was not smiling, but there was a calm serenity about his face as he said:

"Dr. Hawke, there is a passion for inquiry in your nature. I don't deny its nobility. To doubt and to desire to know, are the well-springs of all knowledge. It is only science that has misled you. Facts have no ultimate meaning—believe me. They are the substance of this civilization you live in, but, like the facts it is composed of, it will not last so very long. All facts change, as matter changes. One of these days you may glimpse a realization of the alchemical process of life. But to conquer and control the material forces of our existence is not the victory of life. You are building Towers of Babel all around you. One of these days they will crumble and totter and fall, and the meaning of your civilization will vanish as completely as false civilizations have vanished before. Be advised by me and make no effort to understand what has happened in this house to-night. Facts are all that you can appreciate. Then take the facts and let it pass at that. Claude Weaver has killed himself. That was as it should be. His life was of no consequence. It was misused. I have this manuscript. It was given me of her own free will by this lady, who understands the immortal forces of life better than you in that she has not resisted them. On the face of it, it is all very simple. Claude Weaver is dead. His wife belongs to you because of an emotion which, even though you are conscious of it, you do not understand. You have every reason to be content." All this he said, and neither I, nor Juniper, nor Mrs. Aubrey Weaver said a word to interrupt him. In silence, as we stood there in the hall, we watched him go to the place where his black sombrero hat was hanging. In silence he took it down and went to the door. He did not turn again to look at us. The clock at the foot of the stairs struck the hour of one. He opened the door and went out. As he closed it, I strode across the hall and opened it again. Had I the impulse to call him back? If I had, it turned to nothing. A flame that blew out the moment it was lit. On the doorstep I stood there in silence, watching his tall figure as it passed down the drive.

One o'clock at night. Where was he going? What place at that hour would take him in? Did he want any shelter? Did he want a place to sleep? He had in his possession the thing he had come for. What was sleep to him?

Against a white bush of syringa lit up in the moonlight, I saw his black sombrero hat as he turned a corner of the drive. Then he was gone.

I was never to see Gollancz again.

I knew that.

THE END